CHECKPOINT

books by CHARLES W. THAYER

fiction

CHECKPOINT

MOSCOW INTERLUDE

nonfiction

GUERRILLA

DIPLOMAT

THE UNQUIET GERMANS

BEARS IN THE CAVIAR

HANDS ACROSS THE CAVIAR

RUSSIA (*with the editors of* LIFE)

a novel by

CHARLES W. THAYER

CHECKPOINT

HARPER & ROW, *Publishers*

New York, Evanston, and London

CHECKPOINT

I TO THIS DAY, NO DOUBT, THE KREMLIN'S INTEL-
ligence services believe that Geoffrey Schuyler's assignment as U.S. Representative in Berlin was a subtle move in a
sinister plot against the Russians and their position in East
Berlin. However, the fact of the matter was that his assignment was a last-minute expedient to forestall the appointment of an incompetent political hack.

I was in Washington at the time, having come back
from Europe for the funeral of Geoff's wife, Millicent. I
had been best man at their wedding fifteen years before
and knew what a shock her sudden death must have been
to him, so when I got the news I closed up my chalet in the
Bavarian mountains and took the first plane I could get out
of Munich. I'd been home about three weeks staying at the
Cosmopolitan Club. It is about as gloomy a place to stay as

there is in Washington, but I dislike hotels and I had sold my little house in Georgetown. I had no need for it after I resigned from the service following my spectacular row with a certain Secretary of State who shall be nameless, not because I want to protect him—quite the contrary—but simply because I still dislike even to write his name.

I had done what I could to help Geoff with the funeral and to dispose of his house and Millicent's things. He was now busy getting ready for his next post, as ambassador to Italy. Naturally he was pleased to get his own embassy after twenty-five years in the service, and his only regret was that Millicent was not to enjoy the luxury and charm of Villa Taverna, the gem of our ambassadorial residences, high on a hill overlooking Rome.

The elections the year before had thrown out the administration, including the Secretary and his minions, and the antipathy I had long felt for the sprawling new State Department had more or less been dissipated, especially since many of my old friends were now back in positions of responsibility. The new Secretary, John Lane, for example, I had known right after the war in Austria. Old Nelly Larsen, after years of exile in Djakarta, had recently been summoned to take over the job of running the department as Lane's Deputy for Administration. His task was to try to restore some order and morale among our career diplomats after the chaotic "reforms" of the previous administration.

Nelly's real name was Norris E. Larsen. He was the senior officer in the Foreign Service, having entered it shortly after the First World War, and he was generally looked up to by the old career diplomats as the staunchest defender and most loyal member of that much-maligned group. He had been the counselor of the Berlin embassy back in the thirties when Geoff and I, fresh out of college, had been assigned there as vice consuls, and ever since I had looked up to him as my first mentor and as a kind of service godfather.

As soon as I had a free moment I called up his secretary, made an appointment, and for the first time in five years entered the pompous new State Building in Foggy Bottom.

Recalling the old State Building next to the White House, I felt a wave of annoyance as I walked into the pretentious lobby. Old State was probably the ugliest building in Washington, its high-ceilinged corridors and checkered marble floors and impossible lighting as unfunctional as possible, but there was something friendly and old-fashioned and tranquil about it. Outside the doors of the great had sat gray-haired old colored men beside tables piled with doubtless secret papers they were waiting for equally elderly messengers to pick up. To know and be known by these ancient guardians was the ambition of every new Foreign Service officer. For all its inadequacies and ugliness it was a place that inspired awe, tranquillity, and statesmanlike decisions.

And now it was replaced by this atrocity, doubtless far more efficient, more functional and "modern," apparently designed by some architect who thought diplomacy was a disease and should be housed in an up-to-date hospital. As I wandered down its endless white, antiseptic, windowless corridors I had the feeling I was in a mental institution and half expected one of the doors to open and a rubber-gloved hand to seize me and pull me in or a wheelchair to emerge with some lunatic strapped to it. In fact, the harassed expressions of the young, black-suited men who raced along it suggested that they were rushing to nervous breakdowns.

At last I came to a door above which was a wooden plaque with Nelly's name in gold letters. These plaques at least were the same as those which had once hung above the offices of the great in old State. With a feeling of relief I hurried in. Nelly was in his outer office talking to his secretary, and immediately he invited me into his room.

He was a small, thin man with a short, gray mustache, a sharp-pointed nose and quick, nervous gestures. As he peered over the disorderly pile of papers on his desk, he looked like a ferret standing on his hind legs in the tall grass looking about for a mouse. But his most striking features were his eyes, steel blue and sharp, but tired and buried deep in brownish-gray sockets. They were the badge of the overworked, harried government servant, who spent his days wrangling with budget officials and politicians and his nights poring over the endless reports, appropriation requests, and efficiency records of a vast corps of equally overworked diplomats scattered around the globe.

He led me to a leather couch and sat down beside me.

"Been reading your stuff everywhere," he said enthusiastically. "I'm delighted you're doing so well." It wasn't precisely true, for my magazine sales had been slim in the past months and my books too were selling rather slowly. "Liked your last article on Tito in the *Post*."

"*Harper's*," I corrected and hastily changing the subject asked about his problems.

"Not so good, Harry, to be frank. The biggest worry is personnel. The old crowd are disgruntled and discouraged and the new people who have been let into the service are inexperienced and—well—undisciplined is probably too strong; let's say they're a little spoiled and not quite as responsive to orders. They're apt to protest to their congressman whenever they miss a promotion, and when they're assigned to some stinking post in Africa they think they're being discriminated against. It's not what it was in the old days when the promotion board consisted of half a dozen semiretired diplomats who usually met in the dim religious atmosphere of the Cosmopolitan Club and whose decisions had the authority of those of the Delphic Oracle."

He lit a cigarette nervously and smiled.

"Nowadays it's all done by machines and punched cards. They're supposed to be impersonal and impartial. I daresay they are but they're also arbitrary, insensitive and often downright stupid." He smiled bitterly and puffed awkwardly on his cigarette as though he had just taken up smoking.

"For instance, every job, every position, has its classification card and its special punched holes, and the fellow who fills it has to have exactly the same holes in his card."

I clucked sympathetically. Just then the light on the intercom, the bane of every intelligent conversation in the department, flashed on. Wearily Nelly went back to his desk and pushed the button marked "The Secretary." I got up to go but Nelly waved me back into my seat.

"Yes, Mr. Secretary," he answered.

"Larsen, have you filled that Berlin post yet?" I recognized at once the high-pitched, intense voice.

"I have the papers on my desk now, Mr. Secretary, and I'm looking around for the right man."

"What about Judge Laughton?"

Nelly grimaced. "It's impossible, sir. You can't take him."

"Why not? The President is feeling a good deal of heat on his behalf, three senators in as many days."

"It's much too important a job, Mr. Secretary. We have to have someone there who won't go off half-cocked."

"Why should Laughton go off half-cocked? He was a general once. Served in Berlin even. He should be able to get on with our military."

"It's the Russians he's got to get on with, not our own generals. Besides, Laughton's no soldier. Got a National Guard commission from his governor during the war, if I'm not mistaken. Actually he's a lawyer."

"What's wrong with lawyers?" Lane's voice sounded a trifle sharper and Nelly grimaced again. Until a few months ago Lane had been the senior partner of a famous New York law firm. Poor Nelly, ever since I'd first known him twenty-five years before he had had a way of putting his foot in it with his superiors.

"What I mean, Mr. Secretary," Nelly explained, "is that he has no diplomatic experience."

"Is that so damned necessary? Haven't we got the facilities to control him from here? And if not why not?"

"Our communications with Berlin are as good as any in the world, Mr. Secretary." Nelly's voice was a little sharp now. "You can push a button on your phone and they'll get you through to headquarters in Clayallee within a minute. But that's not the point. We need someone there who can give us answers, not just ask questions and take orders. How can we tell him what to do unless we know what's going on?"

There was a long pause before the Secretary answered. "Well, Larsen, as I said, the heat from the Hill is on and the President is beginning to feel it. I daresay if you don't take Laughton you're likely to feel it yourself when you're next up there."

"I'm used to that, Mr. Secretary," Nelly replied quietly. "It's an old congressional tradition. The Foreign Service doesn't elect senators or representatives, so why should they bother to treat us civilly? If we raised hogs or peanuts or something, it might be different. But to them we're just a bunch of dirty foreigners or, worse still, expatriates—and expatriates don't make a very effective lobby."

Lane seemed to chuckle. "I guess you're right and perhaps I'd better get ready to take some of their guff myself."

"They'll be kind enough to you, sir. At first anyway. Cabinet officers usually get a few months of grace. But for us permanent officials, it's open season all year round—like varmints in a game preserve."

Lane chuckled again and when he replied his voice was quiet and mild. "O.K., Larsen, but let me have a man for Berlin soon." There was a click and the light on the intercom went off.

"Laughton!" Nelly spluttered contemptuously. "He could never handle it. Nominally, of course, he'd be subordinate to the military commandant," he went on. "But in actual fact he'd be the boss—in one of the most ticklish spots we've got. Last week the Russians tried to pick up one of our patrols on the boundary. Just a couple of days ago there was that shooting at the Brandenburg Gate." Nelly paused, looking down at his desk in disgust at the thought of Laughton. Then he looked up at me again: "What do you know about him?"

"All I know is they used to say he was so dumb other generals began to notice it."

Nelly laughed. "I'll have to tell that to the Secretary." He pushed a lever on the intercom and repeated what I had said. There was a peal of laughter and then Lane said: "Wait till I tell that to the President."

Subsequently I often wondered whether that silly joke was not responsible for killing Laughton's appointment and thus for all that followed.

When he switched off the intercom Nelly swung round in his swivel chair, turning his back on me, and looked out onto the parking lot which provided his only view. Then he swung back to face me.

"What brings you to Washington?" he asked. "I thought you had abandoned us for the Bavarian Alps."

I told him I had come back for Millicent Schuyler's funeral.

"Geoff is one of my oldest friends. We joined the service together," I added.

"I know, I know," Nelly said with the irritation of all old men who think their memories are being impugned. Then he swung round again and stared at the sea of parked cars.

"Geoff Schuyler," he murmured. "He'd do for the Berlin job."

"But the President has just named him for Rome," I protested.

"I am aware of that," Nelly said wearily. "It would be damned unfair. But then who have we got except Laughton? And the worst of it is that Pate, the present U.S. Representative, has just come down with ulcers and they're about to cut his insides out at Walter Reed. And, on top of that, his deputy who's been there five years already just sent me a report from his wife's doctor saying if she doesn't get out of that Berlin climate at once she's in for serious lung trouble. She's had TB once already." Once again there was a weary sigh and Nelly shook his head.

I felt sorry for him, and suddenly said: "Of course Geoff would be disappointed if he didn't get Rome, but if you put it to him I'm sure he'd take it."

Nelly's eyes flashed. "Of course he would! He's not one of these new types around here who think they can choose their own posts. I'd fire half of them if they'd let me," he said angrily.

"Now, Nelly," I said soothingly. "They're not as bad as all that—and we old-timers weren't as good. You remember when you sent me to Harbin under that old bastard what's-his-name and I cabled and asked for a change of assignment. Do you recall your answer?"

Nelly laughed. "I think I told you that vice consuls don't choose their consuls general."

Nelly's tired eyes wandered up to the clock behind me. I rose hastily and said good-bye.

"Don't say anything to Geoff until I've had time to think it over," he said as I went out.

The caution was unnecessary, for I didn't see Geoff

that evening since he was going to dine with the Italian ambassador. The next morning I was about to go down to breakfast when the phone rang. It was Nelly's secretary asking if I could stop in later in the morning.

When I entered his office he seemed a little more relaxed than on the previous afternoon.

"I talked to Geoff," he told me. "He wasn't very enthusiastic about my idea but he took it like a soldier."

I could imagine how disappointed Geoff was and began to blame myself for ever having mentioned his name.

"He had just one question," Nelly went on, "but I think we may be able to fix that." Then he reached over to the intercom and pressed the Secretary's switch. There was a grunt on the other end and Nelly said, "Mr. Secretary, I have Mr. Harding in my office, if you're free." He switched it off and, rising, asked if I wouldn't go down to Lane's office for a moment. Taken by surprise, it didn't even occur to me to ask what was up.

As Nelly led the way down the long corridor on the seventh floor I noticed a mahogany plaque on every second or third door.

"Looks like this is the VIP ward," I said.

"The Secretary calls it the bridge," Nelly admonished. "He's a yachtsman." A moment later we were ushered into the big, paneled office of the Secretary of State.

Lane greeted me warmly and waved me to a chair by his desk. Nelly took a seat at the opposite side.

"A long time since Vienna," Lane began affably. "And you're still a bachelor? I remember that blonde countess you had in those days. Whatever became of her?" I

grinned foolishly. "She took off with one of our occupation generals," I said. "After all, the soldiers, not the
diplomats, ran the PX's in those days—and still do."

The Secretary smiled. "You're probably damned lucky.
But then you always were." He paused and began doodling
with his pencil. I realized he was fumbling for a way to
broach whatever it was he and Nelly had cooked up.

"And now you're a highly successful author?" he went on.

"A writer," I corrected, "and not all that successful."

"Living in Bavaria?"

"Yes," I said. "It's cheaper. Besides I've lots of friends
there. That's where I was when I crossed swords with your
late, unlamented predecessor." Lane smiled but said nothing, as though he did not want to appear prejudiced against
the previous Secretary.

"Ever think of getting back into the service?" he asked.
His voice was just a trifle too casual.

"Good God no!" I said. "I walked the plank once and
I've no intention of climbing back on this ship."

The Secretary smiled. "Not even temporarily?"

Bewildered, I looked at him and then at Nelly.

"What's this all about?" I said a little uneasily.

The Secretary smiled again: "Just this; I'll be frank and
brief. We want Geoffrey Schuyler to go to Berlin. Naturally he's disappointed at not getting Rome and no one
blames him. He deserves his own embassy if anyone in the
service does. But the situation in Berlin is so damned
tricky we've got to have a first-rate man there. In the end
he agreed to take it, but with one stipulation."

Nelly broke in. "I wouldn't call it a stipulation, Mr.

Secretary. Schuyler's an old hand and he'll go wherever you send him without making any conditions. You might call it simply 'a request.' "

His tone was emphatic as though he were trying to make a point both with the Secretary and with me.

"I stand corrected," the Secretary said, smiling. "The old hands go wherever I send them. But the point is, Mr. Harding, he asked if he couldn't have you as his deputy."

So that was it. My first reaction was resentment.

"Why me, for God's sake? You have plenty of competent men to be his deputy!"

"I'm not sure myself," the Secretary said. "But he said Berlin was a pretty grim post. He mentioned the fact that his wife had just died. He said he'd known you longer than anyone in the service. He also said a great many very complimentary things about you. But what I gather is he wants someone around he can rely on. Someone he doesn't have to train or to test."

"You know why he'd want you," Nelly broke in impatiently.

It was my turn to get impatient. "But what about me? I'm settled. I've work of my own, and even if it's not very lucrative I manage pretty well. Besides, I've got a book I'm under contract for and I've got to finish that. Furthermore, to be just as frank as you, Mr. Secretary, Berlin is the last place on earth I want to go to."

"It was your first post," Nelly said. "And as I recall you had a pretty good time there." I didn't like the sly implication in his voice.

"And that's precisely why I've never been back since," I said.

The Secretary looked puzzled. "You've been living in Bavaria all these years and you've never been back to Berlin? Why not?"

I gave Nelly a hard and what I intended to be an unkind glance.

"It's a purely personal matter, Mr. Secretary. It's not important to anyone else." The Secretary looked inquiringly at Nelly, but Nelly knew he had already touched a sore spot and said nothing. The Secretary shrugged. "Well, if it's a personal matter . . ."

I began to feel like a petulant child and smiled. "It's not all that important, Mr. Secretary—just one of those shades of a private past."

"O.K., but how does it affect your decision?"

"I have made no decision yet," I said, half in desperation. "But," I added strictly to myself, "I'm certainly feeling the pressure."

"As for your other objections, the job would only be temporary. We can easily work out the mechanics with Larsen's personnel people. How long will it take you to finish your book?"

"About three weeks, if I work like hell."

He started to tell me about my salary, my title and status, but just then a light flashed on his telephone and he picked it up. "Yes, Mr. President?" he said. I couldn't hear what was said on the other end, but then he went on: "Another letter? My God, that man Laughton's got a lobby like the China crowd. But, Mr. President, we're working on the Berlin problem right now and I think we've got a solution." He paused and looked up at me. "Have we?" he asked, holding his hand over the mouthpiece and looking straight into my eyes.

I knew then that I had had it and meekly nodded.

The Secretary smiled a warm thanks at me and returned to the phone. "Yes, sir. We're sending Mr. Schuyler." He paused while the President said something. "Yes, I know. He's pretty disappointed, but he's a good soldier, sir—like all of Larsen's old hands." Another pause.

"I knew you'd appreciate it, sir. And I'll tell him what you've just said." Then he hung up. "Well, that's that." He sighed. "Thank you, Mr. Harding, I am very grateful and I know the President is too. I guess you and Larsen can work out the details." As we rose and left his office my knees felt flabby and unsteady.

Outside I started to turn on Nelly but he held up his hand, smiling: "Now, now, don't say anything. After all, you were brought up to be a good soldier too."

That evening Geoff and I had dinner together at the Cosmopolitan. The big red room upstairs by the bar was empty except for old Mr. Williams, who had been Chief of Personnel back before the war. Fortunately he was reading the papers at the far end of the room and did not recognize me when I came in and ordered a drink. A few minutes later Geoff appeared.

Ever since I had first known him twenty-five years before, Geoff had been a handsome, impressive person, tall, erect, lean, and incisive in his movements. Now his jet black hair had receded, leaving a prominent widow's peak. His face was long and thin and his brown eyes were set well apart beneath heavy black eyebrows. He had a small mouth and his lips though thin were mobile and usually gave an impression of kindliness. His chin too was long, but ended in a firm, square jaw. When he was worried or irritated the muscles under his cheeks tightened and rippled, but except for that he seldom let his face reveal what was going on in his agile, sensitive mind.

He looked a little weary and discouraged as he sat down beside me, his long legs stretched out in front of the big fire. From anyone else I would have expected some expression of gratitude for what I had agreed to do that morning. But from Geoff I expected none and got none. That was understood. Obviously he already knew about it for he said with a thin smile:

"Well, Harry, I guess we've both had it." And with that he dismissed the subject. Oddly enough I was flattered, for it showed that Geoff felt that he considered me still a part of the team, that close-knit little band of professional diplomats, and as such bound by its rules to go where I was told.

It tickled my pride to know that he of all people considered me a teammate, for ever since I had met him I had looked up to him. Though we had both been equally lowly vice consuls then, I knew from the start he was far more qualified than I. He was one of the best-educated people I knew. As a child he had been taught to speak French and German fluently. He had a scholarly knowledge of the classics from the ancient Greeks to the present, and his grasp of history, especially European history, had always made me envious, for my own education had been more conventional and superficial.

I do not want to give the impression though that he was

a dried-up scholarly type. On the contrary he had one of the warmest and most sensitive of natures and was always ready, even eager, to help his friends when they got themselves into jams—as I was one of the first to discover in Berlin. This sensitivity, not only to his friends but to complete strangers, coupled with a shrewd penetrating eye, his "political eye," I used to call it, made him one of the best political observers and reporters in the entire diplomatic service.

After his apprenticeship in Berlin he had served briefly in the State Department and then had been sent to Moscow, where he had quickly become fluent in Russian. He had served there for four years and later had returned for a second assignment at his own request, for, like everyone who has made an effort to understand the Russians as individuals, he had promptly fallen in love with them. By the time he left Moscow he was one of the very few real experts who not only knew the Communists and their strange patterns of thought but the history of Russia from the days of the Tartars, their literature and poetry, their folklore and their unpredictable national psychology, if one can call it that.

Early in the war, his brilliance and wide knowledge had attracted the attention even of the White House, notorious under every administration for its hostility to career diplomats. As a relatively junior officer he had accompanied the President to several of his wartime conferences and after the war had played an important, if unpublicized, role in the rehabilitation of Western Europe. He had, for instance, been the key man in settling the

Trieste dispute and subsequently in getting the Russians to agree to the Austrian treaty ending the occupation of that long-suffering country. Since then he had risen to the top of the career service and had served all over the globe as what the press always calls a "trouble shooter": in Korea and then Saigon, and in Iran during the oil crisis.

But throughout his career his real love had remained the Russians, whose sufferings under Stalin's tyranny had touched his heart. Toward the Germans he always had had an ambivalent attitude. On the one hand, he admired their industry and the scholarly approach of their intellectuals, and, perhaps because they were the first foreigners he had got to know during our assignment together in Berlin, he often showed a real affection for them, especially after Hitler started to terrorize them as Stalin had the Russians. On the other hand, he often expressed contempt for their lack of civil courage, for what he called their pusillanimous servility to their masters, whether it was Bismarck or Hitler or more recently Adenauer. Their political ineptitude too offended his intellectual sensibilities. But, above all, he disliked and distrusted their frenzied lack of restraint whenever they were released from their self-imposed rigid discipline. "When Russians get drunk," he often said, "they get maudlin and feel sorry for themselves and everyone else. When Germans get drunk they go berserk and hate themselves and everyone else."

I was not surprised therefore when, after ordering a drink, Geoff turned to me and said in his low, quiet way: "You know I think I'd prefer Addis Ababa to Berlin. The Ethiopians are the only people in the world who dress from the waist up." I smiled, recalling a picture he had once shown me of a group of Abyssinians with voluminous shamas draped across their shoulders and chests, leaving the lower parts of their bodies uncovered.

"But at least," he went on, "the Ethiopians know they're backward. The Germans are usually well covered, but when they strip they can be damned ugly."

His exaggerated gloom was understandable. After all, for weeks he had been preparing himself for his Rome post, and in his intense, conscientious way had been learning the language, studying back reports, reading endless histories and current studies about Italy and her neighbors. Now suddenly his orders had been changed. He must have felt like a skipper who had been preparing for a luxury cruise to the Mediterranean and suddenly found his destination changed to the North Sea. All the cargo he had so carefully stowed had to be taken out and an entirely new cargo assembled and loaded. The charts in his cabin had to be changed. Even his white tropical uniforms had to be replaced by heavy clothes for the cold northern climate. And on top of it all, instead of being the captain he was to be only the navigator, for the post of U.S. Representative, at least nominally, was second to that of the Military Commandant in Berlin.

There was, however, no point in letting him feel sorry for himself. So I reminded him that he had had a pretty good time in Berlin twenty-five years before. "You were practically in love with it then," I said.

He smiled mischievously: "Perhaps. But not quite as actively as you, Harry. I saved my virginity for Russia."

I laughed but felt my face flush at the remark and for a moment we neither of us said anything. When the waiter brought his Scotch and soda he took a long drink before he broke the awkward silence.

"Tell me, Harry, have you ever heard from Annemarie?"

"Not a word since those letters from Stockholm in 1940," I said.

"And you haven't tried to look her up since?"

"I tried to get the Stockholm embassy to find her but after we got in the war I realized it was hopeless." I paused for a moment and lit a cigarette. "I've heard she's back in Berlin now."

"You've heard? You mean you haven't been back to see her?"

"No. I deliberately never went back to Berlin. I don't believe in trying to revive old—" I hesitated, seeking an inoffensive word—"old friendships."

Geoff looked grave. "I hadn't realized you felt that way, Harry, when I asked for you to come with me. I'm sorry—"

"Skip it, Geoff. I'm not all that emotional. I guess it's inevitable we'll meet. But it's all over the dam now as far as I'm concerned, and she too, I guess." And then to change the subject I said something about Berlin's problems and the Wall. Geoff was obviously as eager as I to change the subject, for he at once launched into a monologue about Berlin, and the Berliners.

"The trouble with Berlin," he concluded, "is that everyone there seems to think he's taking part in some sort of crusade to defend the faith."

I objected that in a sense that was exactly what they

were doing—defending the Western democratic faith.

"Perhaps," he answered, thinking out loud. "But it tends to confuse their judgment. They get involved in moral and emotional issues instead of sticking to political realities."

I suggested that with the war, the Russian invasion, the raping and starvation, the blockade and finally the Wall, the Berliners had considerable justification for getting a bit emotional now and then.

"But it's not just the Berliners," Geoff said. "It's everyone who ever goes there, the West Germans, Americans, even Englishmen. The German ambassador here was telling me the other day that whenever they send an official from Bonn to Berlin to represent the West Germans, within a few weeks he becomes an advocate, not of Bonn, but of Berlin." He raised his hands in a gesture of helplessness.

"Look at the Americans right here in Washington who served in Berlin during the blockade: Jim Stevens or Johnny Hale or Rebecca Wells. Whenever you try to discuss Berlin with them they act as if they were born on Unter den Linden."

I suggested that it was nothing new for a diplomat to get attached to his post and exaggerate its importance. "Localitis," we had called it in the service.

"Remember old John Wister when they sent him from Warsaw to Panama? He once wrote me saying Panama was the most vital post in the world."

Geoff laughed. "John was always a special case. Besides, Berlinitis is a much more virulent disease than localitis. The difference between double pneumonia and a runny nose."

When we went upstairs to the dining room on the top

floor we continued to talk of Germany and Berlin.

"The difficulty is, they're all so emotional about it that they can't deal rationally with the Russians," Geoff said.

Uneasily I asked what he meant. He knew the Russians himself and he knew how difficult it was to deal rationally with them under the most normal circumstances.

"Yes, of course they're difficult. But if you understand them and try to see their legitimate interests, there's a chance they'll reciprocate. At least that's the only chance I see of fixing things."

I looked at him questioningly. "Fixing things?"

Geoff smiled. "I had a long talk with the Secretary this morning. He was pretty cagy. He started by asking if there was anything to be done to take the heat off in Berlin and I told him I thought we might make some reasonable arrangements with the Russians if we went about it the right way. And then he suggested that I take the job." Geoff paused and stared out the window at the lights of Washington. Over the treetops we could just see the roof of the White House a block away.

"They're expecting me to straighten out the mess," he said half to himself, and from the direction of his eyes I knew exactly who he meant by "they."

It worried me even then. If Geoff had a fault it was his compulsion to fix whatever he found wrong. Probably it sprang from his sensitivity to injustice, but it had been nurtured by the long string of assignments since the war to trouble spots all over the globe. But Berlin was not just a trouble spot in the ordinary sense. It was the focal point of our differences with the Russians and I suspected that neither Geoff nor anyone else was going to "fix things" in Berlin. That was a job for the Kremlin and the White House alone. Uneasily I remembered Nelly Larsen once saying, "The only trouble with Geoff is he personalizes his job too much."

But I said nothing. Geoff suddenly broke the silence:

"What do you know about Bureau X?" he asked sharply.

"Practically nothing," I said. "I told you I haven't been in Berlin since the war. What one hears down in Bavaria is that it's a sort of secret society which hopes to force the Russians out of the East Zone by sabotage and terror. They burn warehouses, wreck trains, and even try to assassinate East German Communists, hoping to provoke a general uprising that will scare the Russians out. As a matter of fact it sounds so silly to me I rather doubt if the group even exists except in the minds of some ultra-nationalists."

"I hope you're right, but I doubt it. Germans are like that. They get so worked up they get hopelessly irrational. Anyway, we'll have to put a stop to it if we ever hope to come to terms with the Russians."

We had finished dinner and Geoff announced he was going home to bed, so we walked down to the door, where we parted. As we shook hands he seemed unusually solemn. He asked what my immediate plans were and I said I was returning to Bavaria next day. Then he said, "Do me just one more favor, will you?"

I said that of course I would.

"Try to be in Berlin when I get there," he said. "And plan to stay with me." And then after a pause he added,

"It's going to be a bit lonely there at first."

I knew what he meant but there was nothing to say and I turned and went inside and ordered a stiff nightcap. As I drank it I had a feeling I was getting into something bigger than I had bargained for.

II

THE DAY BEFORE GEOFF WAS DUE TO ARRIVE in Berlin I set out by car from my place south of Munich. Except for a mile or two it was autobahn all the way and the little Fiat rolled along easily at eighty miles an hour. Nevertheless, it was getting dark when I reached the border point at Hof in Northern Bavaria, and the West German police strongly urged me not to try to cross the Soviet Zone after dark.

Unlike the Helmstedt-Berlin autobahn the Hof stretch was not authorized for official U.S. use, but until I reached Berlin and was sworn in I was still a private citizen and as such could get an East German visa permitting me to use it. However, the police pointed out there was practically no traffic on the autobahn at night and no one to help me if I had a breakdown or ran into trouble with the Vopos—

the surly, tough East German police. Besides, they said, I would not be allowed to stop even to get dinner along the two-hundred-mile stretch.

Reluctantly I turned back to the town of Hof, got myself a room in a shabby little commercial hotel, and made arrangements to leave early next morning.

A heavy fog had arisen during the night and by the time I reached the East German checkpoint traffic was almost at a standstill. It took me over an hour to get my visa, change my money and pay my toll fees, and it was nearly noon by the time I finally set off along the long, lonely highway to Berlin, which lies like an oasis in the heart of a hostile desert.

By now the sun had burnt off the morning fog and the fields glimmered gold and russet brown in the bright autumn light. As I pushed on as fast as the Soviet speed limit allowed, the countryside at first seemed little different from that on the far side of the border. But I soon began to notice the little telltale signs that I had left the West and had entered the Communist world.

In the fields peasants were digging potatoes and I noticed that most of them were women—a phenomenon common to the Marxist world, where the men have left the field work to the women. The traffic was light and composed chiefly of open trucks—again just as it was even in Moscow, the heart of the Communist empire. The few passenger cars I passed were either shabby old prewar models or else they bore license plates showing that they too came from the West. Each time I passed one of the latter I felt as though I were meeting an ally behind enemy lines.

It was midafternoon when at last I reached the exit point at Berlin. A sullen Vopo searched the car carefully lest I had picked up some East German and was trying to smuggle him into West Berlin. Finding nothing, he grumpily opened the barrier into West Berlin and waved me on.

A half hour later I drove up to the U.S. Representative's villa in Dahlem, a western suburb of Berlin where most of the American installations were located. It was a big, pretentious villa of gray granite, built in the Victorian era—a cross between a neo-Gothic cathedral and a miniature medieval fortress.

The door was opened by a white-coated, cadaverous-looking creature with tiny eyes sunk in deep purple sockets, sallow, hollow cheeks and a bald head. With a stiff bow he introduced himself as Matusek, the butler. Though he looked more like a corpse than a living human, he managed to carry my heavy suitcase from the car.

I had never been in the U.S. Representative's house before, and when the butler disappeared upstairs with my bag I wandered through its great cavernous rooms trying to imagine what sort of person would have chosen to build so pretentious, uncomfortable and gloomy a home.

The main hall beyond the foyer was a big high-ceilinged room designed to resemble a baronial hall in a feudal castle. On one side a great stone fireplace took up most of one wall. Opposite it a wide oak staircase led upward at right angles to a gallery that ran around the entire second floor. The ceiling was supported by heavy oak beams from which was suspended an enormous chandelier made of stags' antlers. The newel posts at each turning of the heavily carved banister resembled great acorns, and from each sprouted a wrought-iron lamp. Halfway up the staircase was a big stained-glass window which cast a yellowish light into the gloomy cave.

Just off the hall, at the right of the front door, was a library paneled in walnut, its walls lined with deep book-cases. It too had a fireplace, smaller than the one in the hall, and beside it on each side were two heavy leather chairs. In one corner the books had been removed from the shelves to make room for a makeshift bar. As I poured myself a drink I recalled a weird tale about this very house that had come out at the Nuremberg trials, to which I was assigned after the war. When the Americans had first taken over the villa after the occupation of Berlin, the security police had discovered that this library was studded with microphones concealed in the bookshelves and connected with an elaborate recording mechanism installed behind the paneling of the master bedroom upstairs.

At the pre-trial interrogations of the Nuremberg Tribunal, a prominent Nazi had revealed the reason for these odd devices. Apparently at the time of Hitler's coming to power the villa had been confiscated from its owner, a wealthy Jewish textile manufacturer, and turned over to a minor Nazi official, a certain Herr Schimmel. Herr Schimmel, the investigators at Nuremberg were told, was a man of no great talent, who had nevertheless managed to survive Hitler's frequent purges almost to the very end of the war, when he was killed by an American bomb as he was crossing the garden from his mistress's house next door.

Herr Schimmel, according to his Nazi colleagues, had

installed the listening devices himself. It had been his practice to invite fellow Nazi party members to dinner, feed them elaborate meals, and then as they sat relaxed in the heavy library chairs, smoking cigars and drinking liberal servings of brandy, he encouraged them to unburden themselves of their complaints and criticisms of their Nazi superiors.

After they had revealed their doubts and troubled thoughts about even the Fuehrer himself, Herr Schimmel would throw a switch and play back to them the recording of their treasonable indiscretions. Then the gracious host would set his price in lieu of hush money: the denunciation of some superior standing in his way; the covering up of some blunder of Herr Schimmel himself; the surrender of some blonde who had caught Herr Schimmel's eye; or even, on one occasion, the liquidation of a Nazi colleague who had begun to suspect Herr Schimmel's method of operations.

As I sat in one of those heavy leather chairs, resting from the strenuous drive and sipping my Scotch, I tried to imagine the anguished expressions of Herr Schimmel's victims sitting in the chair opposite. A shiver ran up my spine at the gruesome picture I had myself evoked and, hastily finishing my drink, I rose and started upstairs.

As I crossed the gloomy baronial hall it annoyed me that, with all the gay, modern, pleasant homes in Dahlem, the most inappropriate for a man in Geoff's depressed state had been chosen as the U.S. Representative's house. But then I remembered the first U.S. Representative during the occupation, a man of little feeling, no taste, and soaring pretensions, who doubtless had been as impressed by its pseudo-baronial splendor as the textile maker who had originally built it.

Matusek followed me upstairs and showed me to my room, where to my annoyance I discovered he had unpacked all my baggage, including my briefcase, the contents of which were carefully laid out on the desk. As I started through the papers looking for some galley proofs of the book I had just finished, Matusek hovered by the door.

"Will there be anything you need?" he asked in a heavy Slav accent, and I made no effort to hide my annoyance when I told him he could go.

Despite three weeks' hard work I had not finished correcting the galleys, and since the publishers were impatient for them I had brought them along. While I waited for Geoff to come back I set to work going over them. Correcting galleys is probably the most boring and time-consuming of a writer's jobs, and I was delighted when after an hour or two I heard Geoff's voice downstairs. I left my papers and hurried down to see him.

Geoff looked tired. He had arrived on the morning plane direct from Washington and all day, accompanied by the American commandant, General Patman, he had attended briefings by various sections of the military and civilian staffs. Whatever he had learned had not seemed to cheer him up.

Apparently the only light spot in their gloomy day had been at a briefing by Patman's security officer, Colonel Ulysses Samson, whom I had known when he was serving in Munich. He was a short, corpulent little man with horn-rimmed spectacles, a face like a moon and a stomach that he vainly tried to conceal behind a tightly buttoned, wrinkled tunic.

As soon as Geoff mentioned his name I smiled: "They used to call him Humpty Dumpty in Bavaria."

"I don't mind his being a simpleton," he said. "What I object to is his illiteracy." As Geoff went on to describe the colonel's briefing I had little difficulty imagining how the garrulously inarticulate soldier had rubbed the meticulous diplomat the wrong way.

Pseudo-psychologists often speak of a person's powers of total recall. I have seldom known anyone with this miraculous faculty, and Geoff's ability to repeat a conversation word for word without missing a single intonation or gesture was the result of no supernatural gift but of endless training during his twenty-five years of diplomatic service. As a scholarly student of diplomats' memoirs he had as a young man learned the importance of repeating a conversation with absolute accuracy, and when reading a colleague's report of an important conversation he had an uncanny faculty for knowing what had actually been said and what was the product of zealous wishful thinking or a bright afterthought or witticism that had occurred to the reporter after the event.

As he described Colonel Samson's briefing, I could easily imagine myself sitting beside him in the underground supersecret operations room on Clayallee.

The squat colonel stood, pointer in hand, by a curtained map and announced, as though he were a cadet at West Point reciting his daily lesson, that his subject was "the security of Berlin in all its facets, intelligent and counter-intelligent." After admonishing Geoff and the general that his remarks and the information behind the screen were classified as "top secret" he had with a dramatic gesture pulled aside the curtain, revealing a map of Berlin which, as Geoff said, could have been bought at any tourist agency.

"The paramount point to be made about the present, actual and current situation in West Berlin is that the situation is, in a nutshell, fraught." He glanced at the commandant as though only they and certainly no newcomer like the civilian Geoffrey Schuyler could appreciate the profundity of the remark.

Street by street he traced the boundaries of the city—boundaries which Geoff knew all too well, for he had helped trace them himself at the interallied conferences in London which set up the postwar occupation. Then he pointed out the Wall, dividing the city almost in half.

"The enemy," he went on, "occupies this area," and he pointed to the East Sector. "Our positions are here," and he tapped the Western Sectors with his pointer. He looked down at Geoffrey with a benevolent smile. "You will pardon these military nomenclatures," he said, "but we here are military men.

"Across this line which we in Berlin call the sector boundary," he went on, "repetitive attempts at what we call in top-secret intelligence parley penetration, infiltration or simple transgression are repeatedly made. These maneuvers are in the bigger majority subterraneous—that is underground, or to put it in layman's language," and he smiled again to Geoff, "sub rosa."

Addressing the commandant again he went on, "But I

must stress, without blowing on anyone's horns, that all such enemy operations—at least since I've been in Berlin—have," he paused a moment for emphasis, "aborted."

The colonel had then gone on to describe what he called his own "counter-transgressions," which he maintained had penetrated every corner of the Soviet Sector and Zone.

After listening only half attentively to his rambling description Geoff finally interrupted him.

"In all these operations, Colonel, have you ever come across an organization called Bureau X?"

Colonel Samson started and looked anxiously at General Patman as though pleading for instructions.

The general looked impatient: "Go ahead, Colonel. I told you that Mr. Schuyler is fully cleared and that you should tell him anything he wants to know, no matter how highly classified."

Samson turned back to Geoff. "Actually we have some information on Bureau X, sir. They are a group of patriotic Germans devoted to the democratic ideal and the liberation of the East Zone from Communist domination."

Obviously annoyed by the colonel's political loquacity, Geoff cut him short. "Precisely what are they doing, Colonel?" he asked impatiently.

"At the moment they might be called quiescent. Their last action about four weeks ago was the blowing up of the East Berlin radio station—it was only a partial success and failed to put it out of action."

"What else?"

"Two months ago they killed a member of the Central

Committee in Leipzig and almost got a Soviet deputy minister of trade. It was very bad luck. Just before that they
set fire to the party headquarters in Dresden and wrecked
a train in Frankfort-on-Oder, carrying machinery to the
Soviet Union. In all, they've succeeded in about two
dozen operations in the past six months, I would estimate—
a pretty good record, all things considered."

Geoff frowned. "Are you or your people cooperating
with them in any way?" he asked.

Once again the colonel looked unhappy and cast a glance
at the general, but Patman this time remained silent, annoyed at the colonel's hesitancy.

"We've merely penetrated them," the colonel said at
last.

"You mean you have Americans in their organization?"

"No, sir. A German—Herr Schmid. He's the Berlin
representative of the Bonn intelligence outfit. He's in contact with them, and of course he's hand-in-pockets with us."

Patman interrupted at this point. "Colonel, I think you
should make clear to Mr. Schuyler that Schmid is only his
cover name."

"Yes, sir," the colonel said, a little abashed. "Schmid is
his *nom-de-guerre*, you might say. We don't know his real
name."

"Are you sure this Schmid tells you everything?" Geoff
asked.

The colonel drew himself up and his answer was indignant. "I can stake my intelligence reputation on my
agents," he said.

Geoff leaned over and whispered in Patman's ear: "Tell

me, Dick, what precisely is the colonel's intelligence reputation?"

The general laughed and the colonel, suspecting that whatever Geoff had said was at his expense, looked bewildered and angry.

"I guess that'll be all," the general had said rising. "I've told Mr. Schuyler to feel free to consult you on any questions that may occur to him later," he added to the colonel as he and Geoff left the hot, stuffy room.

When Geoff had finished his story of the briefing he sat silent for a moment.

"Why is it that most security officers are so stupid, Harry?"

"It's an old army tradition," I answered. "I think it's chiefly due to the fact that you can't make a career in the security branch. Old-time officers don't even consider security a specialty. It's just a slot they have to fill on their staffs and they usually pick the officers who can't do anything else or those who think the title of intelligence officer confers gifts God denied them at birth. But why does Patman put up with Samson?"

"I gather he hasn't much choice. In some quarters of the Pentagon, that childish prattle passes for erudition. I only hope Humpty Dumpty doesn't fall off the wall. And anyway Patman's well aware of his deficiencies."

Geoff stopped and looked at his watch. "By the way, Patman's coming for dinner. Should be here any moment."

Promptly at seven-thirty the general arrived.

Dick Patman was a tall, wiry, vigorous man with prematurely white hair and an open, good-natured, round

face. Soon after the war he and Geoff had gone to the
National War College in Washington together and had
been close friends ever since. He was obviously fond of
Geoff, for after dinner he took me aside and questioned
me about his state of mind. Did I think he was happy in
his new job? What had been the effect of Millicent's sudden death? Was there anything he or his wife could do to
help him?

I told him what I knew of Geoff's selection and added
that he probably knew as well as I how a man as devoted
and intense as Geoff would react under the circumstances.

"It's an awkward situation for both of us in a way,"
Patman said. "Nominally I am the boss, but the job's not
a military one—it's purely political—and that's Geoff's func-
tion. I told him this morning that as commandant I'm supposed to give the orders, and if everything goes all right
I'll get the medals. But Geoff has to call the shots, and if
anything goes wrong his knuckles will get rapped."

It was such an unusual remark for a general to make
that for a moment I looked at him, wondering whether he
was simply trying to impress a person he knew was perhaps Geoff's closest friend. But his expression was so sincere and his words so straightforward my mistrust vanished.

"I also told Geoff," Patman went on, "that as far as
our personal relations were concerned he is the boss. I'll
see to it that our military are ready to do what's demanded
of them. But he's got to tell me what's needed. And the
military staff will back him."

"Does that go for Colonel Samson?" I asked skeptically.

Instead of being angry at my remark Patman laughed.

"Old Samson's a problem, all right, but I think I can handle him."

Geoff broke into the conversation at that moment.

"We were talking about Samson," Patman explained to him.

Geoff smiled sourly. "He's a perfect caricature of a West Point cadet sired by a Prussian Junker."

"As a matter of fact, he's never been near West Point," Patman said. "He's not even a regular but a temporary reserve officer."

"Why's he here then?" Geoff asked.

"He was foisted on my predecessor back in the days of the great witch hunt. At that time he was some sort of administrative assistant to one of those Midwestern senators who saw Commies under every bed except their own. To take the heat off itself after the Zwicker hearings, the Pentagon gave him a commission and sent him here to Berlin. Been here ever since. I have several times hinted that he's due for a transfer, but apparently he likes it, and among certain quarters in the West, the Birchers and all, he's looked upon as the man who's keeping Berlin safe for democracy or something similar."

"Has he any qualifications for the job?" Geoff asked.

"If he has he's keeping them under cover, as he would say. You heard him talk. I doubt if he ever finished eighth grade myself."

"Was he telling me all he knew about Bureau X?" Geoff asked.

"I hope so," the general said. "So far as I know they seem to be a rather quixotic bunch. What are you worried about?"

Geoff scowled. "I've a feeling they're not all that innocent. There's always been a school of Germans who think they're the only ones who understand the Russians and know how to deal with them—and either they make wars on them or make deals with them. Both methods have invariably proved fatal—and not just for the Germans."

"But how could the Germans in their present condition start a war with the Russians?" Patman asked.

"They could provoke them to attack us," Geoff said. "And then where would we be—and particularly yourself, Dick, with your six thousand troops? That's why I'm afraid of these Berliners with their fanatic crusading zeal."

As soon as coffee had been served Patman excused himself and went home. After he had departed Geoff explained that Patman's only obsession was fitness and that he insisted on being in bed by ten o'clock.

I suggested it might be a good idea if we followed his example for once and went up to bed.

Undressing, I thought to myself how lucky we were to have Geoff as our diplomatic representative in this ticklish Berlin situation. A man with less instinctive feeling—less intuition if you will—could easily overlook the dangers in this situation—the shoals and hidden rocks—until we ran aground. But Geoff had always looked far ahead, had always spotted the obstacles in good time to avoid them—though his warnings had not always been heeded.

I remembered his showing me a memorandum he had written years ago in which he had predicted that, when World War II ended, the U.S. would be left alone to defend the free world against a powerful, aggressive Russia. The date on the memo was December, 1941—the month we entered the war. He had shown it to his mission chief, who had urged him to destroy it. To suggest at that time that our brave Russian allies were not trustworthy was considered little short of treason.

III

THAT FIRST WEEK GEOFF AND I WERE both so busy going through the endless bureaucratic procedures of getting installed that we scarcely saw each other except in the evenings. There were security cards and commissary cards and PX cards to get and safe combinations to memorize. Geoff arranged for me to occupy an office adjoining his secretary's room. He offered to get me a secretary but I said I would hardly need one. As his deputy I was entitled to a diplomatic passport, and he insisted I make out an application and send it to Washington, for only the State Department is permitted to issue a diplomatic passport. He also suggested I get official license plates for my Fiat, but I flatly refused, knowing how complicated it would be to get back my old West German plates when my temporary assignment was over.

Fortunately Geoff's subordinate staff was fully familiar

with the routine office work. And Geoff let them all continue as they had before I arrived so that I would be free to handle any special jobs he might have for me.

After I had been photographed and fingerprinted and was installed behind a desk, there was still plenty for me to do just studying back reports and getting to know the staff members. They were a highly competent group but what struck me most was their enthusiasm, amounting almost to fanaticism, about Berlin and its problems. I remembered what Geoff had said in Washington about Berlinitis. He had not, I soon discovered, exaggerated.

One young man called Bill Harmsworth impressed me particularly. He was a short, scrawny fellow in his middle twenties. His reddish brown hair was always in need of combing, with a cowlick on the back of his head that stuck up like a coxcomb. He had a thin, solemn face, but his eyes were bright and twinkled incessantly as though he found life very agreeable. When he grinned two deep dimples showed on his drawn cheeks, and a gap in his upper teeth where a front tooth had been chipped off gave him an almost schoolboy look.

He told me he had come to Berlin as a student at the Free University, and after he had graduated he got a job with the Central Intelligence Agency, which in turn had assigned him to Geoff as a sort of private intelligence assistant. In his free time he said he was still doing postgraduate work at the university, specializing in political science. When I mentioned him to Geoff he commented rather laconically: "He's a live wire all right. I only hope he doesn't short circuit."

If that first week was full for me it was hectic for Geoff. He was still determined to "fix things" in Berlin and insisted on crowding all his routine chores into his first days so that he would be free to tackle his major tasks as soon as possible. That meant calling on his British and French opposite numbers, making a ceremonial appearance at the Rathaus to meet the governing mayor and the city councilors, or senators as they call themselves in Berlin, receiving the senior members of the staff and finally, at Patman's insistence, inspecting the American garrison and observing their maneuvers as they went through their various exercises.

The first really free moment we had was on Sunday. It was one of those beautiful warm autumn days for which Berlin is famous. The air was clear, the sky brilliant blue, and the bright sun lit up the russet leaves of the beeches in Geoff's garden.

In the old days before the war we would have driven out to one of the lakes beyond the city limits or taken an excursion to one of the old towns in Brandenburg. But now the zonal boundary confined not only ourselves but all the two million West Berliners to the Western Sector hermetically sealed off by the Wall and the high barbed-wire fences.

After breakfast Geoff suggested a walk in the Grunewald. We strolled down through Dahlem, across Clayallee and into what once had been a forest of tall pines. During the Blockade in the forties much of it had been chopped down for fuel, and the new growth, though thick, was only a few feet high.

The paths that meandered through the park were crowded with Sunday strollers. They were of all ages: young couples walking hand in hand pretending that they were alone in the forest; old couples with equally ancient dogs on leashes; children rushing through the crowded paths bumping into their ill-tempered elders.

We had only been out an hour when Geoff stopped suddenly and said, "This is giving me claustrophobia." He suggested that we take a cab and drive down to the Kurfuerstendamm, the main street of West Berlin.

As we drove toward the center of town Geoff peered curiously out the window, trying to orient himself and identify old landmarks, but most of them had been destroyed and what remained were either ruins or had been rebuilt in unrecognizable forms. Several times he asked the taxi driver where we were or what a passing ruin had once been.

"You're new to Berlin?" the taxi driver asked at last.

"I left before the war," Geoff said, "and haven't been back since."

"You haven't missed much," the taxi driver remarked laconically and Geoff laughed aloud.

He told the driver to drop us off at the Brandenburg Gate. Just in front of the gate a double barrier of barbed wire had been strung. On the west a British tommy was standing guard and behind the wire a group of Vopos were strolling about. As we walked up to the barbed wire they watched us intently through their field glasses.

Geoff pointed to the flattened ruins of a large building just to the right of the gate and east of the wall.

"The good old Bluecher Palace," he said nostalgically. Before the war the Bluecher Palace had housed our embassy and we had both spent many tedious hours in its code room deciphering cables. But ironically now only a few feet of its old walls remained standing and formed a portion of the new Wall dividing the city.

"I wonder—" Geoff began to say, but stopped short. Then he turned around and I followed him into the Tiergarten.

Like the Grunewald it had once been a forest of great elms and beeches, but now it was scarcely more than a garden of shrubbery. Here and there you could still see the gnarled trunk of one of the old trees, scarred by shell fire, its branches stumped and twisted.

Before the war Tiergartenstrasse had been the most fashionable street in town, lined with Victorian villas set far back in private gardens of their own. But most of the villas had been completely destroyed during the Battle of Berlin and only jungles of weeds remained in their once formal gardens.

At the far end of the park we turned into Rauchstrasse and headed south toward the canal. At one point I stopped and peered through a barrier of overgrown shrubbery and brambles at the remains of a burnt-out villa. Its walls were still standing but the roof was gone and the windows were blank holes. Through them we could see weeds and even small trees sprouting from the interior ledges. The lintels were black and charred. As we stood there staring at the ruin I tried to imagine how it had looked that day when it had burnt, the flames first consuming the heavy gold brocade curtains inside and then breaking through the glass and curling outward and upward seeking more timber to consume.

I pointed up at one of the second-story windows. "That was her bedroom," I said, and my voice suddenly sounded strangely hoarse. As though to break the spell, Geoff hurried on across the canal toward the hideous stump of the Gedaechtnis Kirche.

The Kurfuerstendamm was crowded with Sunday strollers just as it had always been. Many of the buildings were new but the names of the side streets and the stores were the same. The beer gardens and sidewalk cafés were teeming with fat Berliners drinking coffee heaped with whipped cream, while others in their fashionable clothes were window shopping or carefully examining the clothes of their fellow strollers.

We went into one of the big beer gardens, took a table near the sidewalk and each ordered a glass of beer. We drank silently and for a long time not a word passed between us. Geoff sensed where my thoughts were and refrained from intruding into the memories evoked by that charred old ruin in Rauchstrasse, where Annemarie had once lived with her widower father.

When we were assigned to Berlin in the late thirties, the Nazi regime had been in power for several years. The once cosmopolitan, often brilliant international society of the capital had long since been pushed into the background by the coarse, arrogant Nazi hordes. Many of its most prominent members had been forced into emigration because their genealogies were not purely Aryan. Others, revolted by their new masters, had retired to their estates, where they lived in lonely, shabby grandeur. The few who had stuck it out clustered about the foreign embassies like bees, sucking up the foreign luxuries—whiskey, coffee, even butter and cream, which, despite their wealth, Hitler's autarchic economy had deprived them of.

Soon after our arrival Geoff and I were invited to a reception by the ambassador—the first and last time in the years we were there that we set foot in his house. He was a parsimonious old history professor, who considered diplomacy a rather nefarious profession and to show his contempt for it spent his days proclaiming his dislike of everything German in general and everything Nazi in particular—which did not make him the most successful ambassador in Berlin.

Born and raised in a small college town, he found diplomatic entertainment an awkward chore because, I always suspected, he had little social charm and found any conversation not involving American history either boring or frightening, like swimming beyond his depth, for he was basically, despite his brave denunciations of Germany, a rather timid little man.

When Geoff and I went up to pay our respects he was cordial enough and offered us each a cocktail. He watched me curiously as I took a sip and asked me how I liked it. Though it tasted like stale canned fruit juice I managed to say that it was excellent.

"Eight parts pineapple juice and one part gin," he said grinning slyly. "If you know how, you can handle a couple of hundred guests on one bottle of liquor."

As quickly as we could Geoff and I slipped off among the guests. In the next room my eye was caught by a tall, black-haired girl of about twenty, whose wide brown eyes met mine with a frank, self-assured gaze. I went up and introduced myself.

Annemarie was not perhaps beautiful, but she was remarkably handsome in an almost masculine way. She wore her black hair almost shoulder length, so that it framed her oval face and emphasized her clear, pallid skin. The points of her high cheekbones were a bright red. Above her big, dark brown eyes, a thin line of carefully plucked black eyebrows swept in an oriental curl across her smooth, round forehead. Her gestures were vigorous and suggested a determined self-confidence. Her words were no less forceful.

Her eyes searched the crowd around us with a scornful look.

"If you'll excuse my rudeness," she said in perfect English, "your ambassador can collect the weirdest assortment of people in all Berlin." Slightly embarrassed, I only smiled, for I was after all our host's humble servant.

"I can't blame him for not inviting the government crowd. My father won't have a Nazi in his house either. Neither would I. But where does the ambassador find those frowzy old ladies and those awful schoolteacher types with bad breath?"

She tasted the cocktail and made a wry face. I grinned and barely restrained myself from repeating what the ambassador had just said about its ingredients.

Suddenly she gave me a pleading look. "Let's get out of here," she said. "Have you a car?"

I said I had and we slid toward the door as unobtrusively as possible.

When we climbed into my car, I looked at her questioningly.

"Let's go to my house. My father can mix a marvelous martini."

So we drove to Rauchstrasse, where I met old Herr Dahlmann for the first time. At least he seemed very old to me then, but I daresay he was barely past fifty. He was a big, heavy-set man with a red and good-natured face and sparse sandy hair. At Annemarie's suggestion he fixed a pitcherful of excellent dry martinis. He took one himself and then left us, saying he had some work to do in his study.

When he had gone, Annemarie told me he was a banker and represented some big Swedish financial institutions. Her mother, she said, had died when she was a small child. Ever since she could remember, she told me, he had had a mistress whom she referred to as "Tante Viktoria." Tante Viktoria apparently did not stay at Rauchstrasse but at a small villa Herr Dahlmann had inherited on Mueggelsee, a large lake in the eastern suburbs of Berlin.

Annemarie was obviously devoted to her father and only with difficulty did I manage to turn the conversation to herself. Self-deprecatingly she told me she was studying law at Berlin University.

"Not that law plays much of a role in this Nazi-ridden place," she said bitterly. "But when we get rid of them I think we'll need some lawyers about, if only to remind us what laws are for. And anyway," she added after a moment, "it gives me something to do."

It was after seven when I rose to go, but when I went in to say good-bye to Herr Dahlmann he insisted I stay for dinner. He was obviously something of a bon vivant, for the food was excellent, which was unusual in Berlin in those days, and he opened a very good bottle of Burgundy, explaining he had laid in a large stock just before Herr Hitler had shut off all luxury imports.

During dinner he questioned me closely about immigration into the United States. I explained to him that, because of the flight of Jews, the German quota was full and the waiting time for visas was several years. He seemed surprised that the quota applied to non-Jews as well as Jews.

"You mean we so-called Aryans have to wait too?"

Annemarie burst into laughter. "What did you think, Papa? That your Aryan blood entitled you to certain privileges?"

Her father smiled guiltily. "I suppose I did. That's what happens to you after a few years of Nazi propaganda."

"And why this sudden interest in American visas?" Annemarie went on.

"Well, I was just thinking if things get much worse here. . . ."

"Don't be ridiculous, Papa. You know perfectly well you'll never leave Berlin no matter how bad it gets. You've always said you were born at Mueggelsee and are going to die there."

Shortly after dinner I said good-bye but not before I had made a date to take Annemarie to dinner several nights later. Back at the apartment which Geoff and I shared, I told Geoff about Annemarie. I tried to be as casual as possible and act as though she were just another of many young ladies I had met in Berlin. But I must have made a poor job of it. At any rate Geoff smiled knowingly and warned me to control my enthusiasm, because in those days Foreign Service officers were practically forbidden to marry foreigners—especially Germans. At that time they occupied about the same position in American public opinion as the Russians do today.

Despite Geoff's warning I saw Annemarie frequently from then on. Once she gave a cocktail party at Rauchstrasse to celebrate her twenty-first birthday and insisted I bring Geoff. All the other guests were young Germans, mostly in smart military uniforms. Their wavy blond hair and erect, arrogant bearing and Teutonic good looks rather irritated me, and when I asked Annemarie if she planned to marry one of them she burst into roars of laughter. "Those poor simpletons?" she said. "All they can think about is their horses and their regiment. They still think they're in the nineteenth century. They bore me to death. What's more they'll all be killed when the war finally comes and I have no intention of being left a widow at thirty."

But one of the guests was not in uniform and the reason was obvious, for he walked with a marked limp. Nor did he look like those handsome young Aryans in uniform. He had a round, moonlike face and his ears stuck out almost at right angles from his skull. He and Geoff had struck up a conversation and I asked Annemarie who he was. She told me he was a neighbor and childhood friend. Presently he was studying law with her at the university. I felt a twinge of jealousy until she said:

"Poor Max. I'm afraid he's always been a little in love with me. I'm very fond of him and he's terribly bright but he's hardly my type." She took me over to introduce me. His name was Ebers, and as I shook hands I noticed he was wearing a Nazi party button. He must have caught my glance because he laughed. "Don't worry, Mr. Harding. I'm not really a dreadful Nazi. I simply had to join the party to be admitted to law school. Annemarie as a girl is luckier. All she had to do was prove she was Aryan, as we say here."

Later Annemarie told me more about Max Ebers. He was from an old East Prussian Junker family. His ancestors for several generations had all been generals and he too had been destined for the army, but he had crushed his foot in a riding accident when he was a child. "He'll never get over it," Annemarie said. "He's frightfully patriotic—a nationalist you would say—even though he hates the Nazis. Seeing all these empty-headed young fools in uniform must hurt him dreadfully, but he insisted on coming."

He and Geoff had taken a liking to each other, and when the party broke up the four of us went out to dinner together. Max suggested a little bar off Kurfuerstendamm called the Bird Cage. It was small and crowded and the dance floor was hardly larger than a Persian prayer rug. But the food and drink were good and the music excellent. The proprietor, who also tended the bar and occasionally took a turn at the piano, was a huge, athletic-looking man with a great unkempt mop of curly brown hair. His name was the same as mine, Harry (it is oddly enough a fairly common name in Berlin). And he seemed to know practically all his clients by name, which was all the more remarkable because Harry was stone blind. Max explained that he had an uncanny faculty for remembering voices and could almost invariably tell where a person came from simply by his accent.

After he had placed us at a tiny table in the corner he went back to the piano. Max called to him and asked for his theme song. With a flourish he began to play a popular tune of that time, "A Tisket, a Tasket," and as he did so many of the guests joined in the chorus:

> A Tisket, a Tasket,
> Put Hitler in a basket.

Geoff and I exchanged nervous looks, for diplomats are not supposed to associate publicly with rebels. Max laughed. "Don't worry. Practically everyone here loathes the regime. It's a regular anti-Nazi hangout. They seem to think Harry's blindness is a protection, and as a matter of fact it is. The Gestapo have always been suspicious of the place and they've questioned him about his clientele several times, but he claims he doesn't know who they are because he can't see."

We had a pleasant evening. When Geoff danced with Annemarie, I had a chance to talk to Max and found him a sensitive, clever and articulate young man. As Annemarie warned, he was an ardent nationalist but not disagreeably so and not at all arrogant or boastful.

It was past midnight when I took Annemarie home. She asked me in for a nightcap and explained that her father was staying the night, as he often did when business was light, at his place at Mueggelsee with Tante Viktoria. When finally I kissed Annemarie goodnight she took me by the hand and without a word led me upstairs.

That was the first time I ever slept with her. Next day

was Sunday. It was a warm spring day and together we drove out to Mueggelsee and had lunch with Herr Dahlmann and Tante Viktoria. She turned out to be a very dignified lady in her late forties, tall, gray-haired, with a long, slender neck, an unusual, handsome face and that soft complexion you see in women who grow up in mild northern climates.

After lunch Herr Dahlmann took us for a cruise in his speedboat. We rode around the lake and then up the Spree River and through a network of canals, arriving back at the Mueggelsee just before dark. As usual Herr Dahlmann mixed us a martini before we started back to Rauchstrasse, where I dropped Annemarie. When I finally returned to the apartment Geoff looked relieved but discreetly asked no questions.

From then on I saw Annemarie almost daily. On weekends we sometimes went to Mueggelsee and spent the night in a little room Annemarie had fixed up above the boathouse. Herr Dahlmann and Tante Viktoria seemed to regard our relationship as the most natural thing in the world, but he alluded to it only once, when he said to me alone: "After all, Hitler's going to get us into a war sooner or later and then everything will be finished. So I want Annemarie to get all she wants out of life while she still can."

Occasionally we spent the weekend at Schloss Marquardt, an old country estate which had been taken over by Kempinski, the Jewish restaurant owner, and fixed up as a luxurious weekend hotel where Berlin couples came on their honeymoons or with their mistresses. Kempinski himself had of course been dispossessed by now, but the Nazis who had been regular clients before they came to power kept the manager and continued to run it.

Many of the Nazi bigwigs still came, but we seldom saw them for we usually spent the day walking through the woods and parks and dined early. But one evening we lingered a little longer than usual over dinner. The dance band was playing when Dr. Ley, Hitler's Labor Minister and a particularly lecherous old man, came into the dining room with his aide. He caught sight of Annemarie and stared at her for a full minute before he took his seat. He was talking loudly and was obviously drunk.

We were about to leave when his aide came up and told Annemarie Dr. Ley would like to dance with her. Annemarie declined as quietly but as firmly as she could, but the aide persisted. Eventually I pointed out that Annemarie was not dancing and suggested the man leave. We rose to go but Dr. Ley, who had been watching, headed us off as we made for the door and caught Annemarie by the arm. Flaring furiously, she swung round and gave him a resounding slap on his fat, florid cheek. Dr. Ley withdrew a step, but the aide pushed forward and I just managed to get between him and Annemarie. He spluttered and threatened to have us arrested, until I pointed out that as a diplomat I was immune from arrest. Finally he cooled down enough for us to get away and up to our room.

Annemarie seemed completely calm and unruffled when we finally went to bed, but the incident worried me and I scarcely slept. After all, Annemarie had no immunity. As a German she could be arrested by the Nazis whenever they wanted. Furthermore, it was no problem to find out from the management who she was. There was only one way I could protect her and get her out of the country. That was to marry her. Till then I had never seriously thought about our future. Our relationship had all been so natural and simple. We had never discussed marriage. I knew it would mean the end of my diplomatic career, but then there were plenty of jobs I could get back home.

When the dawn began to seep through the drawn curtains, Annemarie was lying in the crook of my arm, apparently sleeping peacefully. As I looked down at her face, her eyes opened and she frowned. "Stop fretting," she mumbled. "Nothing's going to happen to me."

At breakfast I broached the subject of marriage. She burst out laughing: "And let you give up your career? Are you mad? What sort of a life does that leave me? Every time anything goes wrong or your job gets too boring, who will there be to blame—just little Annemarie. No thank you, silly. And stop worrying. Those brutes won't dare bother me for fear of the scandal. Thank God no one in the restaurant saw it."

Later when I told Geoff about the incident he was worried, but when I said I wanted to marry Annemarie he frowned and tried to dissuade me. When I stuck to my decision, however, he smiled gently. "I suggest you let Annemarie make the decision," he said.

For the time being, both Geoff and Annemarie turned out to be right. She refused to consider marriage and the Gestapo left her alone. At least there were no immediate repercussions to the aide's threats. The very lack of action emboldened her and encouraged her to be even more outspoken against the regime. At about that time she seemed to have established contact with what had survived of the old German Socialist movement. She seldom referred to them and then only half jokingly. I think she was afraid I would interfere, as indeed I would have had I known how deeply she was involved, for I was well aware how thoroughly the Socialist underground was infiltrated by the Gestapo.

Once she asked me to talk to one of her friends, and when I came to Rauchstrasse I found a gray little man with pince-nez and a sallow, pinched expression, which looked as though it had been acquired in a concentration camp. He asked me whether it would be possible to get in contact with my government and obtain some sort of assurance from it if the Socialists staged an uprising to oust Hitler. After checking with Nelly Larsen, who was then counselor of the embassy, I told him that the United States government could have no association with any anti-government group or give it any sort of assurances. Annemarie was upset with this reply and scolded me for not being more determined. I retorted that she did not fully understand how little influence vice consuls had in the counsels of the great in Washington.

A few weeks later she asked me to exchange several thousand marks for dollars. Again I had to tell her we were strictly forbidden to exchange currency except through official channels, and again she was angry.

Shortly after that we dined one night at the Bird Cage, and when we left I noticed several truckloads of young men roaring through the streets. A few minutes later the sky lit up and someone said a synagogue at Marienfelde had been set afire. I started to drive toward it, but on the way we came across a gang of young toughs raising havoc in a row of small Jewish shops, breaking windows, looting and beating up the protesting owners. Though several policemen were watching they did nothing to stop the riot.

Blind with anger, Annemarie leaped from the car, though I warned her not to, and began upbraiding the young men. A small Jewish boy—he could hardly have been twelve—was weeping on the sidewalk while his father was being beaten and kicked by the ruffians. Then one of the men turned to the boy and began kicking him. He fell screaming to the ground just as Annemarie and I reached him. I held off the tough while Annemarie seized the child and dragged him to the car. Several of the tough's companions were soon on top of me, and the next thing I knew I was lying on the pavement with a very sore head. A policeman was bending over me. He had my diplomatic identification card in his hand and was asking me where I lived, obviously concerned that a foreign diplomat had been beaten up.

By the time I got to my feet I saw the car was gone and realized that Annemarie had had the good sense to get the small boy out of the riot. When the police finally drove me home I telephoned at once to Annemarie and then Geoff drove me over to Rauchstrasse. Annemarie was beside herself with indignation. She had dressed the little boy's cuts and put him to bed and was trying to get in touch with his parents. A little while later a terrified Jewish woman, wrapped to her eyes in a shawl, rang the doorbell to claim her son.

The pogrom, now known as the Crystal Night, actually

lasted for three full days. Several synagogues were burned to the ground. Every Jewish store in town, including some of the largest department stores, was looted and wrecked, and thousands of Jewish families were more or less severely beaten up, some of them killed and others carted off to concentration camps.

From then on Annemarie made no secret of her feelings for the Nazis, despite my protests and those of her father. Only when an anonymous friend telephoned her and said she was about to be arrested did she show any concern. Herr Dahlmann by now was terrified for his daughter. He immediately got in touch with a young, ill-paid police official whom he happened to know, and, armed with a large packet of Reichsmarks, he managed to get Annemarie a passport. But when he tried to get an exit visa he was firmly rebuffed. He did succeed, however, in getting a visa to Sweden through his banking connections.

Meantime, Geoff and I had persuaded Annemarie to move to our apartment, where she enjoyed a certain degree of safety, since the police were reluctant to enter diplomatic quarters even in search of German citizens.

We had just finished dinner one evening when the phone rang and I answered it. It was Herr Dahlmann and his voice sounded strangely casual as he asked if by any chance Annemarie was with us. Since he knew very well she was I asked if he was alone. He told me that some friends of Annemarie had called and wanted to know when she would be back. Obviously the police were at Rauchstrasse waiting for her. Assuming that our phone was tapped I said that Annemarie would be home in about an hour.

Five minutes later Annemarie and I were heading north

on the autobahn to Hamburg in my Mercedes. Behind us Geoff was following in his Fiat sports car. There was no speed limit on the autobahn; even if there had been I was in no mood to dawdle and kept the Mercedes wide open. The Fiat easily kept pace. It was well past midnight when we by-passed Hamburg and took the road to the Danish frontier. There was not a sign of a car following us and we thought we had given the police the slip.

We said little during the drive. Annemarie was grim now, and though she showed no signs of fear she was determined to get away. There was no more flippant talk as there had been a few weeks before about the quiet of a concentration camp. She was in a fighting mood.

We were hardly twenty miles from the frontier when Geoff signaled with his lights that a car was following him. Although we had left the autobahn now and the road was narrow and winding, I stepped on the accelerator and drove the car as fast as it would go. But soon I could make out the lights of the car following Geoff. Fortunately we had anticipated being followed and had carefully planned our strategy before we left the apartment.

Annemarie was holding the map in her lap and reading it with the aid of a flashlight. A sign reading ten kilometers to the frontier flashed past. Then in the rear view mirror I saw the car behind Geoff overtaking him. Knowing they could catch us, I slowed and let the car, a big Horch, speed on past us. I guessed that they wanted to get in front so that they could halt us at the frontier. Since both our cars had diplomatic plates it would have been illegal to stop us elsewhere. For all its brutalities and stupidities, the Gestapo was still a stickler for protocol.

The red tail lights of the Horch had disappeared ahead of us when Annemarie spoke.

"Another half kilometer, I make it," she said, her voice low but steady.

Another sign indicating an intersection caught the glare of our lights.

"Now," Annemarie said. I slammed on the brakes and just managed to skid around onto a dirt country road which according to our map led to an isolated frontier station ten miles east of the main one on the highway. A moment later I saw Geoff's lights still following. So far everything had worked according to plan, but the tricky part was still ahead. The road was bumpy and twisting and I had to slow to barely forty miles an hour. We still had seven kilometers to go. Geoff had slowed down now and I could hardly make out his lights far behind.

"Three kilometers," Annemarie said as we crossed an iron trestle bridge scarcely wide enough for two cars. "Just what Geoff's looking for," I murmured as we clattered across it. On the far side I stopped and hastily Annemarie crawled into the trunk compartment behind. I kissed her and slammed the lid shut.

Behind me I could see Geoff's lights, and my heart sank as I saw another set of lights coming over a hill half a mile behind him. As I started up I heard Geoff's brakes screech and saw his lights veer off the road.

A couple of minutes later I saw the steel barrier of the customs station ahead. A single German guard was standing idly by it.

As I drew up I handed him my diplomatic passport. Slowly and diligently he looked at it, turning page by page just the way all frontier guards do, even when they can't read. I tried to control my impatience and seem casual. At last he handed it back to me, saluted and moved toward the barrier. He was about to raise it when the sound of another car could be heard coming up behind.

Before I knew it their headlights were glaring in my rear view mirror. It looked as though they would be on us in a second. But then someone shouted at the guard and he turned belligerently and motioned him to be quiet. One does not shout at officials in Germany. Deliberately he raised the barrier. The Mercedes was already in gear and I shot through. A moment later a Danish soldier raised the barrier on his side of the frontier and motioned me to stop. From the commotion thirty yards down the road at the German station he must have guessed what was happening. With a sly grin he handed me back the passport and waved me on.

That evening I saw Annemarie off on the ferry to Sweden and next day I drove slowly back to Berlin. Geoff had preceded me. The Fiat was in the garage with a crumpled fender where he had rammed the iron bridge. For several days we waited fearfully to be summoned to the counselor's office and be told we had been declared persona non grata by the Germans. But all that came was a curt note from the Foreign Office saying that the police had reported Vice Consul Schuyler for drunken and reckless driving in the neighborhood of the Danish frontier. The Gestapo never liked to admit failure.

I had never seen Annemarie since. For some months we had corresponded regularly. She had found an apartment in a Stockholm suburb and was busy working, though she never told me what sort of a job she had. Then I was transferred back to Washington and a few weeks later the war broke out. I tried to keep in touch with her through our embassy in Stockholm, but our overworked staff there apparently decided that their wartime tasks took precedence over the love affairs of vice consuls.

IV

I WAS STILL THINKING OF ANNEMARIE when Geoff rose abruptly. Hastily I finished my beer and we took a taxi to Geoff's office on Clayallee. It was a habit of twenty years' standing that, except on one of his rare vacations, Geoff stopped at his office at least once a day whether a workday or Sunday to go over the latest cables. It was a sort of addiction with him, like smoking cigarettes, and until he had gone through the stack of yellow sheets in the code room he was always uneasy and restless.

I left him at the office and drove the few blocks to the house. I let myself in with a key and went to my room to do some work on the galley proofs of my book. But as I picked up the first uncorrected sheet I realized something was wrong. Though I had left them untouched since the night before I remembered exactly where in the story I had stopped, and now I found a different galley on top of the pile. I checked the numbers and discovered that galley No. 89 was missing. Carefully I went through the entire heap, checking each page, but No. 89 was not among them.

Annoyed, I searched around the room, suspecting a breeze might have blown it off the desk. I looked behind the chairs and under the bed. I even rolled back the rug, thinking it might somehow have slipped under it. Perhaps it had been blown out the window, and I started to go down to the garden to look, but then I saw the windows were all fly-screened.

Thinking I might have accidentally stuffed the sheet I was working on in a drawer I took out all the drawers of the desk, but still no galley. By now I was thoroughly angry, though I couldn't decide what or whom I was angry at—except myself for being so stupid as to lose a sheet of printed paper three feet long.

I was on my hands and knees starting to roll back the carpet for a second look when I was conscious of someone standing in the doorway behind me. I wheeled around and found Matusek, looking more corpselike than ever, staring down at me with those deep-sunk little eyes.

Jumping up I explained to him about the missing galley.

"Was it very secret?" he asked, speaking German in a Slav accent.

"It wasn't secret at all," I snapped. "It was a passage from a book that is about to be published." He seemed relieved that I was not just a mad carpet chewer.

"It can't be far," he said. "I am the only one who has been in here except yourself." Then he joined in the search and once again we tore the room apart but without result. We had just about given up when we heard Geoff come in. So we abandoned the search and I joined Geoff in the library while Matusek went off to get the lunch.

Not wanting to worry him with my personal problems, I said nothing about the missing galley, but I did ask him about his strange butler. He told me that he had been engaged by the personnel office of the U.S. headquarters and that he was a refugee from Czechoslovakia. Beyond that and the fact that he was a competent butler, he knew nothing except that he had been carefully screened by the U.S. Security Branch.

"He has a rather funereal air," Geoff admitted. "But it seems to fit into the atmosphere of this tomb."

After lunch Geoff suggested we make a tour of the Wall—the iniquitous barrier the Communists had erected across the whole of Berlin to keep their exasperated subjects from escaping to the West. He telephoned Bill Harmsworth and asked him to take us around. "I'm told he knows Berlin better than any other American here," Geoff said.

Harmsworth showed up a few minutes later and suggested we ride in his car, a dilapidated old Jaguar. As he drove he told us how the East Germans had taken the Americans completely by surprise when they put up the Wall that August night in 1961.

The stream of refugees that had been crossing into the West ever since the Blockade had been relatively constant, he said, until July, 1961. Then the Russians began threatening a quick settlement of the Berlin problem by force, and the inhabitants of the East Sector and the Zone panicked and came across in droves.

"They were coming at the rate of several thousand a day by the beginning of August, and it was obvious that unless someone stopped them there'd soon be no one left in the East except the people who couldn't walk.

"The only effective way to stop them was to build a fence, but that wasn't so easy. As you'll see, the boundary between the East and West Sectors is a crazy zigzag line through the heart of the town. It runs through the middle of parks and squares, and even cemeteries. In some places the front door of a house opens on the East Sector and the back door on the West."

The idea of running a fence across the city therefore seemed to the Americans in Berlin almost too absurd to be possible. "As for Washington, those guys apparently never even thought of it," Harmsworth said contemptuously.

An impatient grunt from Geoff, who was sitting in the front seat beside him, made him pause and turn questioningly to him. "That is not entirely accurate, Harmsworth," Geoff said sharply.

Harmsworth realized he had stepped on someone's toe and looked worried. "I only meant that was the impression . . ."

"Well, the impression was wrong. Perhaps the CIA thought that way but at State we always reckoned with the possibility."

Like most older diplomats, Geoff considered the CIA a mixture of necessary evil and amateur incompetence. Bill Harmsworth for a moment looked unhappy but then went on.

"Well, I guess our boys here should have got wind of

it but they didn't. The first people who did were the taxi drivers. Around three in the morning that Sunday some of them coming back to the West Sector from taking late fares into the East reported to their offices by radiophone that something strange was brewing. They said that unusually large numbers of Vopos were being assembled along the border and that they were bringing up tanks and truckloads of barbed wire. The cab companies warned their drivers not to take any more fares across the boundary, but they never thought of notifying us."

"By the time we got up on Sunday there was a wire fence right across town manned by Vopos and police dogs. It wasn't too effective at first. Within the first couple of days hundreds of people got through. But little by little the Commies stopped the gaps and replaced the wire with a six-foot concrete wall. And they also began to shoot to kill."

We had arrived at the northernmost point of West Berlin, where the boundary meets the outer perimeter of the city bordering on the Soviet Zone. Here the boundary ran through fields and meadows, for although Berlin is one of Europe's greatest cities almost half of it consists of parks, forests and even farmland. We drove up a well-paved road which Bill explained was once a main highway to northern Germany. Suddenly we reached a deep ditch across the road with a high mound beyond it. To both right and left barbed wire stretched across the fields. We got out and Geoff jumped across the ditch onto the mound.

"I wouldn't do that, sir," Bill warned. "Those bastards are pretty careless with their triggers." But Geoff paid no attention and stood looking out over the fields. Suddenly from nowhere two men in the gray-blue uniform of the Vopos appeared out of a concealed dugout just beyond the wire. One of them trained his field glasses on Geoff. The other with a loud click slipped a cartridge into the chamber of his rifle.

"Please, sir," Bill pleaded. "It's really hardly worth it."

Geoff stared angrily at the dirty-faced, ill-uniformed men opposite him as though to defy them, but then he thought better of it and jumped lightly back across the ditch.

Making our way south we came across an area of small gardens—scores of them, each enclosed by a little fence and each with a tiny shack—where for generations Berliners had cultivated their flowers and vegetables and in the summer months spent their weekends. The boundary ran straight through this patchwork of plots. On the far side of it, the enclosures had been flattened by bulldozers and the little shacks razed. Here and there the charred remnants of debris lay black and rotting. Halfway across the devastated strip of no-man's land ran a deep trench, and from time to time we could see the head of an East German soldier poking above the breastwork and examining us through field glasses.

Further south in the built-up areas the fence became a high concrete wall surmounted by strands of barbed wire or broken bottles set in cement. In places the boundary ran along the western curb of the street so that we had to leave the car and squeeze between the blocks of cement and the houses across the narrow sidewalk.

At Bernauerstrasse in the French Zone, the boundary coincided with house fronts on the eastern side of the street. Almost every window was sealed with bricks, and Harmsworth explained that in the first days of the Wall hundreds had escaped by leaping from the windows and even from the roofs. We passed a heap of funeral wreaths on the sidewalk and he told us that it marked the spot where an old man had died jumping from the roof.

At the end of the street the Wall crossed the road and there a crowd of schoolboys were standing taunting the Vopos on the other side. Suddenly a smoldering stick arched over the wall and landed at the boys' feet. Laughing they ran back a few yards as the stick exploded with a sharp report and belched out a white cloud of smoke.

"Get to windward," Harmsworth warned. "That's tear gas."

Further on we came to where a railroad bridge crossed the River Spree connecting West and East. At the far end a group of Communist railroad police in their somber black uniforms were standing guard.

"Those are the real bastards," Bill told us. "They always shoot to kill."

"And the Vopos?" I asked.

"At first they only shot occasionally and either they couldn't or they deliberately didn't aim," Harmsworth answered. "But now," he added, "they all aim."

Just after they built the Wall, he said, a young East Berliner had tried to swim the Spree at this point. The Vopos on the bank had fired volley after volley all around him as he bobbed about in the water but none had come close to him. Then the railroad police had started shooting, and with a few rounds had killed him.

Our next stop was at the Brandenburg Gate. Back of the wire the Vopos once again fixed us with their field glasses as we walked up to the barrier. Geoff pointed to the ruins of the Bluecher Palace and asked Harmsworth: "Has anyone ever tried to reclaim that?"

Harmsworth looked puzzled till Geoff explained that the ruin was our old embassy.

"I never knew that," Harmsworth said. "I don't suppose there's anyone in the whole headquarters who has ever thought about it."

Geoff grunted. "Well, it's American property even if it is on the wrong side of the Wall," he said.

Back in the car we drove around Potsdamerplatz, past Checkpoint Charlie on Friedrichstrasse, and on southward. Then Harmsworth stopped the car again at a spot where the Wall made a U-bend eastward around a small churchyard separating it from its church, which was in the East Sector. Harmsworth told us that several people had escaped by jumping from the church windows until the Communists had closed it.

"They say that if we'll give them the churchyard they'll reopen the church," he added.

"Why don't we?" Geoff asked sharply. Harmsworth looked surprised.

"But, sir, we can't give away any territory to *them*. That would be appeasement. Besides, the churchyard's full of graves and you know how sentimental Germans are about their ancestral remains."

Geoff grimaced but said nothing and strolled thoughtfully back to the car.

"I've had enough of this," he said finally as we took our seats. "Let's go back home."

Matusek had left us a cold supper in the dining room and Harmsworth joined us. It was a dreary German supper —slabs of cold ham and cheese and salad with a watery dressing. Geoff and I were both depressed by our day's excursion and we spoke little. Harmsworth too was silent and we hardly noticed he was there at all.

Drearily my mind wandered back over the depressing route we had traveled that day: the little church cut off from its churchyard; the Brandenburg Gate and the ruined Bluecher Palace; the charred remains of the weekend bungalows, the Tiergarten and that empty window in Rauchstrasse.

Suddenly I heard myself asking Harmsworth: "Do you know a Fräulein Dahlmann here in Berlin?"

He started a little and I thought it was just because of the suddenness of my question.

"You mean—?" he began.

"Annemarie Dahlmann," I said.

"Dr. Dahlmann, the lawyer?"

I nodded.

"I don't know her but I know her daughter."

I would like to think the clatter of my knife and fork against the plate as I laid them down was my own imagination. I saw Geoff's head jerk up as he glanced at Harmsworth.

"Daughter?" I asked at last.

Harmsworth looked bewildered as though he had made

a *faux pas*. As I lowered my eyes to my plate I could feel Geoff's eyes steal a glance at me. But then I recovered myself.

"How—how old is the daughter?" I asked, trying to make my voice sound calm.

"I'd say Christl is about twenty-three or four," Harmsworth said. "We were classmates at the university. As a matter of fact we still take courses together in the postgraduate school." He paused for a moment and then added: "She's a very nice person. I see a great deal of her." As I looked at him his face flushed a little and he smiled, embarrassed. I was doing a hasty calculation while he chattered on as though hiding his own confusion. "She was born in Sweden early in the war. As a matter of fact she has a Swedish passport still. It's a great help getting through the checkpoint. You see they won't let West Berliners into the East Sector, only foreigners and people from West Germany. It's a stupid, arbitrary kind of system."

There was a long pause and at last I spoke again.

"About her mother," I started. "What does she do now?"

"Oh, Dr. Dahlmann's almost a legend in West Berlin—a sort of Joan of Arc you could say, especially among the university students."

Geoff and I both looked at him questioningly.

"She runs a refugee center for those who escape from the East and she's always helping them get jobs in the West and legal aid and that sort of thing. She even sends packages to the families they left behind." It seemed a rather mild occupation for a Joan of Arc and he must have thought so himself for he hurried on.

"But she's really much more than that. You could say

she's the spearhead of the reunification movement in West Berlin. Before the Wall went up she was always needling the politicians at the Rathaus to do more about reuniting the city, and the whole country for that matter. Since the Wall, she's constantly making speeches and starting campaigns to get it torn down. As a matter of fact, she's a bit of a thorn in the politicians' sides. Your predecessor," he went on, addressing Geoff, "found her pretty hot to handle."

Geoff laughed. "We might have known that," he said turning to me, but all I could manage for a reply was a rather sickly grin. He must have noticed what a shock Harmsworth's innocent revelations were to me, for he abruptly changed the subject.

"Tell me, Harmsworth, what do you know about Bureau X?"

"You mean is Dr. Dahlmann behind that too? Well, to tell the truth I've often wondered—"

But Geoff brusquely cut him short. "No. Let's skip Dr. Dahlmann for the time being. What do you know about Bureau X?"

Again Harmsworth looked confused as though he had unwittingly offended one of us.

"Actually I don't know too much about Bureau X, sir. Colonel Samson handles all our contracts with them. I gather they're a pretty extreme group aiming at organizing a resistance movement in the East. They seem to think they can drive the Russians out by using terror."

"Does that make much sense to you?" Geoff asked somewhat less belligerently.

"No, sir. I can't say it does. But then some of the ultras are a pretty desperate crowd."

"How active are they at present?"

"As a matter of fact they've been quieter lately—at least that's my impression. You can't be too sure, because of course the Commies accuse them of everything that goes wrong. If a grain elevator burns down they say it's Bureau X, or if there's a train wreck it's Bureau X. Sometimes I think they get credit for more than they actually accomplish. But there hasn't been too much mention of them in the last month or two."

"Why, do you suppose?"

"I have a hunch it's because they can't get their people and their equipment across."

"You mean because the Wall is getting so tough to cross?"

"Very tough indeed. You must know from our reports that in the first months it was pretty easy. Ducking through the wire, running trucks through the Wall itself, getting through windows and the sewers—but that ended after about six months. The Wall itself was made stronger and higher and the guards were more carefully screened. Then, you remember, they caught on to the sewer racket and pretty much closed the sewers off. They even forbade moving dead people from the East Sector. The mother of an acquaintance of mine died about four weeks ago and the children wanted her buried in the family plot in a West Berlin cemetery. But the East German authorities refused permission."

Geoff frowned unhappily.

"And then came the tunnels," Harmsworth went on.

"But you know all about them. They've been written up in every newspaper in the world," he added bitterly.

"Why was that?" Geoff asked. "Why couldn't they keep them quiet? That was one thing I never understood. They'd spend weeks digging one and after a handful of people got out it would be in the headlines."

Harmsworth nodded his head vigorously. "Don't I know! I guess the trouble was most of them were dug by students, and once they'd made it through to the East Sector they couldn't keep their mouths shut. But the journalists were partly responsible—one or two of them at least. Anything for a scoop. And as soon as the Russians were tipped off they started developing some pretty sensitive equipment that could detect any tunneling."

"So the tunnels are pretty much out of action now?" I asked.

Harmsworth hesitated a moment before replying. When he began again his voice had dropped almost to a whisper. "Well, there's still one the Vopos don't know about. But the trouble is the fellows that dug it struck an underground stream and they only managed to get a few people through before it flooded. They call it the Water Tunnel."

"Is it still flooded?" Geoff asked.

"Yes. It could of course be pumped out but your predecessor forbade it. Said it was too dangerous. Of course if you . . ."

"No," Geoff interrupted. "It's going to stay flooded," he said with finality.

Harmsworth looked a little crestfallen and there was a long silence before Geoff spoke again: "Tell me something about the students who dug the tunnels. I've been reading about them in the reports but I still can't make out why they take such risks and spend such a lot of time trying to get people through the Wall. You seem to know them pretty well. What's your opinion?"

Harmsworth thought for a moment before replying.

"They're a mixed crowd," he began. "A few of them, as you know, did it for money—charged so much a head to get people through. But there weren't many like that and the rest of the students soon put an end to their business."

"And the others?"

"Well, I guess some of them did it just for the kicks, you might say, for the excitement and the glory if they succeeded. But I'd say the majority of them think it's their duty. Dr. Dahlmann's had a lot to do with making them do it. And then a lot of the people they got out were once their fellow students at the Free University. Some of them, the best of them, are convinced that Hitler and the war and everything that's happened since was because their own parents didn't do enough to fight the dictators, Hitler and Stalin and the rest. They swear they'll never make that mistake again. Of course you might call them fanatics and idealists if you want but they're a pretty sincere, determined bunch."

"I'd like to meet some of them," Geoff said. "Could you arrange it?"

"Easily. One of the best of the lot is a big Bavarian peasant type we call Sepp. He'll give you an earful. I'll ask him around if you want."

"Fine," Geoff said. We had finished our supper, but just

before Geoff rose from the table he turned again to Harmsworth: "So it's your view that the tunnels are out; that the Wall is just about impenetrable now?"

"Not entirely," Harmsworth answered. "There are some foreign diplomatic missions in the East Zone, mostly satellites themselves. They have pretty easy access across the checkpoint, and occasionally they smuggle people through in their cars for a very handsome price. You know, they tie them to the bottom of the car or hide them under the seat, that sort of thing. But as often as not as soon as they collect the fee they turn the escapees in to the police. Not a very satisfactory method," Harmsworth said smiling.

"So that about closes the Wall?" Geoff asked.

"Just about. Of course you get a screwball escape every now and then, but it's so risky that the only people who try it are half crazy. For a regular courier service, such as the Bureau X needs, there's no reliable channel. And that's, I think, why the Bureau has been so quiet lately."

"You said a moment ago that foreigners could cross at the checkpoint," I said. "Does that apply to all foreigners?"

Harmsworth nodded. "Except of course for us Americans. But that's our own fault," he added, with a slightly bitter look at Geoff. "Since we don't recognize the East German regime, those of us with diplomatic passports are not allowed to show them to the Vopos, and in turn they won't let us through."

"But if you have an ordinary nondiplomatic passport?" I asked.

"Then you can show it and, aside from a little searching, the Vopos let you across."

I turned to Geoff. "Would you mind if I withdrew that application for a diplomatic passport?" I asked. "It seems to me it might be useful for me to go across now and then." Geoff thought for a moment.

"Perhaps you're right," he said at last.

Geoff asked no more questions and sat thinking about what Harmsworth had told him. Finally Harmsworth himself rose and said goodnight. A few minutes later both Geoff and I went up to bed.

As I followed him up the gloomy old staircase, his shoulders seemed to droop.

"What a benighted place," he muttered as he turned to say goodnight.

The remark surprised me, for it was unlike Geoff to get discouraged. He had had some pretty grim assignments in the past and had survived them well. But Berlin was different. Anyone would be depressed by the utter hopelessness of the people in the East and the impossibility of doing anything to help them despite the fact that they lived only a short distance across that monstrous Wall.

But after what I had learned about Annemarie and her daughter I was hardly in a mood to cheer him up, and I was about to turn to my room when he clapped his hand on my shoulder and smiled.

"Now don't get upset about her," he said as though reading my thoughts. "Let nature take its course. Of course we're bound to see her soon."

"But this Christl, Geoff, her daughter. Twenty-three or four. That's just how long it's been—"

"Now, Harry, don't start imagining things. It could

have been someone else. Didn't that cripple, what's-his-name Ebers, follow her to Stockholm?"

"Max Ebers?" I asked astonished. "I never heard that."

"I don't know who mentioned it to me," Geoff said a little evasively, and I began to suspect he was making it up to stop my fretting. "By the way, they told me today that he has surfaced too. Down in Bonn with the German intelligence." He turned toward his bedroom. "Anyway, goodnight, and don't worry about it."

But naturally I did worry and it didn't help at all when I switched on the light of my bedroom and saw on the carpet at my feet that missing galley, No. 89.

V

PROBABLY I SHOULD HAVE TOLD GEOFF ABOUT the mysterious galley then and there. After all, if there was a spy in the house the sooner we found out the better. But I was reluctant to do so and hesitated for several days. The whole purpose of my coming to Berlin with Geoff was to lighten his burdens, not add to them. However, in the end I felt obliged to tell him. As I had anticipated, Geoff was disturbed and immediately summoned Colonel Samson and asked me to repeat my story to him.

When I had done so Geoff asked whether the colonel was satisfied that the servants in his house were reliable. Could one of the maids or even Matusek himself be employed by some intelligence agency, and if so which one?

Samson said emphatically that it was quite impossible. But he seemed to me a bit unhappy and gave me a look which was not entirely friendly, as though he suspected I was intentionally making trouble. Nevertheless he promised to look into the matter at once.

A day or two later the colonel telephoned and asked to see Geoff, and Geoff called me into his office.

When the colonel showed up, Geoff asked at once what he had found out about the servants at the house. The colonel somewhat sheepishly said he had not yet turned up any information. His investigations, he said, were still continuing.

Geoff looked annoyed.

"It was something else I wanted to tell you," the colonel said, and looking at me added, "very confidentially."

Obviously whatever was on his mind was not for my ears. But Geoff simply smiled.

"Look here, Colonel, there's one thing we might all get straight. Mr. Harding has been performing missions for the government for years, and has security clearances for any information you or I might discuss. So shoot—what did you want to tell me?"

The colonel aimed a rather forced smile in my direction as though welcoming me to the fraternity, but not with much warmth or enthusiasm.

"It's about Schmid, sir." Geoff looked puzzled.

"You know, I mentioned him the other day, the Bonn intelligence representative here in Berlin—the contact man with Bureau X."

Geoff nodded. "Yes, now I remember."

"Well, sir, he's disappeared."

Geoff's head jerked up. "Disappeared? What do you mean? Has he gone back to Bonn or something?"

"I'm afraid not," Samson said, and hesitated a moment. "Getting right down to brass facts, sir, he may have defected—to the East."

"What makes you think so?"

"The guard at Checkpoint Charlie reports a man answering his description walked across the boundary last night."

"But how could they be sure it was Schmid, particularly at night?" Geoff seemed annoyed at the assumption.

"He is not an easy man to miss," Samson explained. "You see he is pretty easy to identify. He has a rather unusual face. His ears stick out." Geoff frowned impatiently as though this were all too absurd, but Samson went on. "And he has a bad limp—something wrong with his foot. He told me once it was a riding accident when he was a child."

I wheeled around and stared at Geoff. But Geoff's face was expressionless.

"Colonel, you said Schmid was his cover name," I broke in. "Do you know what his real name was?"

"No, I don't. He was pretty careful about it."

Geoff gave him an impatient, scornful glance, indicating precisely what he thought of Colonel Samson's intelligence, military and human.

"Well, try and find out. And if there's any definite word that he did defect, let me know at once." Samson, considering himself dismissed, started for the door, but Geoff stopped him.

"If he has skipped, Colonel, how does that affect your organization? How many of your people are compromised? How much of our information could he have taken with him?"

"Fortunately not much from us, sir," Samson said. "He

probably has a good deal of dope on the Bonn government's intelligence operations. And then, of course, Bureau X—he knew all about it."

Geoff let out a deep sigh. "Oh, Lord. This isn't going to make things any easier for me." Then he waved Samson out, calling after him: "I want answers to my questions as quickly as possible."

We did not have long to wait. The East German news broadcast at noon had the whole story. A senior official of the "Fascist" intelligence bureau in Bonn, it announced, had defected, giving as his reason his disgust with the political regime. Though he called himself Schmid, his real name was Max Ebers.

I have never been able to understand how a sane person could defect to the East on purely ideological grounds, but judging from the East German communiqué this was exactly what Ebers had done. Geoff seemed to share my bewilderment, for he said: "I wonder what's behind it. I don't blame him for being fed up with those Bonn politicians, but that's hardly a reason to defect. Or has he simply let those complexes he always had get the better of him?"

I suggested he might have got in some sort of trouble and had been blackmailed.

"I doubt if it's blackmail. Whatever he was Max was brave enough," Geoff said. Then he told me of an incident I had never known about, for it happened after I had gone back to Washington.

It was the 3rd or 4th of September, 1939, Geoff said. Hitler's invasion of Poland was well under way and the

British and French, to the amazement of the German public, had just declared war. Goebbels had tried to stir up some enthusiasm among the Berliners and had marched several divisions of German troops down Unter den Linden with bands playing and flags flying, but the Berliners had just stood on the sidewalks and watched glumly, almost resentfully. Hitler had promised them he would get his ends without war, but now they were at it again.

The Gestapo had quickly noticed the general apathy and had tightened up every form of security precaution against any displays of defeatism or sabotage. Foreigners' phones were put under not just intermittent but constant surveillance. Geoff's relations with individual Germans were practically ended. Even his apartment, he felt sure, was thoroughly wired with microphones. In short, any contact with foreigners had become dangerous in the extreme.

And then suddenly Max Ebers had turned up at the apartment and suggested he and Geoff go for a stroll in the Tiergarten. Geoff managed to give the Gestapo man who was following him the slip—they weren't very expert yet—and met Max up near the zoo. For three hours they walked among the old elms and lindens on the neat, carefully raked paths and talked treason—from Max's position, the most blatant, obvious treason.

He had started by saying he was in close contact with the underground opposition—the opposition that was finally destroyed in the fatal 20th day of July putsch. Max said they were ready to start an uprising for, as Geoff knew, the German population at that moment was bitterly disillusioned and frightened by the prospect of another war.

Would the United States, Max had asked, support such an uprising? Would it recognize a revolutionary government if they managed to set one up in competition with Hitler? Could we provide arms? Naturally Geoff was, as the Germans would say, *uebergefragt*—overquestioned—but he promised to find out and afterward reported to Nelly Larsen. In reply to their message to Washington they got a short and very peremptory answer instructing them to make no promises to any German groups. Apparently, even then, the idea of a "good German" as opposed to a "bad German" received little support in government circles.

Max and Geoff had arranged for a second rendezvous—this time out in the country on the banks of the Spree. Again they had walked and talked for hours. Max was naturally dismayed at Geoff's answer but they continued to explore other possibilities of staging a revolt. In the end, however, they had to admit they were pipe-dreaming.

"The whole episode," Geoff said to me, "looks rather childish now. But it wasn't then. Our emotions were all pretty keyed up. And the Gestapo's activities, once war broke out and martial law prevailed, were nothing to laugh about. Whatever you say, Max's talking with me then called for real courage and a real sense of principle. There really were 'good Germans' then and I guess there still are."

The defection of Max Ebers was of course a major news story. The Bonn government was badly shaken—and so indeed were Washington, London and Paris, for no one knew how much secret information Ebers had managed to take with him. (He was carrying a large and obviously heavy suitcase when the MP's saw him crossing at Checkpoint Charlie.) But for some reason Geoff was not too upset and in his cables to Washington he played down the whole episode. "Any statements or speculation now," he cabled, "would, I urgently suggest, be most premature."

The East German press staged a press conference, where Max went through the usual ritual of denouncing the Bonn government as warmongers, but both Geoff and I had the impression that his performance was even less convincing than in previous cases of defection.

Nevertheless, reading Max's statement I was infuriated by his apparent treachery.

"The son of a bitch," I said when I finished it.

"I'm not so sure," Geoff said quietly, and reaching into his breast pocket he pulled out a small envelope addressed to him.

"Read this," he said, passing it to me.

"Dear Schuyler," it read. "Make no judgments about me until all the facts are in." It was signed "Your old friend, Max."

"How did you get this?" I asked.

"It came in this morning's mail. The curious thing is it was mailed in the West Sector. Obviously someone must have smuggled it across."

"What do you make of it?"

"On careful consideration, I think it's good advice, and I intend to follow it," Geoff said.

For some days the Western press speculated gloomily about the consequences of Ebers' defection and, of course, the East German press trumpeted its triumph in fat headlines. But eventually Western newspapers turned their attention to later sensations and even the Eastern press ceased to boast about their latest hero.

While the affair did not directly concern us, since Ebers was technically from Bonn and not from Berlin, Geoff was disturbed by it on personal as well as political grounds. What upset him most was its effect on his long-planned schemes for coming to terms with the Russians. While the affair was at its height he was reluctant to make any approaches in that direction despite the great importance he attached to developing contact with the Soviet authorities in Eastern Germany.

For me too the defection of Max had personal consequences. Ever since Bill Harmsworth had told me of Annemarie's presence in West Berlin, I had known I would eventually have to look her up. My reluctance to do so sprang from a not very admirable fear of opening old wounds. Though my deep affection for her as a young woman had faded away in the intervening years, I dreaded the possibility that it might revive again. While the sensation Max had caused lasted, it served as an excuse to postpone the inevitable encounter.

At last one morning—it seemed like months after my arrival, though in fact it was hardly a matter of weeks—Geoff came grinning into my office to tell me he had finally arranged an appointment with the Russian military headquarters in Potsdam.

"And when you talk with Russians a witness with a good memory is a must," he added. "We'll be leaving in half an hour."

Before he had left Washington, Geoff had, of course,

thoroughly discussed his ideas on "fixing things" in Berlin with all the so-called German experts and with the Secretary. As a result they all believed that they had reached a complete understanding on what Geoff could and could not undertake. The agreement did not, however, connote a complete meeting of the minds on what should be done. The department, and particularly the Secretary, thought some of Geoff's ideas a little too bold. Geoff, naturally, felt that the agreement limited him more than was necessary. But at least they seemed to be agreed.

I must, however, stress the "seemed." With personalities as strong as Geoff's and the Secretary's, compromises are seldom, if ever, so binding that they cannot be stretched in one direction or another to accommodate strong views vigorously held. That is particularly the case when the parties to the compromise are separated by three thousand miles of ocean.

Nevertheless, in one respect there was complete and real agreement: Geoff was to make clear to the Berliners that they were not the center of the universe and that Berlin's problems were only a part and in many cases a relatively minor part of the whole East-West conflict.

State had also agreed, a little reluctantly, to Geoff's proposals for coming to terms with the Russians, at least on local issues. For some time past there had been practically no contact with the Russians, particularly since they had withdrawn their nominal commandant. Now Geoff was authorized to renew contact with the Soviet military authorities at Potsdam, but not with the Soviet embassy in East Berlin, as that might imply a recognition of the East

German regime, which for the time being at least the department wanted to avoid. Just how far these contacts were to go was much debated. Geoff, as I have said, had a deep respect for the Russians as individuals, and in his personal contacts he had always hankered for genuine friendship with them.

Like many others he went a step further and, associating the Soviet official with the Russian individual, was reluctant to accept the thesis that, apart from the physical identity, there was nothing in common between the two. Many of the Soviet officials' peculiarities he ascribed to a sense of inferiority vis-à-vis Westerners. But chiefly, he felt—and I use the word "felt" rather than "believed" intentionally—that, if he could by demonstrating his understanding of their background, history and psychology gain their confidence and dispel their distrust, he could uncover the Russian man under the Soviet official shell. Once that was accomplished he was confident he could reach rational understandings with them.

The Secretary of State and some of his colleagues in the department, recalling others who had shared these views—not least among them President Roosevelt—were somewhat skeptical of Geoff's guarded optimism. Consequently they shied away from his more far-reaching proposals for getting a lasting settlement. They believed that Communist officials were by training and constant discipline as divorced from the Russians' more human nature as a dead body is from its soul.

Nevertheless, they saw no objection to Geoff's re-establishing normal contacts with them, at least socially, and agreed to give Geoff his head if and when these contacts produced tangible results in minor disputes that now caused much of the friction around Berlin. However, they warned Geoff against making any substantial concessions simply for the purpose of producing cordial relations.

As soon as the repercussions of the Ebers affair had died down, therefore, he sent word to the Russians that he would like to call. A cordial enough reply suggested he go to the military headquarters at Potsdam to see the military commander, General Soloviev. The barrier between the American Sector and the Soviet Zone, the Russians said, would be opened to facilitate his journey and avoid the necessity of traveling all the way round the city.

Geoff had urged General Patman to accompany us, but Patman had insisted that since the matters to be discussed were purely political it was best to confine the talking to the Political Representative. It was an unusual attitude for a general to take and Geoff reluctantly deferred to it.

As we crossed the bridge out of the American Sector, a neatly turned-out Russian officer stepped forward and greeted Geoff with a friendly salute and handshake. Two motorcycle escorts moved out from the curb, signaling us to follow. I could see Geoff was encouraged by these small courtesies, though he knew the Russians too well to think this implied a change of heart rather than a change of tactic.

At the Soviet headquarters building another officer was waiting on the steps and led us into a large, ornate waiting room. In one corner a round table, covered with green baize, was equipped with ash trays and boxes of Soviet cigarettes. We sat down and in a matter of seconds General

Soloviev walked in, erect and resplendent in a uniform covered with medals. He shook hands with Geoff, who introduced me as his deputy.

Soloviev, whom I knew only from his photographs, was something of a war hero, and among the medals on his chest I spotted the order of Lenin and the star of the Hero of the Soviet Union. He was well over six feet tall but lean and brisk in his movements. His bullet-shaped head was practically clean shaven and his craggy, weather-beaten face was friendly and open. The high cheeks and the big mouth, and the small but bright eyes, were typically Ukrainian. But I suspected that behind the plain, bluff manner lay all the calculating shrewdness and wiliness of the peasant.

Behind him followed another officer wearing a colonel's insignia. Soloviev introduced him as his assistant, Colonel Alexeiev. He was of quite a different stamp. He wore his curly blond hair long and brushed back from a high, unfurrowed forehead. His blue eyes were large and pale, his cheeks plump and rosy. Unusually handsome, he moved gracefully and with perfect ease as though he had been brought up in just such a salon as the one we were now occupying. Hardly waiting for his chief to be seated, he pulled out a chair and draped himself into it. Reaching forward he passed the cigarettes, asking in fluent but accented English if we smoked.

Then the big double door opened again and a thin little man in a gray suit slipped into the room. Off-handedly, Alexeiev pointed to a straight chair, hardly a stool, beside me and indicated the gray little man's place.

"This is Herr Klein, of the Berlin city administration," Alexeiev said.

Geoff frowned and Soloviev noted his annoyance at being seated at the same table with a member of a regime our government had repeatedly refused to recognize.

"Herr Klein is also Alexeiev's assistant for administrative affairs," he said hurriedly and, smiling at Geoff, added, "Let us consider him present in that capacity, not as a German official." Geoff evidently decided not to let a mere matter of protocol spoil this first effort of his and nodded his agreement.

Then Soloviev turned to Geoff and, speaking Russian which Herr Klein interpreted into German for my benefit, made the usual blunt remarks which in Soviet practice take the place of a speech of welcome. Hardly less formally Geoff returned the compliments. For several minutes the conversation turned on the weather, the palace the Russians occupied as headquarters with evident pride, the quality of Soviet cigarettes, and at last the unhappy state of the world.

As Klein translated I found myself more intrigued by him than by either of the two Russians. He was, as I have said, a small man, with a sharp, thin face and a slightly tanned complexion that suggested a sun lamp rather than the sun. His thin hair was reddish brown and neatly swept back over a domed brow. His blue eyes were keen but friendly and his nose and mouth, in contrast to the heavier features of his companions, were delicate and finely shaped. His hands too were thin and the fingers long. His nails I noticed were carefully polished. His movements were graceful and his voice gentle and refined. I began to wonder how a man of such polished outward appearance could be connected with a regime so notorious for its coarseness and brutality. It was a question that was to bother me almost to the end.

Geoff, the general and more and more Alexeiev were still exchanging banalities when a white-clad waiter appeared with a tray of vodka and caviar. Soloviev proposed a toast to the American President. Geoff returned the compliment with one to the Soviet Chairman. Then they drank a third to better relations between each other. Geoff always disliked drinking in the middle of the morning and firmly turned down a fourth glass.

Then Soloviev pushed aside his own, straightened himself in his chair, tugged down his tunic and indicated that, the social amenities having been complied with, it was time to get down to business.

"What is it you want?" he said bluntly. Alexeiev looked unhappy at his superior's abrupt manner.

Geoff explained he had only come to pay a courtesy call and to make the general's acquaintance. He hoped, he said, the general would do him the honor of visiting him in Dahlem. The general grunted noncommittally.

"But you must have something on your mind," he insisted and Alexeiev squirmed again.

"I had not intended to discuss any business," Geoff said, "but if you would like to, I have several suggestions to make for the purpose of improving the relationships which we have agreed are not as close as they might be." The general nodded and Alexeiev leaned forward intently.

"Well?" said the general, obviously impatient to get down to cases.

"One small matter I have been turning over in my mind is the poorness, indeed the total absence, of channels of communications between our headquarters. As you recall, my first message to you took several days to be delivered. It did no harm, of course, because there was nothing urgent. But with the state of things existing in Berlin today matters of far greater urgency are apt to arise at any time. If we can talk them over quickly, many can be settled. Otherwise I fear trivial misunderstandings might easily become inflated just while we are trying to get in touch with each other." He paused and the general grunted, "And so you suggest what?"

"Why don't we have our communications people set up a direct telephone line between your office and mine?" Geoff said, and watched for a reaction on the general's face. The general instinctively looked at Alexeiev. His expression was puzzled as though Geoff were suggesting some sort of a trap. But Alexeiev seemed perfectly casual and said, "An excellent idea." Then he turned to Klein. "Remind me to have our signal people get in touch with the Americans." The general looked relieved that the responsibility for this perplexing question had been taken out of his hands.

"Anything else?" he said to Geoff.

Geoff hesitated a moment as he calculated his chances of pressing ahead without provoking a rebuff.

"I understand you are interested in a slight border rectification at the Sankt Jakob Church," he went on at last, referring to the graveyard we had visited with Harmsworth.

"Not particularly," the general said. "The East German parishioners have complained that they wanted the church reopened, which of course we could not permit so long as the boundary ran along its walls."

"But if you got the churchyard you would reopen the church?" Geoff said.

Soloviev nodded. "In that case we would have no objection."

There was a momentary pause and then Geoff abruptly changed the subject.

"Are you familiar with the location of the Bluecher Palace?"

To me it was obvious what he was driving at, but the others looked startled and suspicious.

The general said he did not know of the Bluecher Palace but Herr Klein quickly produced a map of the Brandenburg Gate area and Geoff pointed to the location.

"It happens to be American property," he said casually. "In fact it was our embassy when Mr. Harding and I were vice consuls here before the war." Soloviev and Alexeiev looked surprised and a little incredulous but Herr Klein quickly confirmed Geoff's statement.

"What about a trade, General?" Geoff said. "We'll straighten the boundary to include the churchyard. You give us access to our Bluecher Palace through the Wall."

"But why do you want the palace? It is nothing but a ruin."

Geoff smiled. "Now it is, but eventually we'll want to rebuild it. The division of Berlin, I am sure you agree, won't last forever, and meantime the architects could survey the foundations and make plans."

Soloviev and Alexeiev exchanged questioning glances.

"We will consider it," Soloviev said at last. "Have you any other proposals?"

"I have several others, but I don't want to take them up now."

"For instance?" the general persisted.

"Well, General, without going into the rights and wrongs of it," he said, "we all know that the Wall has caused great hardship to many people on each side of it." He paused. The general frowned again, but said nothing. Alexeiev's eyes seemed to grow closer together as he leaned over the table, but he said nothing either.

"I hope that in the course of our future talks we may be able to relieve some of these hardships." Geoff was obviously reluctant to go into these more delicate matters until he had prepared the ground more thoroughly and demonstrated to the Russians his understanding and sincerity. Without that he would run into precisely the obstacles that had thwarted his predecessors.

But the general insisted on pressing ahead. "What sort of steps have you in mind?"

"It seems to me," Geoff said, "that regulations for crossing the border could be modified. After all there are many frontiers in the world, but few so rigidly controlled that the local inhabitants can't cross with relative ease."

"Do you mean local inhabitants or your spies, Mr. Schuyler?" Alexeiev broke in with a sly smile, self-satisfied at his own wit.

Geoff stiffened. "Not our spies or yours, Colonel," he said sharply. "I am talking about the ordinary people—you call them the workers—the Berliners. Do you know that not even a corpse is allowed out of the East Sector?"

The general looked up. "Corpse? What do you mean?"

Geoff repeated to him what Harmsworth had told us,

without, of course, identifying the persons concerned.

The general listened intently, frowning and obviously disturbed. "But that's absurd," he said, turning to Alexeiev as though the colonel himself were to blame. "That's ridiculous. Why didn't I know that?" he said still more crossly to his assistant. Alexeiev started to speak but the general cut him short and turned to Klein.

"Set up a procedure at once whereby corpses can be exchanged across the boundary without any delay—and none of your German bureaucracy either. You better supervise it yourself, Klein," he added, half threatening, "because I shall hold you personally responsible."

Then he turned to Geoff and smiled as though to say "See how nice I am?"

But Geoff was not taken in. The Russian tactic of conceding trivialities in order to win more important points was an old trick.

"I only mentioned the corpses by way of illustration, General. Other restrictions are far more cruel—families split up, friends divided, sick parents separated from their children. These are more urgent than dead people," he said.

"I have always said that if the Germans themselves would get together these difficulties too could be ironed out," the general retorted.

"But you know as well as I that the West Germans, the West Berliners, do not consider the East German officials competent to speak for the East Germans." Then his argumentative tone changed and he added: "But let us not get into that discussion today. We can talk it over sometime in the future when we get to know each other better," and he smiled affably.

"If you ask me," the general said, "the West Berliners won't talk because they're afraid their compatriots will get the better of them."

Geoff bristled again: "They may be afraid, General, but not of the East Berliners."

"You mean they're afraid of us? I'll give you my personal word of honor that any West German who comes to East Berlin on legitimate business will be perfectly safe," the general said solemnly and looked indignant that his honor might have been impugned.

Geoff, anxious to avoid a quarrel at this stage, said nothing as the general glared at him.

"Anything else on your mind?" Soloviev finally said and Geoff shook his head.

"Well, we've a few suggestions, as you call them," he said, and exchanged glances with Alexeiev. Geoff looked uneasy. This was precisely what he had hoped to avoid.

"In the first place, Herr Schuyler," Soloviev began, "we object to the espionage activities of your military liaison group here in Potsdam. They are constantly going about where they have no business to be. Last week an American captain was found with a camera up on the Baltic coast. When we asked what he was up to he said he was merely 'taking a vacation on the seashore.'" The general stopped and watched Geoff for a reaction, but Geoff's face was expressionless. "Herr Schuyler," he went on at last, "am I to believe that you Americans are so rugged that you take holidays by the seaside in November?"

There was a painful silence and I shifted uncomfortably in my chair as Herr Klein translated, for I knew how strongly Geoff felt about the amateur spy activities of some of our military personnel. Like small boys playing at war, they were forever poking about where they had no business, snapping photos out of fast-moving cars, making sketches of terrain they thought might have some strategic significance, or questioning the inhabitants of Soviet garrison towns, hoping to pick up some significant information about Soviet troop strength.

Quite aside from the fact that such information was of little or no practical importance in the atomic age, their snooping merely served to convince the Russian military that we were really planning a sneak attack, whether it was in East Germany or North Korea or Central Asia or Bulgaria.

But Geoff's bland expression was unruffled.

"General," he said at last. "You probably know that I have no authority over the Potsdam military mission. I shall, however, convey your complaint through the proper channels, and I hope we can work out some way of preventing any unjustifiable activities, if, of course, they are taking place."

The general looked anything but mollified. "Of course they are taking place," he said. "But if you cannot control them, there is nothing we can do but control them ourselves. However, don't blame us if our security measures seem severe."

Geoff nodded but said nothing.

The general straightened himself in his chair and once again tugged at his tunic: "But there is another matter of even more serious concern where I believe you have some authority—or at least someone should have authority." Geoff looked up questioningly.

"I refer to the activities of the so-called Bureau X." I tried to detect a reaction in Geoff's face, for he had frequently expressed his own concern over the activities of this group. But his face was relaxed and his expression unruffled.

Then the general continued: "They are nothing but a band of murderers and terrorists and they openly admit their anti-Soviet attitude. They have assassinated at least three German officials; they have even attempted to assassinate a high Soviet official." The indignation in the general's voice was genuine. "I do not even mention the trains they have wrecked, the buildings they have bombed, the food supplies they have destroyed. Do you know that their sabotage of our harvesting activities may well result in severe food shortages for the East German population, for which you show such concern?" The sarcasm was unmistakable.

"Are you implying that I am responsible for these alleged activities of this so-called terrorist band, General?" Geoff said, his voice hard and cold.

"I imply nothing, Herr Schuyler. I know—and you know—that Bureau X operates from bases in West Berlin. And there, if I am not mistaken, you do have some authority by virtue of what you call occupation rights. We Russians are your allies, Herr Schuyler—at least that is the theory of your occupation. It is your duty to prevent anti-allied activities in your area just as it is our duty to prevent anti-American activities in ours. Are your officials being assassinated? Are your factories being sabotaged? Has any American been fired on by terrorists from the Democratic Republic?" He stopped and waited for Geoff to reply.

"Without some proof I can hardly accept your allegations, General. If you have any such proof I should be glad to examine it."

In view of Max Ebers' defection and the information he had about Bureau X I thought Geoff's retort was brash to the point of foolhardiness, and I fully expected the general to launch into a detailed exposé of Bureau X as revealed by Ebers. But he did nothing of the sort.

"It is not a matter of proof, Herr Schuyler. It is a matter of facts. Naturally Bureau X does not provide us with legal evidence of its activities."

For the first time I detected the trace of a smile on Geoff's face.

"Well, General, if and when you get any proof, I'll be most pleased to examine it and take such action as is appropriate. In the meantime I can assure you that I am as opposed to terrorism as you are. I am opposed to terrorism by West Germans and East Germans, by Americans or Russians, by Hungarians or Cubans." Then he rose from his chair:

"But, General, we are going very far afield. I only came to pay my compliments and make your acquaintance. I hope you will do me the honor of coming to call on me. But now I must not take more of your time."

The general looked startled: "You're not going? But luncheon? We must have lunch." He clapped his hands, a waiter appeared, and though Geoff did his best to protest the doors of an adjoining room were swung open, revealing a table covered with dishes of caviar, hams, salads, cheeses and a half-dozen other forms of hors d'oeuvre.

Further protest was useless. Geoff took his place on Soloviev's right, Alexeiev on his left, with Klein and myself at the foot of the table. While Geoff and the two Russians reminisced about Moscow and the ballet and the theatre there, Herr Klein and I discussed more familiar topics, particularly the landmarks of old Berlin. I had been asked to write a magazine story about what was left of the historic monuments of the German capital, and though I could not write it for the time being it seemed to be a good opportunity to get the material for it now.

He offered to take me around the sector and show me all that was left—and of course the great new "monuments," such as Stalinallee, which had been built since. I eagerly agreed, and made a date for the following week.

Our conversation was frequently interrupted by more toasts, chiefly proposed by Colonel Alexeiev, whose handsome face was soon suffused with a warm, vodka-induced flush. It was nearly three o'clock when we finally managed to get away and back to the American sector.

On the drive back we discussed our talk with the Russians. Geoff was more or less pleased with the way it had gone but he was disturbed by Soloviev's charges about Bureau X, for he knew some of them to be true. I told him of my apprehensions when he had so blandly asked Soloviev

for proofs. Had he not assumed that Max Ebers had provided all the evidence Soloviev needed? Geoff smiled.

"Harry, you forget Max's note. Until the facts are in
I'll follow his advice and assume nothing."

I mentioned his offer of a trade of the churchyard for
the Bluecher Palace. "How will that go down with the
West Berliners?" I asked. "Aren't they pretty touchy about
making concessions."

Geoff smiled. "I think we can persuade them."

"But you don't really think that Washington is thinking
about rebuilding the place, do you?"

"Of course not," Geoff said. "But from what Harmsworth was saying about the Wall the other day, it occurred
to me that the old Bluecher Palace might, under certain
circumstances, be rather useful. Not now, of course, but if
the situation changes—" I looked at him, puzzled, but he
returned my look blandly and changed the subject.

He was, he said, pleased with the Soviet officials' affability,
though he was not one of those who thought it meant too
much. He did not suffer from the illusions others before
had entertained that personal charm could win the officials
over, but he did feel, as I have said, that a man who really
understood their psychology and their complexes could
penetrate their official crust.

And he saw himself as one of the first, if not the first,
American official who by reason of his long experience in
Moscow and his thorough study of their history, and
perhaps even more important, of their national literature,
was in a position to make the breakthrough. Geoff was not
a conceited person—his scholarly bent gave him the neces-

sary humility to avoid that pitfall. But that same bent
also gave him an appreciation of the role of fate or chance
in the twists and turns of history. I had long suspected
that he felt himself destined to straighten out the tragic misunderstandings that had prevented the Russians from accepting American offers for a settlement of the conflict.

He was amused by the charade the Russians had put on
for our benefit. The pose of reasonableness—about easing
frontier crossings, for example—the elaborate banquet, and
the ceremonial courtesies provided by the Soviet military
police were old maneuvers which had taken in others, but
for Geoff they were rather shopworn tricks. On the other
hand the very fact that he had established contact and won
their promise to maintain it was encouraging. He was determined to pursue his course cautiously but persistently.

A major difficulty, and one that had plagued his predecessors, was the almost pathological hatred with which
the West Berliners and West Germans regarded the puppets
of the Eastern regime. Having established themselves solely
with the use of Soviet bayonets, without the slightest pre-
text of consulting their subjects, Ulbricht and his crew
had ever since consistently pursued policies for the benefit
of the Soviets and against the most fundamental interests
of the Germans.

There had been various efforts in the past to make contacts with them and to persuade them to modify their brutal
regime, but each time the talks had broken down, and in the
end the German authorities both in Bonn and Berlin had
decided to have no further dealings with the Communist
regime in the East.

Geoff was well aware of their attitude, and in view of their previous experience he could hardly blame them. However, he also knew that the Russians were equally determined to keep in the background and have their East German stooges front for them in taking the blame for the unpopularity of the regime and its measures.

That they were simply stooges no one denied, and in that fact Geoff saw his one chance of success. If he could first persuade the Russians to take a more reasonable line perhaps they in turn would instruct the Germans who represented them to behave more reasonably. Consequently, he decided not to discuss Soloviev's proposals with West Berlin's governing mayor, but to work on the Russians himself.

Geoff was further encouraged when a few days after our visit to Potsdam the Russians sent a senior communications official to arrange for the direct telephone line Geoff had suggested. They not only agreed to link up Geoff's and Soloviev's offices, but went further and proposed direct lines between their private quarters. The American security officials at once raised objections, saying that the diabolical Russians would somehow use these lines to tap into the American phone system. Just how they would do this under the noses of our own technicians was not clear, but somehow, the American experts felt, that would certainly happen.

Geoff impatiently overruled their objections and the two lines were soon in operation. At about the same time West Berlin officials were approached by Klein's office with a suggestion to work out a procedure for transporting the remains of deceased persons across the boundary with no more formalities than a certificate from each side stating that the coffins contained only dead people. The West Germans, like the American communications officers, were at first highly suspicious, but again Geoff persuaded them to take the chance that the Russians would not fill their coffins with subversive literature.

To my surprise and alarm, Geoff's offer of a trade of the churchyard for the Bluecher Palace was also accepted. A new wall was built, cutting off the graves from the Western Sector. Beside the Brandenburg Gate a gap was cut into the wall, giving us access to the old ruined palace.

As I had anticipated, the exchange was not popular among West Berliners. When Geoff informed the governing mayor he was horrified, but eventually agreed to go along. When the trade was made public, however, a storm of angry protests arose from every side. The newspapers accused Geoff of appeasement and "softness." A students' group staged a demonstration in front of Clayallee and a stream of letters poured into the office calling Geoff everything from a fool to a Communist.

"You have sold our fathers' graves for a few square yards of American-made rubble," one of them wrote, alluding to the American bombings which had destroyed much of Berlin even before the Russians had taken over.

Even the American staff was unhappy, and in barely subdued whispers said that Geoff was "selling out" to the Russians and condoning the "salami tactics" by which the Communists were allegedly whittling away Western rights in the city.

Geoff was unmoved by the stream of criticism. When his press relations staff urged him to reply and defend himself he merely brushed them aside and offered no explanation for his action—not even the one he had given me: that one day, if circumstances changed, the old palace might prove useful.

Even to me he only once referred to the criticism being hurled at him. "When they accuse me of selling their German graveyard for a parcel of American real estate they seem to forget that if there is ever to be a solution of their problems their liberators will not spring from their ancestral graves, waving a Teutonic sword, but from the other side of the Atlantic."

Curiously enough there was one German who did not share in the criticism of Geoff and that was the student Sepp. Bill Harmsworth had brought him to dinner one evening and for several hours he and Geoff had discussed the plight of the Berliners and the students' reaction to it.

Sepp was a large, lumbering, heavy-set, square-shouldered Bavarian with a shock of curly blond hair hanging over his big red face, which wore a pleasant, rather simple expression. One look at him made it clear why his fellow students called him Sepp, the nickname Bavarians apply to their more stolid and stupid peasant compatriots. But after a few minutes it was obvious that Sepp was anything but stolid or stupid.

When Geoff opened the conversation by asking him what the students thought about the American attitude toward Berlin, he launched into a long, articulate and forceful harangue on what he would do if he were in Geoff's position. His language was sometimes earthy but invariably polite and he did not fall into the customary German habit of harping on all the Americans' mistakes in the past. For him these were bygones and should remain bygones. What interested him was the future and the role which he and his fellow students should play in it.

He spoke warmly, almost worshipfully, of Annemarie Dahlmann. She more than anyone else had made clear to the students who collected around her what their responsibilities were and what they should do to fulfill them.

"She'd be the governing mayor, the university rector and the chancellor," Sepp said, "if we had our way."

When Geoff himself raised the question of the exchange of the churchyard for the Bleucher Palace, Sepp simply smiled and said: "I assume you know what you're doing and I have a hunch that whatever you have in mind is probably a pretty good idea. You don't strike me as being stupid, Herr Schuyler," he added with a grin that stretched from ear to ear across his big red face.

Geoff asked him why he, a Bavarian, had come to Berlin to study.

"I never knew the Bavarians had any deep passion for their northern neighbors," Geoff joked. "In fact I seem to recall hearing the expression 'Pig Prussian' rather frequently down in Munich."

Sepp grinned again. "As a matter of fact I started at the University of Munich but when they put up the Wall I decided I ought to come here. So I transferred."

"Why? Because it was more exciting here?" Geoff asked, and Sepp looked annoyed.

"I can always find excitement wherever I am, Herr Schuyler," he said curtly. "I came up here because I thought they might be needing some good strong backs. The Communists can draft all the help they need. But on this side we've got to depend on volunteers—and so I volunteered," he said simply.

"As for the Prussians," he began again, "I don't think they acted any worse than the Bavarians under the Nazis. After all Hitler got his first start in Munich—not Berlin. And remember that until he took over the voting booths the Berliners turned him down at every election. Only the Communists ever voted with him here in Berlin."

"You know your Nazi history pretty well," Geoff commented.

"Thanks to Dr. Dahlmann," Sepp answered. "The rest of them, the older people, the professors and the rest, talk as though history stopped suddenly in 1933 and didn't start again until 1945. They seem to think the Nazi era belongs to mythology and that the real tragedy of Germany began with the American occupation." Geoff smiled as Sepp rose from his chair.

"I've kept you up too late, Herr Schuyler," he said putting out his great muscular paw. He gave Geoff's and my hands two powerful squeezes and then, with a friendly nod, abruptly left us.

"Berlin could certainly use more like him," I commented after he had gone.

"Yes," Geoff agreed, "provided of course they're on our side."

VI

THE UNUSUALLY CLOSE FELLOWSHIP
at the time of the Wall between the Western allied officials
and the West Berliners, only recently despised as the
lackeys of Nazism and the mercenaries of Prussian milita-
rism, is a phenomenon that is difficult for outsiders who
were not involved to understand. Yet for those who worked
in Berlin the relationship was a natural outgrowth of postwar events. When the Russians first began to encroach on
the political rights of the West Berliners after the four-
power occupation government had broken down, it was the
Americans who most actively championed the Germans.
Later when the Russian-imposed Blockade came, it was
again the Americans who threw themselves most whole-
heartedly into the Airlift.

It was not just with money and airplanes that the Americans showed their sympathy. Cheerfully sharing the hardships which the Berliners suffered, the Americans for the most part acted as though it were a privilege, indeed an honor, to stand beside the Berliners in those hungry, cold, lightless months when the ceaseless drone of cargo planes overhead was their only link with the outside world.

Many Germans who had now become the elected officials of the city had once worked in one capacity or another with the Americans in the occupation regime and had come to know them intimately. By the time the Blockade was lifted, a bond had been forged between them which was partly sentimental, partly political, and partly the result of close personal association. In the case of the Americans, it was strengthened by a willingness to forget the bitter enmity and hatred of the Prussians during the war years—an attitude that the French and British were naturally and historically less prone to accept.

When Geoff first talked to me of Berlinitis back in Washington and during those first weeks in Berlin, he often found it hard to forget that Berlin was where the Nazis had plotted the destruction of civilization and where Hitler directed his iniquitous attacks on free men, Jews and non-Jews alike. But no one so sensitive and perceptive as Geoff could be completely immune to the sentiments—call them sentimentalities if you will—that service in that beleaguered fortress evoked.

The claustrophobic atmosphere, which came from living crowded together in a ghetto of freedom, the daily tragedies of the Wall, the constant view beyond it of an unspeakable landscape, a Breughel-like scene of a city run by monsters and imbeciles, and the shrill, piercing screams of Communist propaganda, like the wail of wartime air-raid sirens, beat like waves on Geoff's tough, realistic mind.

Among those who had done most to forge the bonds between Americans and Berliners was Dr. Ernst Bell. A refugee from Hitler's Germany, he had emigrated to America, where, despite his age, he had enlisted in the army. When the war ended he was on active duty in the occupation in Western Germany, but unlike many ex-Germans who, as occupiers of requisitioned villas, bene-ficiaries of an opulent PX, and masters of squads of free servants, had "never had it so good" and who had clung to their jobs years after the jobs had ceased to exist, Dr. Bell had forsworn these fruits of victory, and at the first oppor-tunity resumed German citizenship, settled in his native Berlin and resumed his practice as a lawyer.

A small, round man with a comfortable stomach, an end-less smile, twinkling, humorous eyes, and a gift for witty speech which spluttered constantly from his wide, friendly mouth, Dr. Bell combined great charm with the erudition of a prewar German-educated philosophy student. He used both to good effect as a sort of link between his less witty fellow Berliners and his less erudite ex-colleagues in Ameri-can officialdom.

It was in this self-assumed capacity as a link between American headquarters on Clayallee and Berlin's intellectual community that Dr. Bell had invited Geoff and me to meet a group of officials, writers and journalists in his old house in Marienfelde.

The house was an anomaly in Berlin—the manor house

of a village that had existed eight hundred years ago when
Berlin was nothing more than a tiny fishing settlement on
the River Spree. To this day, the village green has been
preserved with its ancient church at one end, the manor at
the other. On either side tall elms line the green, and behind
them stand the low, sprawling farmhouses which once
belonged to peasants who cultivated the fields to the north.
The fields are gone now—all except the flying field of
Tempelhof—and the dwellers in the peasant houses work in
the garages, factories and stores that have replaced them.

The manor house had been damaged during the wartime
air raids, but Dr. Bell had restored it to exactly what it once
had been, using plans and sketches he had found in a local
museum. Outside it was of ancient brick—pink and white
with age. A low, wide door opened into a big hall, the
ceiling beams of which were dark with age and smoke.
Beyond lay the drawing room, low ceilinged but cheerfully
lit, the casement windows draped in flowered chintzes, the
old furniture covered in bright silk.

Dr. Bell greeted Geoff and me in the hall and led us
into the drawing room, where he took us around and introduced us to the other guests. They included a middle-
aged novelist, a well-known radio news commentator, a
Jesuit priest, and an official of the city administration, who,
I knew, was a close associate of the governing mayor.

While our host passed around the cocktails I tried to
identify the role each of the other guests would play in
what I knew was a carefully selected dinner party. The
Jesuit, a lean, rugged-faced man clad in a black suit and
clerical collar, had been chatting with the novelist and he
graciously brought me into their conversation:

"Herr Scholl," he said, indicating the novelist, "is Berlin's unofficial chronicler. He was just saying how few Berliners are really natives in the literal sense."

The novelist, a rotund little man with a pink face topped by thin wisps of silver hair, turned to me: "The fact is that most Berliners are immigrants from the provinces. Few of us were actually born here, fewer still can claim to come from old Berlin families—the way, say, Hamburgers boast of their patrician clans. Berlin is like New York. For over a century it has attracted the more adventurous, or I should say the more aggressive young people from the provinces— Leipzig, Dresden and, of course, Breslau and Koenigsberg."

"Are they still coming to Berlin?" I asked.

The commentator, a heavy-set, swarthy, black-haired man with a pencil mustache, had joined us. His eyes flashed as I spoke.

"The only reason for East Germans to come to Berlin since the war was to get out," he said. His voice was high pitched and querulous. "Now that you've let them build the Wall, no one comes to Berlin any more from the East."

The priest, his voice low and resonant, put in: "That is not entirely true. East Berlin for all its drabness is still relatively better than the provinces."

"And it also offers the top jobs in the regime," the city hall official added.

The commentator frowned, annoyed at the contradiction. "I was not talking of the little opportunists and stooges. I was talking of the types that once gave Berlin its fame."

I asked rather tentatively, "Are the East regime officials all careerists and stooges?" and then I told them of my friend Herr Klein, without of course mentioning his name. "He strikes me as a rather decent type even if he is a fellow traveler," I finished.

The priest drew himself up and looked at me sternly. "There is nothing decent about the fellow travelers. Every breath they draw is indecent." Then he turned to talk to Geoff and our host.

"The only thing they are good for is a bullet—or a bomb," the commentator said.

"Is that the purpose of Bureau X?" I asked.

"I know nothing about Bureau X," the commentator said frostily, but in a tone that clearly belied his words, and he turned away.

I was left with the novelist, and for lack of anything better to say asked, "What do you make of Herr Ebers' defection?"

A pained look came into his eyes.

"I once knew Ebers well," he said, "and I still can't believe it's as simple as it looks."

While we talked, Dr. Bell hovered about us nervously, as most bachelor hosts do, and apologized that there was still one guest missing. Then at last the door to the hall opened. I glanced up just as Annemarie, tall and erect, swept into the room.

For a moment my vision blurred, or perhaps I simply closed my eyes, but as she stepped toward me she appeared exactly as she had that day I first saw her at the embassy reception twenty-five years before. I saw the same bright red points of her cheeks against the soft, pallid skin, the deep, flashing eyes below the carefully marked black eyebrows, the same vivacious, wide, smiling mouth.

She seized my two hands in hers and leaning close to me kissed me on the cheek. "My dearest," she whispered so low that no one else could hear. The blood raced through my veins and I could feel my face flush.

Then she straightened and swiftly turned to Geoff.

Cocking her head on one side, she looked at him intently.

"Older and perhaps wiser," she said, laughing, "but still as handsome as ever."

As she faced about to the other guests, I saw for the first time a bright silvery streak running through her jet black hair. With a sharp jab that flash of silver seemed to bring me back to reality as I realized this was not my Annemarie but another woman, more mature, more tranquil, perhaps even lovelier in an almost majestic way, but not the same Annemarie.

Watching her intently as she moved from guest to guest, the churning sensation I had felt inside ceased. A pull of intimate affection drew me toward her, but it was not that gnawing, passionate longing I had once known.

Dr. Bell brought her a martini and as soon as she had drunk it announced that dinner was ready. As the only lady present, Annemarie, acting as hostess, sat opposite Dr. Bell, and at the place of honor on her right was Geoff. Strictly according to protocol I sat at the far end of the table next to our host. Silently I thanked Bell for his tact in not seating us side by side, but I found it difficult to keep my eyes from straying to the other end of the table. Whenever they did and caught her eyes, a warm smile flashed across her face and her eyelids dropped for an instant, acknowledging my glance.

The conversation was at first desultory as each of us

talked to our neighbors. But then, gracefully and unobtrusively, Dr. Bell gathered the threads of the various conversations together and turned the discussion to the subjects he felt would interest Geoff most. Summing up my impressions of our fellow guests, I began to suspect that if Berlinitis had an intellectual as well as an emotional basis our fellow guests were its brains.

The pink-faced novelist who was sitting next to me was the first to pick up the cue.

"I wonder," he said, "if we are not too concerned about the effects of the Wall. It seems to me that people are fairly normal. If you walk through the streets it is difficult to see any serious deterioration in their spirits."

Geoff listened intently as he described the mood of the Berliners, illustrating his views with scraps of conversations he had had with the "ordinary people," as he called them. His conclusions were, I know, just what Geoff had hoped to hear and he smiled faintly as he listened. But the radio commentator took strong exception.

Only the day before, he said, he had sent his family off to Munich to find an apartment. The rest of the company looked surprised, and realizing their dismay he launched on an impassioned defense of his action.

"I know that as a journalist it is my duty to remain here and I shall. But it is no place for one's children. It is unjust to expect them to grow up in this prison atmosphere. For seventeen years we have struggled—even longer than we suffered under Hitler. We have put up with crisis after crisis, always hoping, always believing that in the end Berlin would be freed. But our friends," and he looked across the table at Geoff, "our friends have been unable or unwilling to carry out their promises. And today we are worse off than ever. It is too much to ask."

Geoff looked a trifle indignant, but his voice was low and controlled as he asked, "What would you have expected us to do?"

The commentator stared at him a moment, weighing his thoughts. "I do not know. It is not my business to advise the allies. All I could suggest would be a little firmness."

The novelist spoke up again. "But if what you say is true would it not be better to seek an accommodation with the Russians—to try to arrange for a little pause, a breathing spell for ourselves and our children?"

The novelist's suggestion was not popular. After the others had expressed their views the Jesuit spoke in gentle, cultivated German. "I do not think we can seek solutions through compromise. The Church too has children, children of all ages, children on both sides of the Wall. To compromise would be to condemn our children in the East to a Godless, faithless, hopeless future." As he talked on gently, persuasively, but always elegantly, the rest listened and nodded agreement.

But when he finished Annemarie broke in: "I agree with you, Father John. But I think there is more to it than the spiritual side. After all we are Germans and Germany is— or at least was—a great nation. Where my family came from and where I lived as a child in Silesia is also Germany, but now it is swallowed up by Slavs. And what of West Germany? It has been not swallowed perhaps, but firmly embraced by the West, by France, England and America.

They are great nations, but they are not Germany. All that remains now of our old Germany is this tiny remnant on the River Spree—Berlin. And of that only West Berlin has a will of its own. It must remain firm, until we can bring our country together again."

Geoff broke in: "We? Annemarie, who is 'we'?"

"We Berliners, Geoff, are primarily responsible. We Berliners must be the nucleus of reunited Germany. If you support us, so much the better." She smiled at Geoff as she stopped.

Geoff nodded, but he said nothing.

The city official had said little thus far, but now he too spoke up.

"Dr. Dahlmann," he said, "I wish I could steal that little speech and give it to my chief, the governing mayor, to use in his next address." He made a little bow and then continued, "I cannot too strongly support the idea that we Germans must take more part in our own fate."

"But how?" Geoff asked.

The commentator broke in, his voice shrill and biting: "By being firm, Herr Schuyler, by refusing to bow to the Russians' will every time they encroach on our rights."

"And provoke a war, a world war for Berlin?" Geoff asked, and I could see that he too was becoming irritated.

"A war for freedom, perhaps, Herr Schuyler," the commentator said.

Dr. Bell raised his hand and intervened. "Gentlemen, I do not think anyone here would advocate a world war. I am sure it is the last thing we want—or at least the last thing before one—slavery."

Geoff shook his head, but said nothing, and Annemarie spoke again: "Geoff, I don't think you understand. In fact I don't think Washington understands how to deal with the Russians."

"For example?" Geoff asked, and there was more than a trace of belligerency in his voice.

"All right, you asked for it," Annemarie said, and her tone too was sharp. "Take your deal with Soloviev on the churchyard and the Bluecher Palace. The Russians give you nothing but a useless ruin—of no value to anyone, unless it has some sentimental memories for you and Harry. But you give them a churchyard where scores of Berliners' ancestors, mothers and fathers and children, are buried; a churchyard that really means something, a symbol. And then you pretend you have made a fair exchange!"

There was a touch of fury in her voice as she finished and a deep murmur of angry agreement swept the rest of the company. I looked uneasily at Geoff and he seemed distressed. He turned to the priest. "I did manage to have the church reopened," he pointed out. "It is not a Catholic church but I think Father John at least would agree that is something."

"Look, Geoff," Annemarie went on, practically ignoring his argument. "I don't want to criticize you uselessly. But I think I know what I am talking about. When the war ended, I went directly to my family's villa here in Mueggel-see. Father and Tante Viktoria were there and I brought my Christl. The Russian troops were swarming all over us. looting, stealing, raping. I went to the Soviet commandant of the local district and told him if the disorder didn't stop at once we would defend ourselves with guns and organize an underground to shoot any soldier caught raping. Do you know that within twenty-four hours there was hardly another case of disorder in the whole neighborhood?" She paused to catch her breath. "That's how to deal with Russians—not by so-called deals."

There was a long silence and Dr. Bell suggested we go to the drawing room. When coffee had been served, Annemarie went on again:

"Geoff, do you realize what is at stake for us if nothing is done? Don't you see what it means to see our rights sliced away, a thin slice at a time—salami tactics, we call it: our rights to move about in our own city. The right of East Berliners to stroll on Kurfuerstendamm. The right of West Berliners to walk on Unter den Linden and sail on the lakes and canals and rivers in the East Sector. The right to move from one part of town to another without being shot and killed—the way that small boy was last week or Peter Fechter, who bled to death under our eyes—without you Americans doing a single thing about it? Don't you see why we feel that at last it is our turn to take part—an active part—even if it does involve some false assumptions?"

Geoff stared at her long and hard, his fingers so tightly linked that the knuckles turned white. Then at last he said: "No, Annemarie, no. I don't see blowing the world apart for Berlin."

Once again Dr. Bell intervened.

"It seems to me that for one evening we have talked enough about Berlin," he said quietly. A faint ripple of laughter met his remark and at once the tension was broken.

For a few minutes longer we lingered and discussed less volatile subjects and then Annemarie announced it was time for her to go home. Geoff and I offered to take her.

She lived in a large modern apartment house in Charlottenburg, and when we reached it Geoff discreetly remained by the car as I took her up the three flights to her little flat.

On the way upstairs I asked when we might see each other again. Though we had spent a long evening together at Dr. Bell's I had not had a single chance to talk to her alone. I told her that on the following weekend we planned to go sailing with General Patman on Wannsee, and suggested she join us. But she refused.

"I've a better idea." she said cryptically, and without explaining she promised she would telephone me soon.

When we reached her door she turned and kissed me lightly on the cheek.

"Dear, dear old Harry," she said. "How I longed to see you again!"

Gently she passed her hand over my head. "It's gray now, and thinner, but it's still curly. For years I thought I'd never get over you, dear. But I did." She laughed and her eyes flashed. I kissed her and left her.

Walking slowly down the dimly lit staircase, I realized that she too had outlived our love.

As we drove home, Geoff was silent. Thinking back over what had been said it was not difficult to guess the reason for his perplexity. I recalled our talks in Washington when he had spoken of the crusading Germans and the danger of their taking things into their own hands. Indeed, some of their remarks at dinner, including Annemarie's, had sounded almost like a veiled defense of the philosophy that motivated Bureau X, which Geoff looked upon as his arch enemy.

Then at last he spoke. "What can I do about them, Harry?" he said. "How can I help and yet not blow up the universe? Granted I must do something, fix things somehow, but how? how?"

He expected no reply from me and got none. Instead I tried to change the subject. It was always the best approach when Geoff got too upset about his personal responsibilities. I told him of my conversation with the novelist about Max Ebers and his evasive reply. "What do you make of it?" I asked.

Geoff shook his head. "I asked Annemarie the same question during dinner. She said that she for one was not going to make any judgments until all the facts were in." He paused a moment as we swung into Miquelstrasse. "Those were almost exactly the words Max used in his note to me," and he turned his tired eyes on me as if searching for a clue.

VII

THE DAY AFTER DR. BELL'S PARTY
I crossed the Wall for the first time to keep my appointment
with Herr Klein in the East Sector. When I reached
Checkpoint Charlie, the American lieutenant in charge
waved me to a halt, took my name and asked how long I
expected to be in the East Sector. I was surprised at the
question until he explained that he only wanted to know
in case I got into trouble and was detained. I told him I
did not know how long I would be gone but that I would
check in before nightfall.

Then I moved across the white line that marks the
boundary. Almost at once a big Vopo officiously shouted
at me to stop again and identify myself. At that moment I
caught sight of Herr Klein standing chatting with a police
officer.

All smiles, he hurried over to me and got into the car. The Vopo officer waved us through and we set out down Friedrichstrasse toward Unter den Linden. Herr Klein had already carefully planned our itinerary. We drove first to where the Lustgarten and the baroque New Palace had once been. The palace, though only partly damaged by the air raids, had been torn down by the Communists as an undesirable reminder of Germany's imperial past, and its site, together with the once shady, tree-filled Lustgarten Park, was now covered with a great sheet of black asphalt to provide the parade ground made fashionable by Stalin in Russsia, where on holidays the workers drearily but dutifully filed past stands of party officials to celebrate whatever joyful event their leaders decreed.

Beside the Marx-Engelsplatz still stood the hideous old cathedral, and somewhat irreverently I asked Herr Klein why the leaders had not torn it down instead of the palace. Herr Klein looked slightly shocked.

"But we cannot interfere with what belongs to the church, only with what belongs to the people," he said.

"And the Schloss?" I asked. "Did you ask the people before you destroyed it?"

"But we represent the people," he said without a smile. "And now let us see the Pergamon Museum," he added, hastily changing the subject. We left the car and walked through the famous collection of Babylonian art with its ancient temple of marble which had been brought piece by piece from the Near East at the beginning of the century.

From there Herr Klein took me into the "old town,"

where narrow alleys wound among ancient buildings which had been surprisingly little damaged compared to the rest of the city. He took me to Sparrow Street and the little Raabediele, the oldest beer tavern in all Berlin. There, in a low, timber-ceilinged room, we each had a stein of beer. Casually Herr Klein asked about the cabarets of West Berlin, and almost before I could reply he suggested that they must be both decadent and impossibly expensive. So I suggested he let me take him to one of the night clubs on Kurfuerstendamm. But he shook his head glumly and explained that unless he was with Soloviev or Alexeiev he was not allowed to cross the Wall. So I proposed we invite Alexeiev as well and he readily agreed.

"Colonel Alexeiev is a most cultured man," he explained. "He knows all the Russian operas and ballets. But he also likes jazz and dancing," he added hastily. "My wife and I have gone out with him several times." Obviously Herr Klein was very proud of his intimacy with the dashing, cultivated Russian colonel.

"My wife would be so happy if she could come too," he added enthusiastically, for the beer had made him lose some of his stiffness. "She loves dancing." From his wallet he produced a photograph of a young woman seated under an artificial cherry tree in full blossom. Her face was round and small but very pretty, her eyes large and flirtatious.

As I admired it he told me they had known each other as children when their fathers worked as stokers together in the municipal power plant. They had married, he told me, when he had been released from prison after being arrested for his anti-Nazi attitude. I asked him how he had revealed his anti-Nazism, and he said he had refused to join the Hitler Youth and had deliberately boycotted the Olympic Games in protest against Hitler. But the immediate cause of his arrest had been getting caught at a Communist meeting to which his brother, even then a Communist party member, had taken him. "I was only fourteen at the time and I served four years. When I got out Ilse was waiting for me and we were married."

"And then?"

"That was in 1939. Then the war started and I was drafted at once and didn't see her again till 1944 when I was invalided home from the eastern front," he explained, and rolled up his sleeve to reveal a long, ugly scar on his forearm.

"I was in the hospital till 1945 when the Russians came. They made me a block warden and I joined the party at once. It was the happiest day in my life," he said, and I could tell he meant it. Ever since, he said, he had lived with his wife in a little apartment in Friedrichshain, back of the power plant where his father had worked. Now he was an official with the Central Committee.

"And you've never regretted joining the party?" I asked.

"You will never know what happiness it has given me," he said. "Today I am safe, sure of a job. I have plenty to eat. But of course that is not the most important. My family is what I live for, Ilse and my son Joseph—I named him after Stalin." I suggested that nowadays Stalin was not so fashionable, but he laughed and said no one need know whom his son was named after.

When we had finished our beer, Herr Klein somewhat

ostentatiously but proudly called for the check and paid it. Then for another hour we tramped through the streets while he pointed out some of the old buildings that had survived and the ruins of those that had been destroyed. When at last we returned to my car I told him there was one more place I wanted to visit—the old Adlon Hotel. In the days before the war the Adlon bar had been the noontime meeting place of the foreign diplomats and the remnants of Berlin's society. Since it was almost next door to the Bluecher Palace I had often stopped there before lunch.

Herr Klein looked troubled. "It is almost entirely destroyed," he explained. Nevertheless I insisted, and we drove down Unter den Linden to Pariserplatz, where the Adlon entrance had once been. As we approached, a Vopo stopped us, and pointed out that the entrance to the Adlon was now on Wilhelmstrasse just around the corner from where it had been.

All that remained of the luxurious old hotel was one single back wing. The entry was dark and shabby and deserted except for an ancient doorman. When I asked for the bar, he shook his head gloomily. He told us the original bar I had known had been destroyed during the Battle of Berlin. Depressed, I turned to go, but then he said there was a little barroom where you could still get a drink and led us down a small corridor to a room facing on Wilhelmstrasse. An equally old waiter welcomed us warmly for there were no other guests.

We ordered some mocha coffee and as we drank it I chatted with the waiter. He had, he said, been one of the barmen in the old days and when I mentioned the names of some of the prewar habitués his face lit up—the Bismarck brothers, grandsons of the Iron Chancellor, Baron von Drexler, the Foreign Office Chief of Protocol, Herr Treptow, who had been shot in 1943 for his part in the anti-Hitler plot.

Herr Klein listened silently. Though the people I mentioned were far removed from the Communist leadership he now served, he obviously enjoyed his vicarious association with the names of the once near-great of the prewar era.

When we finished the coffee I insisted it was my turn to pay. However, as I had no "democratic money" as they call the East German marks, I slipped the waiter a five-dollar bill. He was delighted, for foreign exchange was hard to come by in the East. He guided us ceremoniously to the door and urged us to return soon.

"I have few visitors," he said sadly as we departed.

It was already dusk and remembering my promise to the lieutenant at the checkpoint, I drove Herr Klein to his home and then hurried back to the West Sector and Miquelstrasse.

Geoff generally disliked sailing, saying that it made him restless to be cooped up in so small a space. But the following Sunday was another beautiful late autumn day and the only other alternative to staying in the gloomy old villa was another walk in the crowded Grunewald. Patman himself was not much of a seaman and had invited young Bill Harmsworth to help, for Bill, a native of Cape Cod, was an ardent sailor.

When Bill appeared on the dock of the American Forces Yacht Club I was surprised to see him accompanied by a young girl and even more startled when he introduced Christl Dahlmann. Neither Geoff nor Patman, however, showed any surprise and I realized at once that both had known she was coming. Then I recalled Annemarie's remark that she had a "better idea." Obviously they had all had a hand in it. I gave Geoff a resentful glance, but he ignored it, and later I had to agree that it was perhaps the best way to bring us together.

Christl was wearing blue slacks and a loose white sweater, her long blond hair tucked into a stocking cap. You could see at once her likeness to Annemarie despite the fair hair. Had she inherited those curls from me, I wondered uneasily. Her eyes were big and dark brown, her mouth wide and mobile. She had Annemarie's soft complexion too, with tiny balls of red on her cheekbones. But most like Annemarie of all was her self-assurance. Another girl suddenly thrown with two total strangers, literally into a small boat, might well have felt ill at ease, but Christl was not only perfectly natural, she even seemed to enjoy the prospect.

Though this sudden encounter unnerved me, I somehow managed to hide my emotions in the confusion of getting the boat ready and casting off from the dock.

As we tacked out of the little basin we were quickly surrounded by dozens of other sailing craft, motorboats and rowboats, all headed out onto the lake. Time and again we had to tack and twist and turn to avoid collisions. When at last, in the light breeze, we got into the main part of the lake things were only slightly less cramped. Seldom were we more than a few yards from the nearest boat, and frequently a speedboat would cut across our bows, missing us by inches and setting up a swell that made our little sloop bounce and rock in the waves.

While Bill Harmsworth maneuvered the boat I tried to keep out of the way, and found myself sitting with Geoff forward in the cockpit with Christl between us.

"Have you heard the latest?" Christl said gleefully. Geoff and I shook our heads.

"You haven't heard about the bombs?" she said incredulously. "One in the Leipzig Fair buildings in the middle of a huge Communist celebration; one in Pankow, where all the big shots live; and a third on the steps of the People's Assembly. Three in one night!"

"But who did it?" Geoff asked impatiently.

"Why, we did, of course," Christl said, and then corrected herself. "I mean the Germans."

"Bureau X?" Geoff asked and Christl flushed.

"Oh no, that's just talk. It's the East Germans themselves."

"How did you find out?" Geoff said, slightly annoyed that he had not heard about it.

"It's all over town. All the students are talking about it—and of course it's all over East Berlin. They're laughing like mad at the Vopos. If only we have a few more, they'll be doing more than just laughing at them—they'll be throwing stones and then they'll really revolt—at least that's what Mother says and I agree."

She looked at Geoff and seemed hurt that he was not sharing in her jubilation. A long silence followed and finally she turned to me.

"You're Mother's old friend, aren't you?" she said pleasantly, and I nodded. "She told me about you last night when she came home from Dr. Bell's."

Noticing my embarrassment, she turned to Geoff.

"You knew her too, didn't you, in the old days?" and he said he had.

"Tell me something about those times," she rattled on. "I've seen the old villa on Rauchstrasse—or rather what's left of it. But Mother never talks about what she used to do. It must have been interesting, though rather awful with Hitler and all those people."

"She never mentioned me before?" I asked, and I could feel my face turn scarlet.

"No, as a matter of fact, last night was the first time I'd ever heard of you—except of course from Bill," and she waved toward Harmsworth sitting at the tiller.

At that moment a sailboat was cutting sharply across our bows and Bill was frowning.

"Poor Bill." She laughed. "He's such a professional sailor that he loathes these amateurs on Wannsee." Her large eyes looked at him, amused and affectionate.

Geoff was preoccupied with the boat traffic and, half turning his back, watched the sailboats, motorboats and even rowboats that were crisscrossing the lake. Together they seemed like a school of big fish all headed in a single direction, but twisting and turning across each other's path. I thought he looked depressed.

Left alone with Christl, I ignored her question about "those days," for my own curiosity was at least as great as hers. Harmsworth had introduced her as "Miss Dahlmann," which provided no clue to the question uppermost in my mind—her paternal parentage. I thought of Max Ebers and asked if she knew him.

She started when I mentioned his name. "You mean that man who just defected?" she said, and I nodded. She frowned and shook her head. Then abruptly she changed the subject.

"I have a message from Grandfather," she said. "He sends you his best and asks if you couldn't come and see him."

"Is your grandfather still alive?" I asked, for it had never occurred to me that "old" Herr Dahlmann could have survived the war.

"Very much alive. He's living out on Mueggelsee," she said.

"Mueggelsee? But that's in the East Sector, isn't it? I remember the house on the Lake."

"That's it. He moved there when Rauchstrasse was burned and has been there ever since. It always was his favorite home. Old Tante Viktoria lived there with him till she died."

"But Dr. Dahlmann must be pretty old now."

"Yes. He's seventy-five and not too well, to tell you the truth."

"But why did he stay in the East Zone?" I asked.

"I guess you could call it a miscalculation," Christl said. "You see, he loves Mueggelsee and had no place to go in the West. He always thought that if things got too bad he could slip across, the way everyone used to do before the Wall. He even had put his money away in a Swiss bank and was getting ready to move—a bit too slowly as it turned out—when the Wall went up and he was caught."

"But couldn't he have got through?" I asked incredulously.

"At seventy-five it's pretty difficult to scramble through barbed wire or climb over a wall or swim the Spree."

"And now? Is he all alone?"

"Pretty much so. He has a couple of old cronies living nearby. I go over every Sunday to see him and take him what he needs. As a matter of fact, I'll be going over this afternoon when we get back."

"Can you get across the boundary easily?"

Christl laughed. "You see I'm a Swede technically and I have a Swedish passport."

"And your mother?"

"No. She has a German passport and she hasn't seen Grandfather since the Wall went up. It's rather hard on her," Christl said.

We were out in the main part of Wannsee now, and though the traffic around us had thinned a little we were still surrounded by boats of all sizes and shapes. Beside us an excursion steamer chugged past, crowded to the top with tourists, hanging over the rails. Poor devils, I thought. Twenty years ago they could have taken trips on those boats all over the great network of rivers and canals which fanned out from Berlin over most of Germany. Now they were crowded into this tiny last remnant of water in Wannsee.

"Doesn't the fact that your mother is so active politically make it difficult for your grandfather?" I asked. "I'd think the Communists would take it out on him."

"So far they haven't," Christl said. "After all Dahlmann is a pretty common name and they don't seem to have caught on to the fact that they're related. Besides, Grandfather lives practically underground."

"Underground?" I asked. "What do you mean?"

Christl flushed. "Oh, I didn't really mean that—I just wanted to say he lives very inconspicuously."

General Patman had now taken over the tiller as we sailed south down the lake. Bill Harmsworth came forward and suggested to Christl they go up in the bow.

I don't know how much of my conversation with Christl Geoff had heard, but when she had gone he turned to me: "She seems like a damned nice girl," he commented. Ever since I had known him, Geoff had been attracted by pretty women and almost equally repelled by anyone dowdy or unattractive. Indeed, for an allegedly cold intellectual man, he was unusually sensitive to the ladies.

The boat traffic had begun to thin out as we sailed slowly in the light breeze southward. Geoff and I joined Patman in the stern and chatted aimlessly for a few minutes. I noticed that we were suddenly alone on this part of the lake. A hundred yards or so ahead a row of gray motorboats drifted aimlessly across our bows.

Suddenly Bill Harmsworth jumped up from the deck and hurried back to us.

"General, I'd come about if I were you. We're almost across the boundary." Then I noticed a line of buoys only a few yards ahead. The sound of a motor in one of the gray boats, starting up, drifted across the water and, leaving a feathery white wake, the boat abruptly swung around and headed directly for us.

"The water Vopos," Bill said. "They patrol the zonal boundary from here across the lake."

Patman swung the tiller hard and the boat came about, heading slowly northward. The roar of the motor in the police boat dropped to a purr. I watched it resentfully as it turned and swung south again. Somehow it had made me feel as though I were a small rabbit or chicken scurrying for cover when a hawk swooped down on it from some tall, dead tree. Now the hawk was back on its perch, and with arrogant, hooded eyes had resumed its vigil.

By lunchtime we were back at the slip. As Christl said good-bye I asked her to give her grandfather my best regards. She said she would and then she added: "Don't you think you could spare time someday to come out and visit him? He is dreadfully lonely and it would be so good for him."

I said I would come soon.

Then she shook hands with Geoff and said: "Good-bye, Uncle Geoff," and started to laugh. "Mother told me I should call you that."

For the first time that day Geoff chuckled. Then she said good-bye to Patman and turned to me. Suddenly she leaned forward and kissed me on the cheek, her arms lightly around me.

"From Mother," she whispered in my ear. Then she skipped off down the dock, followed by Bill.

Patman and Geoff had turned away and were stowing the gear on the boat when I recovered myself. I knew I wasn't going to be of much help to them and I slowly walked down the dock and out onto the yacht club lawn.

A few minutes later I felt a hand on my shoulder.

"Come along, old boy," Geoff was saying.

Patman suggested a cocktail and I readily accepted.

That evening the villa on Miquelstrasse was more tomb-like than ever. Probably because he knew my own state of mind and wanted to distract me, Geoff held forth at length about the misfortunes of the Berliners confined to their tiny patch of territory.

"It would give anyone claustrophobia," he said. "You can hardly blame them when they gloat over those insane bombings. Somehow we've got to find some way out for them."

My own troubles, however, made me less compassionate and for once I listened with only half an ear. As I sipped my nightcap I could think of little else but Christl and Annemarie. Would Annemarie tell me who Christl's father was? Did I really want to know? Ten years before when I settled down in Bavaria I thought my life was permanently arranged, that nothing again could upset it. But now nothing seemed settled.

At last I went to the phone and rang the number Annemarie had given me. She answered herself and I said bluntly that whether she liked it or not I insisted on seeing her the next evening. After some argument she agreed to dine with me at the Bird Cage.

VIII

IT WAS THE FIRST TIME EITHER of us had visited the Bird Cage since the war. It was practically empty when we came in. I began to introduce myself to Harry but he recognized my voice and cut me short before I could finish.

"Herr Harding," he burst forth and thrust out his hand. Then Annemarie spoke and he turned his blind eyes toward her. "And Fräulein Dahlmann! I always knew you two would come back and see me—as all the others have. But I've waited a long, long time."

Annemarie laughed gaily. "Have so many others come back?"

"You'd be amazed," Harry said. "Of course some were killed in the war. Hitler shot some others but still there are many left." He rattled off half a dozen names.

He led us to a small table in a corner where we had so often sat in those early days. When he had taken our order he went to the piano and in a moment the little room resounded to the tune of "A Tisket, a Tasket." Harry's deep voice boomed out louder than ever with "We put Hitler in a basket." We all laughed, but through the laughter tears welled up in Annemarie's eyes.

Like all such reunions, it fell short of expectations. Annemarie managed to control her tears quickly enough, and when I told her of my meeting with Christl she seemed genuinely happy.

"I knew you two would get on," she said. "Christl was enchanted."

I looked at her earnestly. "Tell me more about Christl, Annemarie."

"More? What do you want to know about her?"

"You know as well as I," I said, trying to avoid the direct question, but she simply smiled and shook her head. Geoff had said that Max had followed her to Sweden before the war and I asked her if it was true.

"You should have asked Max himself," she said evasively, "but it's too late now."

"Have you been in touch with him since the war?" I asked, still probing.

"I have no contacts with Max," she said and the way she said it struck me as odd, for it was not the sort of expression one would use in referring to a childhood friend.

It was obvious that my indirect approach to the question that upset me was not going to get me far.

"Annemarie, you know as well as I what I am driving

at. Tell me please, for God's sake, about Christl." I reached out and squeezed her hand and looked hard into her great brown eyes.

"Dear Harry," she said and pressed my hand in turn. "Of course I understand but I'm afraid I can't help. At least I have no intention of helping. I once told Christl that her father was lost in the war. She believes it and that is all she needs to know, and all I propose to tell her—or you for that matter." Her tone was so firm that I knew that she meant what she said and had every intention of sticking to it.

I threw up my hands in despair. "I suppose you know how this leaves me," I said bitterly.

"Yes, my dear, I know. Once before I refused to do what you asked me because I was not going to rob you of your career. We managed to survive. And now I'm not going to intrude in your present career, which incidentally seems to suit you well." She smiled across the table and reached out and patted my hand. "So let's forget all about Christl's ancestry and talk about more immediate things."

Before I could protest again she went on: "Tell me about Geoff, Harry. His attitude disappointed me the other evening at Dr. Bell's. As a matter of fact it shocked me a little."

"In what way?" I asked, surprised.

"He seems bitter about us Berliners and not really very anxious to help. He's different from his predecessors. They never got very far but they tried. Geoff doesn't seem to want to try even."

"In what way could he help? What can he do? He's tied

by Washington. He's desperately eager to fix things here, but not by force or by threats. He believes the only effective way is persuasion and he's determined to try it."

"But why can't he help us Berliners at the same time?"

"How?"

"In lots of ways. In the rescue work, for example—helping the East Germans to get out. Take one small example: there's still one tunnel the Vopos don't know about, the Water Tunnel we call it. All we need do is to pump it out. But Geoff has given strict orders that it's not to be touched. He's even put a guard on it. If he keeps the guard there indefinitely the East Germans are bound to find out about it and then our last tunnel will have been made useless."

"Under the present circumstances I doubt if anyone is going to persuade him to remove the guard. Of course if things changed—"

"Or if Geoff changed," Annemarie suggested impatiently.

There was a long pause and then Annemarie spoke again. "But doesn't he see that if only we stood up to the Russians—if we made it as uncomfortable for them as possible—that perhaps they would leave of their own accord?"

"You're talking like these Bureau X people, Annemarie. Geoff doesn't think you can frighten the Russians away—and neither, for that matter, do I."

Annemarie flushed and stared down at her plate. When she spoke again her voice was calm and indifferent, and the subjects she talked about were purely impersonal—political developments in Bonn and Washington, the French elections and the latest scandals in London.

We finished our dinner and old blind Harry came and sat down at the table. He was carrying a bottle of old French brandy and three glasses. "For old times' sake," he said as he filled the glasses.

A few minutes later Annemarie said she was tired and I drove her to her apartment in Charlottenburg. On the way home she reminded me of my promise to Christl to visit Herr Dahlmann at Mueggelsee. "He was very fond of you, Harry," she said. "To see you would boost his morale enormously." I agreed to go as soon as I could and asked if there was anything I could take him as a gift.

"I doubt if he's mixed a martini since the war," she said and we both laughed.

A day or two later I picked up Christl for our visit to her grandfather. The weather was cold and nasty. A light rain began to fall as we drove to Checkpoint Charlie.

The American soldiers at the boundary were lounging about drearily in their raincoats. They stopped us just long enough to ask how long we proposed to be gone. As I was about to drive my little car across the line that marked the border between East and West, Christl suggested I put the two bottles I had brought along into the deep pockets of my trench coat. "The Vopos might be thirsty today," she explained.

On the other side an East Berlin Vopo in a long heavy overcoat, cut in the Russian style and about two sizes too small for him, waved me to a halt and then signaled me to drive up a little blind alley where, Christl explained, the East German police screened all visitors. She was evidently thoroughly familiar with the procedure, because as soon as we stopped she hopped out and gave her passport to a young Vopo dressed like the one at the gate, in a long Russian coat, which this time was several sizes too big for him. Taking my passport as well, the Vopo disappeared into a run-down building which had once been a shop and was now converted into a frontier station.

Another Vopo approached in an equally ill-fitting great-coat and demanded gruffly that I open the trunk of the car. He peered into the empty compartment and poked suspiciously behind the spare tire. Then he asked to look under the engine hood, and again I opened it while he stood over me, evidently relishing giving orders to a foreigner and an American at that. Finally he told me to take the cushions out of the back seat. I looked at him in astonishment and began to protest but Christl elbowed me and frowned.

"Just do what he says or we will be here all day," she murmured.

So I complied, and after satisfying himself that I had nothing concealed in the car he asked me how much "democratic money" I was carrying.

I could not help laughing and told the surly Vopo that all the money I had was undemocratic. Annoyed, he at once demanded to see my wallet. Christl must have seen my astonishment at this new affront, for again she poked me with her elbow. "Don't make a fuss. It does no good and can get us stuck here for hours," she said. So, sullenly I handed my wallet to the guard, who after shuffling through its folds handed it back.

"Now get back into your car and wait till you get your passports back," he said and walked off with a self-satisfied look as though pleased at having accomplished his mission of irritating the dirty foreigner.

Indignantly I took my place behind the wheel. "This is worse than Hitler's border guards," I muttered, "and almost as bad as Stalin's."

"The Vopos are descendants of both of them," Christl said smiling.

Ten minutes later our passports were returned and we were told we could go on. Slowly I drove down Friedrichstrasse to Unter den Linden and then turned eastward.

What made the whole procedure so absurd, I said to Christl, was that when I had crossed before I had been met by Herr Klein and had been waved through the Vopo lines like an honored guest.

"Klein?" Christl asked, and I explained who he was. She gave me a sidelong, disapproving glance and frowned. "Of course, if you go around with that sort—" she said and her voice trailed off into silence. I began to feel like a traitor because of my association with Klein.

Our route lay through Alexanderplatz and Christl pointed out the new police presidium which had replaced the bombed-out old prison known as the "Alex" which I had occasionally visited as a young vice consul when stray Americans got put in jail by Hitler's police. The new Alex was in a way even more sinister looking than the grimy old Victorian structure I remembered. It was built of ponderous, rough-hewn granite blocks trimmed with blood-red sandstone, its big windows heavily barred, its iron doors tight shut and guarded by long-coated Vopos. Vaguely I wondered how Klein, on my previous visit, had managed to avoid passing within sight of the big ugly building.

We turned down what had until recently been Stalinallee, with its pompous new apartment buildings—the East Germans' pathetic answer to the handsome Hansa community of houses built in the West Sector.

Though they had been standing only a few years, the buildings, designed in the ornate, pseudo-classical style decreed by Stalin, already looked old and shabby. The ochre-colored tiles were peeling from the walls and great sections of the stucco cornices and trimmings had crumbled and fallen.

Then we turned right past the old Silesian station, now the East station, and I remembered how Herr Dahlmann had once quoted the old proverb that Asia begins at Berlin's Silesian station.

Our route led through the industrial area of Friedrichsfelde, where the tall chimneys of the municipal power plant poured out jets of black smoke produced from the burning of the brown coal. A heavy layer of soot-ridden smog lay over the area, adding to the gloom and dirt.

Christl sat silent beside me, speaking only when she directed me through the winding streets. Obviously she was as depressed by the landscape as I was. But at last we emerged from the smog, and after passing through several miles of workers' communities, came to the more open area on the southeastern edge of the city where it joins the Soviet Zone. Now the blocks of apartment buildings gave way to large villas and occasional parks and woods of birch and pine. Between the trees we caught occasional glimpses of the Spree winding between green banks, a coal barge or two chugging slowly toward the center of the city.

At last Christl pointed the way up a little gravel road through a forest of pines. A hundred yards beyond we came to a community of large rundown villas, their lawns unkempt and overgrown, stretching down to the banks of the Mueggelsee. One of the houses looked vaguely familiar, and Christl told me to stop in front of it.

Almost immediately the front door opened and an old man gingerly came down the broad steps. As Christl threw herself into his arms I recognized the gaunt, aged features of Herr Dahlmann. When I had known him before the war, he had been a big, muscular, vigorous man, athletic and trim, his complexion sunburnt and healthy. Now his face was flabby and gray, his eyes dull, his movements slow.

But he greeted me lustily enough, his old face creased in a big smile. When I produced the bottles of gin and vermouth he roared with laughter and clapped me on the shoulder.

Then he turned to Christl: "Call Fuchs and Heinemann. Tell them there is a guest." He turned back to me and explained almost apologetically: "They are my friends. They live just down the street. Nowadays there are so few people one can trust. In fact they are the only ones. And we have so few visitors from the West that whenever someone comes it is only fair to share him."

He led the way into the house. A smell of coal smoke permeated the air and I noticed a pair of what once had been fawn leather gloves now black with soot. Probably, I thought to myself, they had been part of Herr Dahlmann's elegant race-meeting wardrobe. Dahlmann caught my glance and laughed.

"I've just been trying to get the furnace going," he explained, "but I'm not a very good stoker. Never had any experience until they took our last servants away a year ago."

He led me out onto an enclosed veranda. Just beyond it were the traces of an overgrown formal garden from which a lawn stretched down to the lake shore. In the far corner was the boathouse where he had once kept a speed-boat and a small cabin cruiser. Following my gaze, he said: "Yes, the boats—they took them away two years ago—for a workers' club they said, but I daresay it was for some Russian general or commissar."

As I continued to stare at the boathouse he lowered his voice though there was no one within earshot: "And the little room above it is not used either."

A gate at the side of the garden opened and a well-dressed couple slipped in and up the veranda steps. "This is Herr Fuchs and Frau Fuchs, Mr. Harding, an old friend from the days before the war."

As Christl appeared with a tray of glasses and ice another couple crept in from the garden. "Herr and Frau Heine-mann," Dahlmann said briefly. He waved us to seats around a large table. "And now we are all assembled," he said with finality, as though he were opening a meeting of a board of directors.

Both of the women were dressed in smart, colorful sports

clothes that could only have come from the West. Their hair was neat and combed high in the latest fashion but both hairdos bore signs that they were home-made. The men too were well dressed, in English tweed jackets and bright-colored waistcoats, once the fashion among Berlin's sporting set, a period which had ended when Hitler had banned all imports from England and which had, for the East Germans at least, never been resumed. Obviously the clothes had been unearthed very recently from their chests, for the smell of camphor still lingered on them.

While Herr Dahlmann with a great show of ceremony began mixing the martinis, there was desultory talk about the table. But as soon as he had filled the cocktail glasses and drunk a toast to me the mood of his guests abruptly became more serious.

Herr Fuchs, the youngest of the three men, turned to me: "Tell us, Herr Harding, have you any good news? Is there any possibility that at last something will happen to get us out of this?" and he waved his hand dejectedly at the shabby surroundings.

I told them what I knew, trying my best to be accurate. For the moment at least, I said, I saw no sign of any change for the better. Those who had failed to leave before the Wall went up were stuck. I wished I could have given them some more cheerful news, but on the other hand nothing is more cruel than raising false hopes.

Frau Fuchs seemed to interpret my remarks as an accusation: "But we couldn't leave before they put up the Wall. My old mother was bedridden and so was Tante Viktoria," she added, referring to Herr Dahlmann's old mistress. "Now of course they have both died, but it is too late." I said nothing for there was nothing to say.

"Perhaps you are thinking we should have tried to escape through the Wall," Herr Heinemann said. "But that is only for young men. Perhaps Herr Fuchs could have made it, but what about his four little children?"

Christl broke in: "But I don't think Herr Harding meant to accuse any of you. He was just saying that since the Wall there is not much chance."

Old Dahlmann looked at me sharply: "You were always honest with me before, Harry. Tell me truthfully, have we in the East been cowards? Should we have done more to help ourselves?"

But before I could answer Fuchs broke in: "We tried it once at the time of the uprising in '53. Do you remember, Heinemann, you and me with those bottles of gasoline on Marx-Engelsplatz, when the Russian tanks started charging at us? I ducked into the cathedral and you got behind the grandstands." They both chuckled and their eyes grew bright at the memory. "It was the happiest day in our lives," Heinemann said proudly.

In an effort to change the subject I asked if they had heard the rumor that Max Ebers had disappeared and that the East Germans were searching for him.

At the mention of his name everyone in the room stiffened for a second, and there was an awkward silence as they stared at one another.

Then Herr Dahlmann spoke up, his voice low. "We live very isolated lives, Harry, so we hear no reports—least of all any about Max Ebers."

He rose and began to refill our glasses, but I could not help noticing that his hand trembled and twice he spilled some of the cocktail on the mahogany table. As Christl ran to get a dishcloth, Herr Dahlmann said, "Getting old, I guess. My hand's not as steady as it once was." And he chuckled, but the chuckle was not as hearty as it might have been.

For two hours they plied me with questions, all of them with one gist: what was America going to do to free them, to drive out the Russians? My answers discouraged them. When the last of the martinis had been consumed Herr Dahlmann looked across the table to me as though I had been evading an obvious fact.

"But tell me, Harry, what is the meaning of sending Geoff Schuyler to Berlin? Doesn't that signify some stiffening in Washington vis-à-vis the Russians?"

I looked at him, startled, and I noticed that the others were waiting eagerly for my reply. Noting my hesitation Dahlmann tried to explain his question: "I knew Schuyler well," he began, "and I always thought he knew that we Germans were not all of us Nazis to be hanged like those at Nuremberg. Even as a young fellow he was a man of principles. Certainly you cannot tell me he is prepared to sit by placidly and stare at the Wall and do nothing."

I knew only too well what Geoff had in mind, but I dared not raise hopes by alluding to it. Instead I hid behind rather pompous remarks about Washington's attitude and the fact that Geoff was tied by instructions.

They were clearly disappointed, and I suspected that Dahlmann had been predicting to them that Geoff's appointment somehow signified a change of Washington policy—a ray of hope. I could almost hear him telling them of his young friend, of his courage and conviction, his stubbornness and his brilliance. Now in a sentence or two I had destroyed even that illusion, and their bodies, which had bent tense over the big table, seemed to grow limp, and they all stared at Dahlmann reproachfully.

"But, Harry," Dahlmann persisted, "Schuyler would never have taken the job unless he agreed with Washington. And I cannot believe he is as timid as you seem to suggest—at any rate he wasn't when I knew him."

I resented the remark and answered a little more sharply than I meant to that Geoff was first of all a good diplomat and that his personal views or feelings were not what made policy.

Dahlmann smiled, and staring at his empty glass said to no one in particular: "I wonder."

There was a moment of silence, and idly I gazed out the window to the lake. Just off the dock a black ball was bouncing on the water, but then suddenly, as I watched, it disappeared.

Herr Fuchs began to speak and I turned back to him.

"Then I take it that the Americans are not prepared to do anything for us? They will not or dare not stand up to the Russians? Must we do that for ourselves?" He paused for a moment and then went on, his tone higher, more exasperated, "But how? How can we organize? How can we bring together the millions who think as we do? It is dangerous enough for us three old men to get together as we are now. But it takes hundreds of thousands to be effective. We have no means of communicating, no transmitters, no arms, no organization. Tell me: how? how? how?" His voice had risen to desperation, and I squirmed in my chair at his obvious frustration. The others sat silent, staring at me, waiting for an answer.

But there was nothing to reply. Feeling like a coward, I glanced at my watch and caught Christl's eye. We all rose and as we started toward the door I took one last look toward the lake. It was gray outside and I could just make out the outlines of the boathouse. The last rays of the setting sun seemed to strike the upstairs window and make it glow as though there were a light inside. Herr Dahlmann took me by the elbow and accompanied me to the door.

On the steps Fuchs stopped me and said half apologetically: "Excuse my outburst, but you must know how we feel. What you have told us is bitter, bitter news. But we are grateful because at least we know you have spoken the truth, which is a rare thing nowadays." We shook hands around and I climbed into my car.

It was still drizzling and pitch dark when Christl and I started back toward Checkpoint Charlie. As I switched on the car lights I realized the sun had set a long time ago. Startled, I remembered the reflection on the boathouse window, but then I shook my head. These excursions into the East Sector were straining my nerves and producing hallucinations.

All the way I kept looking in the rear mirror, wondering whether our visit had not been detected, and whether some police car was following us, ready to pick us up when we stopped at the border.

We drove in silence, and I doubt if I have ever been more depressed as I thought back over what those three hopeless, helpless men had said. Geoff's schemes must succeed, but how?

There were few formalities at the checkpoint, and the Vopos waved us through after a cursory glance at our passports. As we crossed the white line marking the boundary and the American M.P.'s checked us off, Christl spoke up: "Whenever I cross back into the West, I feel like a skindiver coming up after a long deep plunge. It feels so wonderful to take that first big breath of fresh air."

Skindiver? Suddenly I remembered that black rubber ball bobbing in front of the dock and then the light in the window. And then I recalled how old Dahlmann's hand had shaken when we talked of Max's disappearance. But again I realized that my imagination was simply getting the better of me.

It was nearly seven when I dropped Christl off at her apartment.

Before she slipped out of the car she leaned over and kissed me affectionately on the cheek.

"You were an angel to come," she said.

My eyes followed her, troubled, as she hurried across the sidewalk. Was I never to know whether she was my own child? With a helpless gesture of despair I turned the car and headed back to Dahlem.

One of General Patman's deputies was giving a cocktail party in Geoff's honor and I had to make an appearance, though after my visit with old Dahlmann it was the last thing I wanted to do.

The party was in full swing when I arrived. The senior officers of the Berlin command in colorful dress uniforms and their wives in low-cut dresses crowded every square inch of the three large reception rooms of the requisitioned villa. Their voices were loud, and growing louder with each fresh glass of bourbon and water which white-jacketed mess boys pressed upon them.

A colonel's wife buttonholed me and asked how she should go about publishing a book of her memoirs which she had just started to write. Somehow I managed to slip away from her but was quickly cornered by Colonel Samson, Patman's Chief of Security.

He too had had his share of bourbon and his weight shifted from one foot to the other in a highly unmilitary manner as he talked: "Have you heard the one about the fellow in the bar who—" he began. Irresistibly my mind wandered back to Mueggelsee as he babbled on. Luckily I subconsciously registered as he finished his story and managed a laugh.

Over the heads of the guests I caught a glimpse of Geoff surrounded by officers' wives, his face blank with boredom. And again I thought of the small unhappy group I had just left behind the Wall. It seemed to me almost indecent even to be present at a party like this after my visit. I pictured them now, sitting glumly at that table in the villa, staring morosely at the empty pitcher of martinis, and thinking in despair of what I had told them.

A young major who worked in the Intelligence Division came up to me and I suddenly felt compelled to talk about

Herr Dahlmann and his cronies. Surely, I thought, an intelligence officer would be interested in this aspect of Berlin. But as I began to describe them and their dismal lives the major excused himself and slipped off to talk to a pretty young woman standing nearby.

At last Geoff caught my eye and signaled to me. I pushed through the crowd and then with him said good-bye to our host and hostess.

Driving home through the rain I told Geoff of my visit and as accurately as I could related the entire conversation, including the many references to himself. I did not try to conceal the hopes his own appointment had raised among Dahlmann's friends.

Needless to say, it distressed him. The picture of the three helpless men huddled together, lonely and despairing, was enough to depress anyone, but the thought that he had been regarded as some sort of a savior upset him deeply.

"Harry, I've got to do something," he said, as we sat before the fire after dinner. "But what? I don't give a damn about the intellectuals' dreams of the great German nation, but to the average Berliners, the run-of-the-mill—especially those in the East—to them we really owe something."

He locked the fingers of his hands together and pounded them on the coffee table.

He had reason to feel frustrated. When he had reported his conversations with Soloviev to the department, Secretary Lane had seemed singularly unimpressed, doubtless recalling the dozens of times the Russians had assumed an air of reasonableness only later to disappoint our hopes. The department had therefore instructed him for the time being not to follow up Soloviev's suggestion to urge the Germans to discuss between themselves ways of mitigating the hardships of the Wall.

"And to make matters worse—take a look at this." Geoff pulled a newspaper from his brief case and tossed it to me. It was an East German paper and across the front page was splashed a headline reading: "Fascist Murderers at Work Again."

Below it an article described a train wreck on the Berlin-Warsaw line in which six people had been killed and dozens wounded. "The police have established beyond doubt that the express was derailed by Fascist saboteurs from the West. Among the debris, they discovered explosive devices made in Munich."

"Do you think it's true?" I asked.

"Of course it's true," Geoff said. "What's more, it's the third time in ten days that Bureau X has pulled something off. Soloviev phoned me this afternoon and called my attention to this one. He said that last Sunday a Soviet official had been shot and seriously wounded during some sort of celebration in Dresden. Of course that one never got into the papers."

"I thought that Bureau X had subsided," I said.

"They had until ten days ago. I asked Samson what he knew but he can't figure it out either—not that I really expected that Prussian mind to produce an explanation."

There was a long silence and I got up and went to the bar to freshen my drink. Geoff continued to sit hunched up in his big chair, deep in thought, his eyes staring at the rug at his feet.

"If only the extremists here in the West would behave themselves," he said, "I think I could fix things in Washington so that the real victims, the real Berliners, could get the break they deserved."

That night as I was going to bed I recalled that revealing remark. Only a few weeks ago in Washington Geoff had seemed determined to put the Berliners in their place. Now his aim seemed to be to rescue them. He was still set on "fixing things," but now it seemed to him that what needed fixing was Washington, not Berlin.

IX

GEOFF'S FRUSTRATIONS ARISING FROM the activities of Bureau X and the cautious instructions he was receiving from Washington were in part compensated for by the progress he was making in his personal relations with the Russians.

A week after our visit to Potsdam, Soloviev had returned his call, and a few days later had accepted an invitation to dinner at Miquelstrasse, which Alexeiev and Klein had also attended. During the course of the dinner Klein, aided by Alexeiev, again hinted broadly that they wanted to see some of the night life along West Berlin's famous Kurfuerstendamm, so I invited them to go out a few evenings later to the Bird Cage, and included Klein's wife in the invitation. I also suggested that Geoff come along, but he thought it would be unwise for him at this early stage in his assignment to appear in public with Russians, to say nothing of East Berlin officials.

The evening we selected was shortly after my visit to Mueggelsee. I had asked Annemarie to come along too but she flatly refused, saying Russian officers were not her favorite dancing partners. So I asked Bill Harmsworth and Christl instead. She too was hesitant, but Bill persuaded her to accept, for he was eager to make contact with the Russians.

At the last moment, I had some misgivings about taking them to the Bird Cage. Perhaps, I thought, they would like something bigger and gaudier, like the Femina, with its huge floor and table telephones, and lots of pretty so-called hostesses. But then it struck me that they would have seen things like the Femina at least in the Hollywood movies, while the Bird Cage was in a sense unique and far more attractive.

Frau Klein, whom I saw for the first time, was a small blonde, and very pretty indeed—even more so than she seemed in the posed, stilted picture her husband had shown me. She was wearing a printed silk dress with a bright flower design which clearly had neither come from nor been designed in the West Sector. Communists, I concluded, observed their own Trading with the Enemy Act. Klein wore a double-breasted blue suit which stirred a vague memory in me which I could not place until I remembered the plainclothes men I had seen in my few visits to Moscow. It must have come from the Soviet military store—doubtless a gift from Soloviev or Alexeiev to their faithful and admiring German aide. Alexeiev himself was dressed in a

practically new tuxedo, which none but an expert tailor
could have cut. Only the slightly crooked bowtie suggested
that he was not entirely accustomed to such elegance. The
fact that no one else in the Bird Cage wore a dinner jacket
did not seem to disturb him at all. In fact, he acted as
though he were the only properly dressed person in the
place.

However, to give the devil his due, this time Alexeiev
behaved very well. He neither drank too much nor talked
too loudly. When Klein got up to dance with his wife,
Alexeiev immediately invited Christl, with whom he twirled
primly around the tiny floor in a way I suspected he had
been taught in some Soviet Army school of decorum. Bill
Harmsworth and I, left alone at the table, exchanged
glances and he whispered to me that the party was already
a success.

Of the three, Klein was, I think, the most enchanted
with the little spot. He constantly looked around at the
chic Berliners at neighboring tables, examining their clothes
intently or staring in open admiration at the elegance of the
red lacquered décor. His wife was hardly less impressed,
and after a glass or two of champagne babbled happily to
anyone who would listen about what a wonderful time she
was having.

Alexeiev was slightly more subdued. I had half expected
him to tell us that in Moscow the dance halls were much
bigger and that the music was provided by a twenty-piece
band and not by a blind pianist. But he said nothing of the
sort, and it was too obvious to conceal that he was
thoroughly enjoying his night out on a bourgeois party.

That he remained so sober was due largely to the fact that he did not miss a single dance, and when Christl finally was too exhausted to take turns with Frau Klein, Alexeiev spent the rest of the evening dancing with the slim little blonde tightly grasped to his chest, her cheek pressed to his in a style I am sure he did not learn at the Russian Army dancing school.

Klein was clearly pleased at the success his wife made, and while she and Alexeiev twined their way around the floor he told us once more what a highly cultivated and brilliant young man Alexeiev was.

"He will make a great career," he confided in me. "Already Soloviev depends on him for all his political decisions. He also has very important connections in Moscow. His brother-in-law is a high official in the Supreme Soviet—" He stopped his eulogy only when Alexeiev and his wife returned to the table at intermissions.

It was well after two when Christl and Bill Harmsworth excused themselves, and a few minutes later, taking the hint, the two Germans and Alexeiev reluctantly said goodnight. Before leaving Alexeiev carefully wrote down the name of the place and its address.

"I shall come back," he said in his heavy Slav accent. "With you," he added, squeezing Frau Klein's bare arm. Herr Klein beamed happily, oblivious of the fact that he had been left out of the invitation.

During the next weeks Geoff's contacts with the Russians slowly became better and more frequent. Both Soloviev and Alexeiev had, it seemed to him, lost a little of their suspicion. They appeared at last to recognize that one could be opposed to the Soviet system yet respect and even admire individual Russians and Russian accomplishments. Personally, they seemed to Geoff to be exponents of the so-called liberal school, as opposed to those remnants of Stalinism that lingered in the Moscow regime, and appeared eager for a freer exchange and some sort of understanding with the United States, which he knew they sincerely admired.

Subsequently Geoff found further grounds for encouragement when the activities of Bureau X, after the flurry of earlier activities, began to subside. This too had been reflected in Geoff's improved relations with the Russians.

Only once was there a flare-up and that, though while it lasted it was nerve-racking, served to clear the atmosphere. The American sector, because of a historical quirk in Berlin's expansion, included a tiny enclave in the Soviet Zone known as Steinstuecken. Early in the occupation, when the allies, East and West, were responsible for feeding their sectors, the U.S. had offered to give Steinstuecken to the Russians, but the offer had been refused. Now, when the Russians no longer fed the population, they demanded that Steinstuecken be incorporated in the Soviet Zone. Naturally, Washington had refused and had assured the inhabitants of the enclave that they would be supported and would have access to the West Sector.

During one of their meetings, Soloviev had informed Geoff that the enclave was an anomaly and must be incorporated into the Soviet Zone. He had been ordered, he said, to close the narrow dirt road leading to it from the American sector. The closing would, he said, take place the following day. Geoff retorted that he would not submit to any such unilateral action and warned the general emphatically that he would keep his promise to the residents of Steinstuecken, by force if necessary. The general looked unhappy, but said he had no choice in the matter. His orders had come from Moscow.

Next morning before dawn Geoff, General Patman and I had gone to the spot where the Steinstuecken road entered the Soviet Zone. A platoon of Soviet infantry had already taken up position across it. American helicopters had reported Soviet tanks concealed on either side of the mile-long road, and Patman had ordered a dozen American tanks as well as a company of rangers to the spot. These movements had taken place with the greatest secrecy, as Geoff wanted at all costs to avoid a public confrontation which might, by raising questions of prestige, stiffen Russian resistance.

Just as light was breaking, Geoff, after a last-minute consultation, started on foot down the narrow dirt road. General Patman had objected strenuously to Geoff's going alone and had insisted on accompanying him. But Geoff pointed out that in case it came to a showdown Patman's place was with his troops, and in the end the general had agreed. I too had objected and said I would go along with him, but to this he retorted that one person was as effective as two.

When the lonely figure strode toward the line of Russian troops we watched him anxiously through our field glasses. As he approached them they closed ranks and stood shoulder to shoulder across the road. A foot from them he stopped and ordered them to make way, but they stood their ground. Then, as previously planned, he turned and signaled Patman. The general nodded to a young captain in battle dress, who in turn assembled a platoon of rangers on the sector line.

"Fix bayonets," he commanded, and I heard the clank of steel on steel.

"Load," he said, and the bolts of a dozen rifles clicked as the cartridges slid into their chambers. Then, taking his place at the head of the double column, the captain turned to face his men: "Now I don't want any shooting," he warned, "unless it's absolutely necessary. Get it? Forward march!"

It was the first time, I think, in the history of the Berlin occupation that a battle-ready unit of American troops had marched into the Soviet Zone prepared for action. An icy chill ran up my spine as I waited for the Soviet response. Behind me I heard the rumble of the tanks as they started up their great diesel engines. Beside me Patman stood grimly, his field glasses fixed on the little band of soldiers, their rifles at the ready across their chests. It seemed like minutes before they reached the lonely civilian standing face to face with the Russian soldiers.

As they neared him, the double column split, one to the left of him, the other to the right. Just as they came abreast of him I heard a whistle from somewhere behind the Soviet line. The rangers' bayoneted rifles were inches from the chests of the Russian soldiers. My hands were trembling, so that for a brief second the field glasses lost the picture, but then I saw the Russian line break open. Geoff stepped through the gap, the rangers on either side of him. As they disappeared behind the Russians, I glanced at Patman beside me. His eyes were still glued to his glasses but I noticed a trickle of sweat running down his cheek though it was a bitter cold morning.

When I looked back up the road, the Russian soldiers seemed to have evaporated into the morning mist. The road to Steinstuecken was open. Ten minutes passed before Geoff's figure emerged out of the fog and a moment later he rejoined us. No one spoke as we climbed back into our cars. Indeed, until today not a word has ever been said about Geoff's march to Steinstuecken, though in a way I wish it had become public, for it would have demonstrated to the Berliners that Geoff was not as "soft" as they imagined. Nor did Soloviev ever refer to the affair, though I noticed a distinct increase in his respect for Geoff at subsequent meetings.

But in one respect Geoff was still pessimistic.

The lot of the Berliners on either side of the wall had not improved at all. I think his discouragement was due to the fact that he was coming more and more into contact with the local people and becoming daily more aware of their tribulations. His antennae seemed to reach out among the crowds around him on the streets, in the theatres and in the parks and playgrounds, registering their fears and griefs, their disappointments and disillusionment.

Rumors had meanwhile grown more persistent that Max Ebers was no longer in the good graces of the Eastern regime. The East German press had long since ceased to refer to his defection, which had so recently been their biggest propaganda coup. Finally a broadcast from East

Berlin confirmed that Max Ebers had been arrested, charged with sabotage, and committed for trial. The trial was to be public. Obviously, the Communists were getting ready to spring some sensations.

That same evening Annemarie telephoned and asked me to stop by her apartment. It was the first time I had been inside. While it was comfortably arranged, it hardly compared to the elegance of the old villa in Rauchstrasse.

Annemarie came to the point at once.

"Harry, I have to defend Max at his trial." I started up, for until then she had persistently said she "had no contact" with Max and presumably had had none since the war. I looked at her questioningly.

"I know. It sounds strange. Don't make me go into all the reasons. You know Max was a childhood friend, my neighbor on Rauchstrasse. I've known him since we were practically babies. If he's in trouble we have to do something for him." The way she emphasized the "we" was unmistakable.

I protested that the East German regime would never permit a Western lawyer to practice in their courts, but she brushed aside my argument.

"On the contrary," she said, "they'll be delighted. They wouldn't stage a public trial unless they were pretty confident of their evidence. Besides, they have always said that they are the legitimate successors of the prewar regime and that their court system is basically the prewar one. Furthermore, East Germans have been permitted to practice in West German courts and they'll be eager to show they are just as bighearted."

"But even if they let you defend him," I protested, "it

would be folly for you to put your neck in a noose. They know all about your activities with the refugees, your speeches and pamphlets. They'll arrest you as soon as you appear."

"Not if the Russians give me a safe conduct."

"But why should the Russians give you any protection?"

"That's where you and Geoff come in, Harry. You've got to persuade Geoff."

"Not I," I said firmly. "I'll have nothing whatever to do with it."

"You're afraid, Harry?" Annemarie asked. "You never used to get frightened so easily." I said nothing, but angrily rose and went over to the window overlooking the great boulevard outside. I was ashamed of my anger, for the fact was that I was afraid, afraid for her, Annemarie. The whole affair of Max's defection had never seemed clear to me. For all I knew this was just a clever trap to lure Annemarie into the East Sector.

Annemarie interrupted my thoughts. "Very well then, if you won't help, I'll do it myself, right now. Is Geoff at home? If so, will you take me to Miquelstrasse? Or perhaps that's asking too much," she said sarcastically.

We hardly exchanged a word all the way back to Miquelstrasse. Geoff was very cordial despite the late hour, but when Annemarie explained her mission he was frankly astonished at her audacity, or as he openly called it her "damn foolishness."

"We're not kids any more, Annemarie," he said, "and we're not just jumping the Danish border. These Communists are playing for keeps."

When she persisted he pointed out as I had that she would be walking into a trap.

"That is where you come in," Annemarie retorted. "You're going to persuade your pal Soloviev."

The more Geoff protested, the more Annemarie persisted. Geoff pointed out it would be highly improper for him in his position as the American Representative to intervene with the Russians on behalf of a German citizen. Furthermore, in view of the publicity the Eastern regime was giving the case, it was very probable that some embarrassing if not damaging evidence was going to be produced. If it ever came out that Geoff had been involved in helping the defense, his position would be much more difficult and his efforts to improve things for the Berliners would be useless.

"Why should it be?" Annemarie retorted. "All I'm asking is for you to talk to Soloviev personally, not officially. Just tell him I'm an old friend."

But Geoff was as stubborn as Annemarie—or almost. During a session that lasted half the night she accused him of obstructing justice by helping to deny Max the right to a proper defense counsel. She said he was contributing to the Soviet's policy of systematically whittling away the rights of West Berliners. This apparently got under his skin and in the end he agreed to talk to Soloviev.

He saw the Russian the following day and told him of Annemarie's request. He also told him that unless Soloviev gave him his personal assurances that Annemarie would have safe conduct and not be molested in the East Sector he would prevent her going. To his surprise, Soloviev agreed to "use his influence" with the East Germans to have Annemarie accepted as defense council. He also solemnly assured Geoff that he would guarantee her safe conduct in the East Sector.

Naturally Geoff was pleased at this indication of co-operation by Soloviev, but he was too old a hand in dealing with Soviet officials to accept the general's word alone. However, he reasoned that not only was Soloviev's personal word as an officer at stake but also, in a sense, the reputation of the Soviet government in the eyes of the world—a reputation that the Kremlin usually took pains to preserve. Under the circumstances, he believed it was most unlikely that the Russians would risk whatever good opinion they enjoyed among the so-called noncommitted peoples throughout the world simply because of a person whom, as far as any of us then knew, they considered a relatively minor figure. On the contrary, he thought, they would play up their magnanimity by every means of propaganda at their disposal. His reasoning seemed to be amply confirmed the next day when the East German radio announced with considerable fanfare that the East German regime was generously permitting Dr. Dahlmann to defend Max Ebers.

Once she had been appointed defense council, Annemarie's first act was to petition the court for a postponement of the trial to permit her to interview Max and prepare her defense. To our astonishment that request too was granted.

Each day thereafter I drove Annemarie to the new Alex on Alexanderplatz, where Max was being held. Each time we went through the Vopo inspection station at Checkpoint Charlie we were treated with great courtesy. In fact, after our second trip, they recognized us and waved us through without even examining our passports.

After my third day of sitting in the prison waiting room all day, and reassured by the correctness of the East Germans, I dropped Annemarie at the prison and drove over to Herr Klein's office on Friedrichstrasse. He greeted me cordially, but seemed uneasy at having me in his office and suggested we go out for a cup of coffee.

He took me to a large modern café, which he said had recently been opened, in the old armory on Unter den Linden close by Marx-Engelsplatz. As we looked out across the platz I thought of my friends in Mueggelsee and their adventures on the square during the 1953 uprising.

"The happiest day in our lives," they had called it.

Now I was with one of those against whom they had risen, and again I felt uncomfortable and disloyal. But Herr Klein was obviously ignorant of my thoughts, for he babbled on endlessly about the architectural improvements about to be made in the city.

At first I thought he was just boasting in his silly little way. Only later did it occur to me that he was talking compulsively to hide his own deep troubles.

"Herr Klein," I said, "do you think that all these great new buildings and monuments you are going to build will help atone for building the Wall?"

The little man's face reddened and his hands lying on the table stiffened.

"I do not understand," he said.

"I mean, how can you reconcile your conscience working for a regime that builds that terrible Wall, and then shoots people who try to cross it?"

For a whole minute he was silent as his fingers played nervously with the coffee spoon.

"You will never understand how it has been, Herr Harding. You do not know what I went through before, and how happy I was with my family. That happiness, that wonderful experience of coming home to my boy and my wife each evening. Compared to that, the Wall and those other things you speak of are of no consequence."

He paused again, his fingers still twitching, his brow furrowed.

"But now," he went on, "I wonder if—"

He didn't finish the sentence and I prodded him to go on. At last he said: "First it is my son. They have taken him into the army and he is no longer with us."

"And the second?" I asked.

His face seemed to droop and his eyes stared into mine as though searching for comfort.

"Yes, and the second is—Ilse."

I must have looked startled for he repeated himself: "Yes, Herr Harding, I am no longer as sure as I was for all those years—"

"But why? Surely she still loves you."

"Perhaps," he said in a whisper. "And perhaps not."

Embarrassed by these intimate revelations, I sipped my black mocha coffee and stared uncomfortably at the table in front of me.

But already Klein had gone so far that he had to go on and pour out his troubles to me. "She is not always at home now when I come back from the office. She does not keep the apartment as she once did. Sometimes I think she spends most of the day away. And when I ask where she has been, she gets angry. Yes, Herr Harding, really angry and begins to scream at me. She never did that before."

"Is there some other man, do you think?"

"I cannot ask. I cannot believe it, but I cannot help suspecting there is someone else, someone more appealing to her than myself, a poor, self-educated bureaucrat."

Contemptible as he was, I could not help feeling sorry for him. But at the same time I was not prepared to spend the day listening to his woes.

Hastily I paid the bill and explained I had to go to fetch Annemarie.

"Ah, yes," he said, "she is the lawyer for Ebers." He shook his head forlornly: "That will be bad, bad, I am afraid."

I asked him what he meant.

"The trial will be bad. It will not help our reputation. Already we are considered not *salonfaehig*, not fit for the drawing rooms of the West. And when the trial is done we will not be considered fit for your kitchens. It is bad and I am sorry. Very sorry and—" he fumbled for the word and his voice again dropped to a whisper—"disappointed."

As I left him he seized my arm. "But, Herr Harding, do not think I am complaining—and of course you will tell no one what we have said." I promised him and hurried off across that hateful Marx-Engelsplatz toward the Alex.

What Klein had told me made me feel even more uncomfortable and sordid, like everyone else around me—the scurrying, drab crowds racing along as though they were being chased, their faces drawn and preoccupied. The crowds in West Berlin hurried too, I thought, but with a different motive, as though they were looking forward to something instead of being driven by something hateful and terrifying.

When I got back to the waiting room at the prison, a guard handed me a note written in Annemarie's hand. Her work was going to delay her, she said, and she would take a taxi home. I had misgivings at first and asked to see her. The guard went for her and she came out, apologizing.

"I've just been told they've rescheduled the trial for the day after tomorrow, so I must get my brief in order," she said. "It is infuriating, but there's nothing to be done about it." She said the police had promised to drive her to Checkpoint Charlie, whence she could get a taxi home. I made her promise to telephone me as soon as she got to her apartment and she laughed: "You are an old worrier," she said, "and always were." Then she kissed me and hurried back to the interview room where she was working with Max.

Geoff and I dined alone that night in the big, dark dining room. I told him of my talk with Klein and his family troubles. Geoff smiled.

"The little swine," he said. "Father John is right. There's not a decent breath in him."

I also told him about Annemarie and the new date for the trial. He seemed troubled and a little uneasy about Annemarie and his uneasiness made me worry even more. We spoke little, and as soon as we finished dinner we went back into the library. Geoff began working over a dispatch he was preparing, and I took a book from the shelves.

When I looked at my watch next it was ten-thirty. Geoff looked at me out of the corner of his eye. "It's pretty late, isn't it?" he said, but I did not want to upset him and merely grunted in response, although I was beginning to be really apprehensive.

Periodically I looked at my watch again, and at eleven I suggested calling Annemarie's apartment. "Perhaps she forgot to phone," I said.

When I called her number I was startled to hear Bill Harmsworth's voice. He seemed embarrassed when he recognized my voice and hastily gave the receiver to Christl. She told me her mother was not home yet. "I thought you were with her," she said. When I explained she sounded alarmed. I heard her talking to Bill.

"We're coming right over to Miquelstrasse, if that's all right with you and Uncle Geoff."

When they turned up at the house Matusek had gone to bed and I opened the door. Christl was looking drawn and nervous.

The four of us talked for several minutes and it was decided that I would drive back to the East Sector to the Alex and see if Annemarie was still there.

The Vopos at the checkpoint, when they saw me, seemed ominously hostile. They searched the car and kept my passport for half an hour before they let me go through. A few moments later I reached the main entrance to the Alex. It was shut tight, but when I rang the night bell, a big policeman opened it and inquired what I wanted. I explained that I was looking for Dr. Dahlmann. Curtly he told me that there was no Dr. Dahlmann there. In fact, he said, there was no one in the interview room where she had been working. I tried to get him to call the officer in charge, but instead he told me to come back in the morning, and slammed the door in my face.

Christl, Geoff and Bill were waiting anxiously when I returned to Miquelstrasse. By then it was nearly three. For an hour we discussed every possibility. Perhaps, Bill suggested, she had gone to Mueggelsee for the night. Perhaps she'd gone to a hotel in the East Sector. Perhaps, though—

Christl suggested Geoff call Soloviev but Geoff was reluctant. After all, we had no proof that anything had happened to Annemarie. Soloviev had given his word of honor that she would be safe, and without more information Geoff hesitated even to hint that his pledge was in doubt. In the end we decided to wait till the following morning.

When he came down to breakfast next morning, Geoff's eyes were heavy and his face puffy. Ordinarily he went to his office at eight-thirty, but now he lingered, waiting for Christl to call as we had arranged. Nervously he paced through the gloomy rooms, smoking incessantly, but saying nothing. At nine o'clock Christl called saying her mother was still not back.

Geoff at once picked up the phone connecting him with

Soloviev's headquarters. But the person who answered the phone told him curtly that Soloviev was not yet available. A half hour later he called again and got the same answer. Russians are late sleepers, and the fact that Soloviev was not at his desk at nine-thirty was hardly surprising, but the tone of the Russian who answered the phone was not re-assuring. Politely but firmly Geoff told him the matter was urgent, and requested Soloviev be asked to call him at his home as quickly as possible.

We waited till ten and still no word came from the Russian headquarters. By now Geoff was deeply anxious and made no effort to conceal it. My efforts to calm him were rather abruptly dismissed, and I sat in silence, trying to concentrate on the morning papers. Except for another article in the East German paper on a renewed wave of Western espionage attempts, there was nothing that could hold my attention.

At ten-thirty Christl showed up. Her eyes were red and her cheeks pale. A moment later Colonel Samson, whom Geoff had summoned, appeared and was told that Anne-marie had not returned from the East Sector the previous day. He was taken aback by the news, as he always was when he was told something. At once he began cursing the Russians for their perfidy. But then he calmed down and by his idle comments managed to convey the idea that he was not really surprised. Was it certain, he implied, that Annemarie had not elected to remain in the East Sector? Geoff did not even deign to answer this question, though Christl's eyes blazed furiously and it was all I could do not to slap his fat face.

Then General Patman and Harmsworth arrived, and

once more we rehashed the entire situation. At last Geoff leaned across the desk in the library, picked up the special phone to Russian headquarters, and announced in hard, sharp words that he was leaving at once to see Soloviev and that he expected the bridge at Potsdam to be open for his car. Beckoning to me he rose, and a moment later we were in his car, headed for the bridge.

A German Vopo, sloppily dressed and insolent, held up his hand and ordered us to stop as we drove up to the bridge. Ignoring him, Geoff beckoned to a young Russian officer lounging at the roadside. He told him who he was and that he was on his way to see Soloviev and in cold, restrained but polite words asked that the barrier be lifted. The Russian seemed genuinely concerned but said he had no instructions. At Geoff's request he went briskly to the little guardhouse at the far end of the bridge, and for ten minutes we waited in silence. Geoff was quite calm now, but the muscles of his jaws worked incessantly and he lit one cigarette after another.

At last the young Russian emerged and signaled the Vopo. The latter sauntered slowly to the barrier and raised it. As we drove by the Russian saluted and Geoff raised his hand in acknowledgment.

At the Soviet headquarters we were evidently expected, for though there was no officer to greet us as on previous occasions, a soldier showed us into the big waiting room and told us that Soloviev would see us shortly. Another ten or fifteen minutes passed and then at last Soloviev came in, followed by Alexeiev. Their faces were grave and their greeting lacked the cordiality of previous encounters.

Geoff had obviously rehearsed his opening words, and in the briefest way told Soloviev that Dr. Dahlmann had not returned from her visit to the East Sector the day before. Soloviev nodded but said nothing.

Geoff seemed a little taken aback and went on: "But you have given me your word of honor that nothing would happen to her," he said, his eyes fixed on Soloviev, his hands firmly gripping the arms of his chair.

"This is purely a matter for the East German government," Soloviev said, and I had the impression that he too had rehearsed his answer.

Geoff stiffened in his chair: "You mean you do not intend to enforce Dr. Dahlmann's safe conduct?"

Alexeiev broke in. "The general," he said, "promised safe conduct to Dr. Dahlmann to prepare Ebers' defense in good faith, and only that. If Dr. Dahlmann engaged in other activities she had no right to expect safe conduct."

I could see that Geoff was having difficulty controlling his anger. Turning on Alexeiev he said in a level, cold voice: "The general's promise, his word of honor, was given; he made no conditions and no conditions were necessary, as Dr. Dahlmann went to the East Sector to prepare the defense and nothing more."

"Yesterday evening Dr. Dahlmann was heard to be discussing something quite different from Ebers' defense, namely the future operations of Bureau X."

For a moment Geoff was silent as he reflected on these ominous words, but his face revealed none of the shock he must have felt. Then, slowly and coldly, he said: "I've no doubt the prosecution will seek to link Herr Ebers to Bureau X. In that case she would have to discuss it."

"That," Alexeiev said," is a matter for the East German justice officials to decide."

"Then she has been arrested?" Geoff said, incredulously.

"You may address your inquiry to the East German authorities."

Ignoring Alexeiev, Geoff swung around to Soloviev: "And you, a Soviet general, are prepared to break your word of honor, a promise given to me personally?"

The way he accented the word "personally" made Soloviev stir uneasily in his chair. His face was grim and gray. Slowly he turned his head toward Alexeiev as though appealing for aid.

Alexeiev began to speak but Geoff raised his hand.

"I did not address myself to you, Colonel," he said sharply, and continued to fix his eyes on the general. A full minute passed, but the general said nothing. At last he rose heavily from his chair.

"I have nothing more to say, Mr. Schuyler," he said, and walked slowly from the room.

X

THROUGHOUT THE LONG DRIVE HOME, across the bridge, back into the American sector and to the headquarters in Clayallee neither of us uttered a word.

My own mind was in a turmoil. Once before Annemarie had been in serious danger—from the Gestapo—but then we had had sufficient warning to permit us to act and to whisk her away across the Danish border. But now she was in their—this time the Communists'—hands. It was too late for escape. What, I asked myself, would they accuse her of? What indeed was she guilty of? Alexeiev had alluded to Bureau X. Obviously they would seek to link her to its insane operations.

And Max Ebers, did he have anything to do with Bureau X? All my suspicions, which until now I had tried to suppress as fictions of an overwrought imagination, suddenly seemed more plausible. His unexplained defection, the curious note to Geoff and Annemarie's odd repetition of it, her statement to me that she had "no contacts with Max," his disappearance in the East Sector, Herr Dahlmann's curious reaction to my questions about him, and finally my imaginings about the boathouse, which I had dismissed as pure hallucinations. Could Max really have been hiding in the same room above the boathouse where so many years before Annemarie and I had passed such blissful hours?

The muscles of my stomach tightened when I thought of Annemarie, now herself a prisoner in the Alex. Though our intimate relationship had long since ceased to exist, another emotion almost as strong had taken its place since we had met again at Dr. Bell's. It was partly admiration, partly pride in our previous association, partly too a sense of loyalty deeper than any physical passion could induce.

There was little comfort in the fact that I had opposed her going to the East Sector. I should have prevented it and I had failed. I had deliberately kept out of the argument between Annemarie and Geoff on the questionable ground that Geoff's decision was a political one, while my motives were highly personal.

Out of the corner of my eye I glanced at Geoff. He was sitting rigidly staring straight ahead, his long, thin fingers clasped together in his lap. He seemed stunned by the shock of the Russians' treachery and unable to grasp at once all its implications. But Soloviev's repudiation of his personal promise was so unmistakably clear that there was no room for doubt that Geoff's hopes for some sort of understanding with the Russians were practically destroyed.

Back at headquarters he shut himself up in his office and told his secretary he wanted to see no one except General Patman. That I, his most intimate friend, was not included struck me painfully at first. But the reason should have been obvious. After all Annemarie had been my friend, my mistress, my love. If he had made a mistake it was I in the first place who would suffer because of it. In such circumstances my reactions, my advice, were not going to help him come to any rational decision. Indeed, it would lead to just the opposite.

I did not see him again until evening when we both went home. He was still preoccupied and silent, but gradually he relaxed and when dinner was over began at last to talk. I encouraged him, hoping it would relieve some of the tension I was feeling.

I shall not attempt to describe my own emotions that evening. That I felt acute pain as I thought of Annemarie sitting in her lonely cell goes without saying. But Geoff's reactions in those critical hours were of a different sort and sprang from other motives.

"I suppose no one will ever really understand those Russians," he said. "Just as you think you have them figured out they do the damnedest things. I remember once when I was in Moscow—" and in a quiet, almost amused way he reminisced about an old peasant who had for years put him up in his hut on shooting trips outside Moscow, and then had suddenly robbed him of a few rubles.

He told of an official of the Foreign Office with whom

he had become friendly, whom he had taken to the theatre and gone on skiing excursions with. One evening he had come to dinner with Geoff and they had sat till long after midnight discussing Chekov, and the next morning during a business call at the Foreign Office the Russian had deliberately tried to filch a document from Geoff's brief case when Geoff's back was momentarily turned.

"You expect them to lie officially and to mislead you on their diplomatic zigs and zags, but somehow—" he paused and looked wistfully into the fire—"somehow, you expect them to respect a friendship and treat you decently —personally, I mean."

The word "personally" was perhaps the key to his perplexed frame of mind. Though he was an official and though his relations with Soloviev were official, somehow he felt that because he had also established personally friendly contacts with him the Russian should respect that friendship in their official dealings.

I do not want to give the impression that Geoff was naïve. He had dealt with Russian diplomats for years and had outmaneuvered them at least as often as they had gotten the better of him. He had studied their political philosophy and their dialectical processes as thoroughly as most of them, and could quote Marx, Lenin and Stalin as glibly as their best ideologues. He knew the weaknesses of their system and despised their regime with a contempt based not on emotions, but on profound intellectual grounds.

I have sometimes suspected, however, that this very intimacy with their history, this knowledge of their family secrets and skeletons, which they knew he had, made him feel somehow privileged and entitled to immunity from the petty subterfuges and deceits with which the Russians had plagued his less knowledgeable predecessors.

And through it all was of course a smattering of sentiment, for no one as discerning as Geoff could be immune to the attraction that the Russians have always exerted on those Westerners who have had close and intimate dealings with them. The *charme slav*, which I do not pretend to understand, for I have only a superficial acquaintance with the Russians, had won his heart as it had the hearts of so many other discerning foreigners who had stayed long enough among them.

But now suddenly his illusions were swept away with a completeness and suddenness that left him without support, like a fisherman fording a rushing stream when he loses the pole he has been using to prop himself against the current. That others had been treated with similar treachery meant little to him. That Annemarie was not the first to have been kidnaped, that Soloviev's repudiation obviously stemmed from political not personal grounds did not mitigate the blow.

And then there was his sense of responsibility to Berlin and the Berliners. Though he had resisted Annemarie's pleas as firmly as he could, he now felt that he alone was responsible for her and to her thousands of admirers in the West.

The news of Annemarie's arrest was not long in coming. That very afternoon the East German papers announced that she had been arrested for complicity in the Bureau X activities and that she would be tried along with Max Ebers.

Within a few hours all West Berlin was talking of nothing else, for as Sepp and Bill Harmsworth had told us before, Annemarie Dahlmann had been a heroine among them—especially among the students. It had been she who had encouraged them to rescue their compatriots behind the Wall. It had been she who had persuaded officials to shut their eyes while the students dug tunnels, opened the sewer labyrinths, and staged raids across the Wall.

When they learned of her arrest their mood was one of frustrated fury. A group of students gathered in front of Clayallee demanding action from the Americans. The fact that Geoff had had anything to do with her volunteering to defend Max was not known. Nor, of course, was it public knowledge that Annemarie and I had once been intimate—or even that Max Ebers had also been involved with us back in the Hitler era.

Nevertheless, Berliners in general had always held the Americans responsible for Russian encroachments more than the French or British, if only because the Americans represented the greatest Western power. But there was something deeper in their resentment when the Americans failed to respond as the Berliners thought they should. For years the Americans had encouraged them to take active political roles, to assume responsibility for their government, to reject the authoritarian methods not just of old Germany, but of the Russian-dominated Germany across the Wall.

The MP's managed to move the demonstrators from the American headquarters with little difficulty, but elsewhere in the city crowds were gathering, and street corner orators shouting.

Around noon the governing mayor telephoned Geoff and told him that the angry mood was spreading. He himself was being pressed to hold a meeting to protest Dr. Dahlmann's arrest. He hoped he would be able to subdue the anger and keep the demonstrators from getting out of hand. A little while later the radio announced the mayor would address the citizens from the Rathaus steps later in the afternoon.

Geoff was talking to Sepp and Bill Harmsworth when the news came over the radio. He had been trying to persuade Sepp to keep the students from taking violent action. His first reaction to the mayor's decision was annoyance but Bill pointed out that it was probably the best way to let the students give vent to their emotions without causing real trouble. In fact Sepp suggested that Geoff himself go to the Rathaus and see for himself what the mood of the crowd was. Reluctantly Geoff agreed but wisely decided to keep away from the officials and merely to mingle with the crowd, which was unlikely to recognize him.

Geoff's chauffeur drove us as close to the Schoeneberg Rathaus as he could, but the police had stopped all motor traffic on all the streets leading to it, and we had to walk the last four blocks. Already crowds were emerging from subway stations, buses and cars, and converging on the square. They overflowed the sidewalks onto the streets, walking fast but silently, their faces tense, and there was none of the banter and laughing one usually associates with Berlin crowds.

Watching them intently, his eyes roving from face to face as though trying to sense their mood, Geoff was unaware of a wheelchair in his path, and stumbled into it. The occupant, an elderly man, grumbled loudly. Geoff apologized, and to make up for his clumsiness offered to wheel the invalid to the square. Carefully he pushed it through the growing throng, but all the time he was looking about him.

Talking in low tones in English, he called my attention to the somber mood. "Hardly the way they behaved twenty-five years ago when they turned out for a Nazi rally at the sport stadium," he said. "I wonder how many of them here were there then." The cripple in the wheelchair must have understood for he twisted painfully in the chair and looked up at Geoff.

"Not I for one," he said in guttural English. "They had me in Dachau, where I lost these," and he patted the stumps of his legs. Geoff looked taken aback, and the old man seemed to regret his outburst.

"But you are right," he added. "A lot of them were there then—and enjoying it." He waved his hand at the stream of people walking beside us. "But they have learned," he went on. "They may not have lost their legs but they've lost lots of illusions—not just about Hitler," he paused, "and not just about Germany." I looked down at the livid gray face inquiringly.

"Your America hasn't exactly lived up to its promises," he said. "Especially these last months." He stared impatiently at me as though expecting me to protest, but I said nothing and Geoff too simply looked stonily ahead.

"Why don't you people do something about Annemarie Dahlmann? Are you afraid? If you stood up to those Russians, they would back down quickly enough. They're no supermen—though you Americans seem to think so."

Geoff made no reply.

We had reached the edge of the square and the old man thanked Geoff for his help and explained that he would roll his chair himself to the special area reserved for invalids under the Rathaus steps. The square itself was packed and with difficulty we made our way to the bus stop shelter directly across the square from the Rathaus.

Several young men had climbed to the roof of the shelter and were waving banners demanding Dr. Dahlmann's release. A squad of policemen pushed through the crowd and ordered them off the roof. "Not allowed on the roof," they shouted, and reluctantly the boys scrambled down.

Geoff looked at me and smiled: "Who was it said they'd never have a revolution in Germany because they'd have to walk on the lawns?"

As I watched the policemen gently herding the crowd and coaxing them into orderly ranks I couldn't help contrasting them with the Nazi storm troopers and brown shirts who had shouted and pushed and bullied the crowds in the old days.

I pointed out a couple of them trying to break up a tight knot of demonstrators. "They seem almost timid," I said to Geoff.

"Let's hope they're not," he commented.

Though the majority of the crowd were young people,

university students and apprentices, there were also a good number of older Berliners: gray-haired women in hats that must have been fashionable in the days of Weimar, and old men leaning on umbrellas. Ahead of me one old lady looking angry and determined was waving her fist toward the Rathaus steps and shouting angrily: *"Feiglings!* Cowards! Do something. Not just speeches!" The people around her smiled indulgently at her spirit. But then suddenly she began to sway and clutched at the man next to her. Slowly she sank to the pavement.

At once a shout for a doctor arose. A Red Cross nurse, followed by two stretcher bearers, pushed into the crowd, which quickly made way for her. A moment later, the old lady was carried off to a first aid truck on the edge of the crowd.

At last the mayor appeared on the steps and stood before a battery of microphones.

"Berliners!" he started, and at once the crowd was silent. "Berliners! Again one of our bravest and most beloved citizens has been kidnaped by those bandits across the Wall." An angry roar rose from the crowd. Geoff looked at me uneasily.

The mayor raised his hand for silence: "But we must keep our heads and show our patience."

Somewhere in the crowd a voice shouted: "Show your courage!" The shout was echoed through the square. Again the mayor, a big, tough-looking man, held up his hand.

"Courage, yes," he said. "But not stupidity!" Then his voice became more soothing as he cajoled and exhorted his audience to remain calm. He was a persuasive speaker and little by little we could feel the response around us. The shouts and catcalls subsided.

"We are not alone," the mayor went on. "We have powerful friends and allies: the Americans, the French and the British stand with us." Somewhere in the crowd a voice shouted derisively, "What are those Ami's doing about it?" Again the shout was echoed with impatient cries.

"They are doing what they can. I have solemn assurances from the American Representative that everything possible will be done to free Annemarie Dahlmann." Geoff looked at me and frowned. Though he had indeed promised the mayor every effort would be made, he had no idea this would be interpreted as a public declaration. The crowd dutifully clapped—as though they appreciated the assurances but did not have much faith in them.

Suddenly a voice shouted, "To Brandenburg Gate," and then the whole mob took up the chant. Protected by the shelter back of us, Geoff watched incredulously as the crowds stirred restlessly. He looked up to the mayor on the steps above: "For Christ sake," he muttered. "Do something! Stop them!" And as though he had heard the appeal the mayor suddenly turned toward the bandmaster below him and shouted something.

A moment later the strains of "Deutschland Ueber Alles" blared out, echoing from the walls of the surrounding buildings. The crowd paused. Then it turned toward the Rathaus, above which the national flag was flying. Immediately in front of us a young girl—she was about

Christl's age—came to attention, her arms stiff down her sides, her hands clenched into tight fists. Raising her chin she repeated the words of the anthem and suddenly the whole square was singing, solemnly, deep-throated and passionate. As she sang, the girl's face became flushed, her eyes sparkled, and two large tears rolled down her red cheeks.

When the singing stopped, there was absolute silence for a long moment and the crowd continued at attention. Then suddenly from overhead the Freedom Bell began to toll, deep, rich and in slow funeral cadence. Except for its boom, there was not a sound, not a motion in the crowd. At last it too ceased, and as the last resonant boom faded in receding echoes, the crowd continued to stand rooted.

The mayor turned and walked from the platform and gradually the mob came to life again. But now anger had gone out of the crowd and within a few minutes it was shuffling off, subdued and almost tame.

For several minutes Geoff stood glued to his place by the shelter, his tense face troubled and anxious. At last he spoke.

"That," he said slowly and emphatically, "was too close for comfort. Thank God for 'Deutschland Ueber Alles.' If it hadn't been for the band there'd have been a real riot."

As we walked back toward the car, Geoff gradually relaxed. "That old cripple is right. They have changed. They still get terrifyingly excited, but it's not that mad hysteria Hitler produced. It's something deeper, grimmer." He paused again and looked at me. "But just as dangerous."

XI

JUST BEFORE THE WAR I HAD SPENT A brief leave visiting friends in our Moscow embassy and had been present at the last of the purge trials staged by Stalin during the Great Terror. It was the trial of the so-called "anti-Soviet block of right-wing Trotskyites," and took place in the Hall of Columns, once the Nobles' Club of Moscow.

With the usual Russian genius for theatrics, the main hall had been carefully arranged to provide maximum dramatic effect. The walls were draped in wine-red plush hangings. A painting of Lenin adorned the wall behind the judge's bench on a dais at one end of the great ballroom. At one side sat the defendants, who included Nikolai Bukharin, once described by Lenin as "the favorite son of the Party," Alexei Rykov, the Commissar for Internal

Affairs in the first Bolshevik government, and Henrikh Yagoda, who had organized the first two purge trials and now at the third was himself in the dock.

André Vyshinski, the state prosecutor, sat or rather stood opposite them most of the time, hurling savage invectives at the condemned men: "mad dogs," a "putrefying heap of human scum," "loathsome hybrids of fox and swine" and "a nest of vipers."

In the main body of the hall sat the spectators—most of them picked followers of Stalin and a handful of foreign diplomats and journalists. Above in the gallery, behind heavy plush curtains, Stalin himself was reported to be watching. Occasional movements of the draperies and from time to time a puff of smoke from a cigarette or more probably from Stalin's pipe seeped through the crack in the hangings.

When, twenty-five years later, I entered the hall where Annemarie and Max were to be tried, the picture of that Moscow trial suddenly came back to me. Here again were all the hangings and pictures of the Communist great, the draperies and the other theatrical props. Apparently we were once again to witness one of those macabre parodies of Communist justice. But this time the defendants were not just names but close old friends. As I took my seat I felt faint and nauseated.

But the difference from the Moscow trials quickly became apparent. In the Hall of Columns the proceedings had been endlessly drawn out, almost leisurely. The speeches and statements were verbose and repetitive as though deliberately to prolong the agony for those in the dock. But here in Berlin all was briskness and bustle. Promptly at nine the judges, a professorial old man and two women took their seats. Then the prosecutor, a young, coarse-looking, heavy-set man, appeared and immediately thereafter Annemarie and Max were led in by two guards.

Considering the circumstances Annemarie looked remarkably well, and her cheeks still had those same red spots. Her black hair was carefully arranged, and her manner composed and calm. Almost too calm, I thought. Her eyes were not the huge, round, dark brown sparks I remembered. Her eyelids seemed heavy, as though she were half asleep.

Max seemed even more dazed as he limped into the dock and sat down. His hair was poorly combed, his suit wrinkled and baggy, as though he had been sleeping in it for weeks. His face was puffed and his eyes small and bloodshot.

The proceedings quickly came to the point. The prosecutor read the charge: "Espionage and sabotage for a foreign power, the United States." Then, in a loud, blustering voice he said that Annemarie had been the principal inspiration and organizer of the notorious Bureau X, while Max had been its operational executive. In great detail he described the sabotage operations that the Bureau had supposedly conducted in the East Sector and the Soviet Zone. He enumerated the names of half a dozen officials who had been assassinated or seriously wounded, the factories destroyed and trains wrecked. I noted that among the names that of the Soviet official of whom Soloviev had spoken was carefully omitted. It would not do to admit that the Soviet comrades were anything but loved by all Germans.

He went on to explain that thanks to the vigilance of the East German security forces the Bureau's activities had been severely curbed during the months following the building of the Wall. When it became impossible to smuggle the assassins and explosives into the zone, Max Ebers had decided to go across himself to the East Sector, where he could better conduct operations.

"Like a sly wolf," the prosecutor said, he had disguised himself as a defector. Pretending to be carrying documents incriminating West intelligence agencies, he had actually brought across a suitcase full of plastic explosives, detonators and other infernal devices. With these the Bureau's agents had once more resumed their fiendish activities. But again the heroic security forces had unmasked the fiend, and now brought him to justice.

Turning to Annemarie, the prosecutor described her activities as the organization's political director and recruiting agent. But her principal role had been as the link between the American imperialists and the Bureau. He promised to produce irrefutable evidence of her taking orders from the West's espionage agents in West Berlin and receiving money and equipment from them, and selecting the targets marked for destruction. When she had come to the East Sector, ostensibly to conduct Ebers' defense, she had actually been laying plans with Ebers for the continuation of the Bureau's activities disrupted by his arrest.

As I listened, my first reaction was one of utter disbelief.

The idea that Annemarie had taken part in what amounted to assassination seemed too absurd to contemplate. It was true, I remembered, that she had not shared Geoff's vehement opposition to Bureau X and its alleged activities. Indeed, she had on occasion attempted to defend the motives behind their actions—the idea that by such sabotage the population of East Germany could be inspired to turn on their Communist masters and eventually make it too costly for the Soviet regime to hang on to its rebellious satellite.

Nevertheless, that had seemed to me a far cry from actively participating in their violent crimes. But now as the prosecutor described her activities, frequently alluding to events I knew had actually occurred and to sentiments I had heard her express, not in the courtroom but in the harmless atmosphere of a salon, I began to suspect that perhaps her support of the idea had indeed gone further than words.

I recalled her earlier behavior under that other tyrant Hitler, her fearless hatred and contempt, her almost reckless defiance of his murderous system. Was it so incredible that she should have gone one step further in her hatred of the Communist regime in the East? Perhaps the very fact she had not taken the ultimate step back in the Nazi era had helped to overcome her natural reluctance to resort to the methods she was now accused of.

As I sat with my eyes fixed on her while the prosecutor ranted on, my respect, my admiration, my deep affection for her and my own helplessness to come to her assistance were almost more than I could bear. I felt my hands tremble as they clenched and unclenched.

Then at last the prosecutor finished with a venomous fury, and the court read what purported to be the confessions Annemarie and Max had signed.

In a way it all sounded plausible enough. But the prosecutor's language and the wording of the so-called confessions were so fantastic, so unlike anything Annemarie or even Max might have said, and so replete with those wornout phrases first used in the Soviet trials of the thirties that it was impossible to believe they were the words of either Max or Annemarie.

Beside me American and other Western journalists smiled and whispered incredulous comments to one another as the clerk droned on. But for me the circumstances were too bitter to strike me as amusing in any way.

Finally the prosecutor told Max to rise and asked him to confirm his confession. Max struggled clumsily to his feet, unaided by the guards standing behind him. He looked at the audience and blinked, his cheeks puffed, his eyes red. Then he turned to the prosecutor and in a barely audible voice said: "I confirm the confession." Then, as though his legs would no longer hold his weight he fell back into his seat.

The prosecutor turned to Annemarie: "Do you, Dr. Dahlmann, confess to carrying on sabotage and espionage in the Democratic Republic on behalf of the American imperialists?"

Every eye in the courtroom was turned to her as she rose slowly to reply. For a moment she hesitated and her mouth seemed to be forming words, but no sound was audible. Then she turned and looked at the audience below her. I had the impression she was under a heavy sedative and that her mind was far away. I had seen the same look among the defendants at the Moscow trials, and a sudden fear seized me that she was about to follow Max's example with a mechanical, meaningless confession.

But then she seemed to start as she stared down at us. I had a feeling, for a moment, that she stared directly at me, but perhaps I imagined it. Her drooping eyelids suddenly opened wide and her great round eyes looked at us, bewildered. Her shoulders stiffened as she turned back to the prosecutor. Everyone in the courtroom leaned forward to catch her words.

"As the principal organizer of Bureau X, and of its actions to free East Germany from Communist tyranny, I am guilty," she said, her voice strong and resolute. I knew then she was speaking the truth. But then she went on: "But that I acted in any way with the connivance or in the interest of the United States, or any nation other than Germany, is a lie." She raised her chin as she finished and stared straight at the prosecutor. But he apparently had dealt with recalcitrant prisoners before and he scarcely faltered.

"You deny your own confession of your dealings with the American authorities?"

Her lip seemed to curl as she snapped back: "You know better than anyone here how those confessions were obtained."

"Perhaps I should refresh your memory, Frau Doktor," the prosecutor said. He motioned to an attendant, who brought forward a recording machine on a small table.

Dramatically, the prosecutor stepped forward and turned it on, and as he waited for the tubes to warm he turned to the audience.

"This is a recording of a conversation between an American intelligence official and Dr. Dahlmann. Perhaps some of you," he added with a contemptuous stare at the section where the foreign journalists were sitting, "will recognize the voice. It is that of Colonel Ulysses S. Samson, Chief Security Officer of the American forces in Berlin." He switched on the machine and suddenly a voice boomed out across the big hall. There was no mistaking whose it was, for Colonel Samson's heavy, American drawl was clearly recognizable.

"It may seem trivial to you," the voice was saying. "But it is important to us—to all of us on this side. Besides, you have a perfect cover—your perfectly legitimate reasons for being over there—"

There was a slight click as though the tape had been cut and then it went on.

"But you won't jeopardize anything. No one will suspect you. You already have the camera. You know how it operates—" There was another split-second pause and then again the colonel's voice.

"Thank you, Dr. Dahlmann. I appreciate your cooperation." To anyone who knew Colonel Samson, the bitter sarcasm mingled with frustration in the voice was obvious. But to a stranger it was hardly detectable. I shifted uneasily in my seat as the tape stopped.

The prosecutor turned to Annemarie, who was still standing rigidly in the dock.

"And now, Dr. Dahlmann, do you still deny that you were sent by the Americans? Do you deny that this conversation took place in your own apartment only six days ago?"

"I do not deny that the recording was a part of a conversation which I had with Colonel Samson. But it carefully omits my complete disagreement with the colonel's rather silly project. From first to last I flatly refused to have anything to do with it. If you would play the whole tape you would know that yourself." She cleared her throat and leaned forward:

"In fact, Herr Prosecutor, you must have heard the whole tape and you know as well as I that you are lying."

The prosecutor raised his hand and tried to break in but she ignored him: "You know better than anyone the extent of your lie. You know what a tragic farce this whole so-called trial has been."

She waved toward Max sitting limply beside her: "You know what drugs were used to break this man who risked everything for his country—and lost."

She paused for a moment and the spots of color on her cheeks grew more vivid. Her eyes were bright and burning. The prosecutor walked across the stage and stood directly before her, his round, short figure dwarfed by the towering, indignant figure above him.

Catching her breath she went on: "It is all a lie but it is just a small part of the wicked tragedy you are perpetrating, you, a so-called German, on your fellow Germans, true Germans. This deceit is only a tiny part of the lie. The Wall, the secret police, the trials that are not staged for the public, the prisons filled with those who have not submitted to your terror."

The senior judge banged his gavel: "The defendant will—"

But with a contemptuous wave of her arm Annemarie ignored his protest and turning toward him went on: "And you, Herr so-called Judge. You are just as responsible for this cruel wicked farce. Why don't you prosecute those despicable Vopos who shoot those who try to escape from this wretched concentration camp you call a 'democratic republic'? Why did you not prosecute the swine who shot Peter Fechter and then let him lie bleeding to death under the Wall for all the world to see?"

The gavel was banging incessantly but Annemarie went right on, her clear voice rising above the noise.

"You too call yourself a German and yet you dare accuse me of treason when you permit those traitors at the Wall to murder your compatriots."

The prosecutor motioned to the guards to take Annemarie from the room. But the two stood transfixed, listening to her impassioned attack.

Suddenly her voice grew calmer as she looked contemptuously from the prosecutor to the chief judge. "I know you will convict me. But that doesn't matter. At least I know I have done my duty here in this court. I accuse you—all of you who work for this infamous regime—of murder, of torture, of betraying your country and your own compatriots, of treason—of the highest treason."

The prosecutor tried to seize her and push her from the room but Annemarie held him off.

"Just one minute, Herr Judge, and then I am finished. The world has accused us Germans of allowing the tyrant Hitler to use us in his criminal attack on humanity. Let no one ever accuse me or my colleagues, all of them real Germans, of permitting a second tyrant to destroy our own nation for the benefit of a foreign conqueror, yes, Herr Judge, of that barbarism called the Soviet system."

She stopped and her eyes were filled with angry tears. Her body seemed to go limp, and slowly she turned and walked from the court, the two guards, still dazed, walking beside her.

XII
AS SOON AS ANNEMARIE LEFT THE courtroom the presiding judge called a recess until the afternoon.

When the trial resumed, the prosecutor called a number of witnesses, chiefly police officials and detectives, who purported to give evidence on Annemarie's and Max's roles in Bureau X. There were vague references to others involved in its activities, but the prosecutor had obviously failed to obtain concrete evidence about them from the two prisoners. The witnesses also testified about Max's plea for political asylum and the generosity of the Communist regime in granting it. While they touched on Max's subsequent disappearance and final arrest, I found it odd that they offered no testimony about his whereabouts or activities between those two events.

When the prosecutor had done his job, expeditiously and efficiently, a sparse-haired, timid little man who had been appointed defense counsel by the court went through some perfunctory gestures which, while in no way refuting the defendants' presumed guilt, attempted to deduce mitigating circumstances.

Then the judges retired briefly. When they returned, toward five o'clock in the afternoon, the presiding judge read the verdict. It was a foregone conclusion and surprised no one in the courtroom. Annemarie and Max were both found guilty of sabotage and treason. Since it was already late Saturday, the presiding judge explained, the court would adjourn and the sentence would be imposed on the following Monday. When he had finished there was a slight commotion as the wire-service and radio reporters hurried from the courtroom. But the rest of the audience sat silent and motionless for several minutes. Up in front two frowzy women wearing thick glasses and caplike hats over their straggling hair started to applaud the verdict. Amid the silence, their clapping sounded like catcalls in the stillness of a hot summer night. People stirred uncomfortably and then, one by one, walked out of the hall.

Numbly I made my way to my car and sat for a minute behind the wheel trying to collect my thoughts. All I could think of was Annemarie back in her cell waiting for the sentence. At the minimum, according to East German law, it would be ten years, at the maximum, death. How could I get to her? I knew they would never let me see her, but perhaps I could send her some sort of message just to let her know she was not alone. It occurred to me that perhaps little Herr Klein could help. I started the motor and drove to his office a few blocks away. The receptionist told me he had not come in to work that day, so I went to the block of apartments where he lived.

It was one of those gigantic piles of cement Hitler had built just east of the municipal power station, four stories high with half-a-dozen identical entrances. Unfortunately I had paid little attention when Klein had brought me there before, and I had a good deal of difficulty locating the proper entrance. For nearly half an hour I wandered about and climbed endless stairs without success, until at last a young man in a leather coat who was hanging about in front of the building offered to help me. He seemed to know Klein, for he at once led me up three flights of stairs, chatting amiably.

"You're from Bavaria?" he asked, and I realized he had spotted the plates of my car. I said I was.

"But you're not Bavarian. You've an American accent."

I nodded noncommittally, for by this time I was thoroughly out of breath from the climb. Besides, I was not particularly keen about establishing my identity too precisely.

At last we reached Klein's door and the young man pushed the doorbell. There was considerable scuffling and fumbling before Klein himself opened the door for us.

"An American visitor for you," the young man said with a smirk. Then he turned and disappeared down the staircase.

Ignoring me completely, Klein stared after him. He seemed dazed and befuddled. As the sound of the young man's footsteps receded down the iron stairs he tiptoed quietly to the banister and leaned over, listening. The entrance door below opened and closed again. Only then did he turn to me and invite me inside, but his manner was anything but enthusiastic.

He carefully locked the door behind him and motioned me into his tiny living room. The furniture consisted of a worn sofa, a few straight-backed chairs, a ponderous carved dining table, its legs and surface scratched and stained, an equally old sideboard filled with brightly colored china, the kind you would find at the annual Berlin junk fair. A smell of stale food and unwashed dishes permeated the little room. Klein must have become aware of the stench himself, for he apologized, explaining that he could not open the one window.

"Wind from the west," he mumbled. I realized what he meant when I looked out and saw a stream of black smoke pouring from the power station's high stacks and blowing in our direction.

He motioned me to a chair and then he dropped into another. From the moment he had opened the door I had suspected something was wrong with him. Generally as fastidious as only a minor German civil servant can be, he was coatless, his sleeves rolled up, his shirt unbuttoned and tieless. His hair was uncombed and his eyes were so blood-shot they looked like slits of scarlet in his puffed-up cheeks. As he leaned across the table I got a strong whiff of alcohol.

"Why did you come here?" he asked, his voice thick and petulant.

I explained that I wanted to send a letter to Dr. Dahlmann.

"I can do nothing for you," he said. "Nothing whatever."

Then he rose. "You better go at once before you cause more trouble." He stumbled and grasped the table.

Taken aback, I rose too. "Are you unwell?" I asked. "Is there anything I can do?"

Suddenly his knees sagged and I grabbed his arm and eased him onto the sofa.

As he slumped down his body went limp and his belligerent look left him.

"Excuse me, Herr Harding," he said. "I am drunk. Very drunk."

The announcement was hardly news to me, but the circumstance frankly shook me. Obviously Klein was going to be no help to me.

He leaned forward and put his head in his arms on the table.

"It is all over now," he whined between the sobs. "Everything is finished. Ilse has left. My home, my little home is ruined. Everything I loved is gone."

It made no sense to me and my first reaction was to leave at once. But somehow I felt sorry for the miserable little wretch. He had been useful to me in the past, and the least I could do was help him now.

I looked about the apartment, and found a tiny, dirty bathroom. I soaked a towel in cold water and wrapped it around his head. Then I went into the kitchen. Among a heap of unwashed dishes I found an empty bottle of Korn—the cheap schnapps popular among Berlin's working people. Rummaging among the dishes I found a coffee pot and a can of coffee which smelt of burnt rye—probably its chief ingredient. I bathed his head while the coffee was brewing, and when he had drunk it he began to revive. He sat up, straightened out his clothes and pushed back his uncombed hair. Then he started to apologize as abjectly as only a deflated little bureaucrat can.

It was all Ilse's fault, he told me again. For the past weeks she had been spending more and more of her time away from the apartment. Sometimes she had not returned home till late at night. The night before she had not come home at all. So he had got drunk.

"There was nothing else to do," he said, spreading his hands.

I asked where and with whom she had been spending her time, but Klein parried the question. "I know," was all he said, "and that is enough."

I asked why he had not done something about it, and his face broke into a weary, helpless smile: "He is not a person I can handle, Herr Harding. Perhaps I could deal with another, but not with him."

I was frankly not surprised that Frau Klein had found someone more interesting than her dreary little husband. I recalled her flirting with Alexeiev at the Bird Cage and for a moment suspected he might be the man, but on second thought it seemed incredible that a high-ranking Soviet officer with a promising future ahead of him would get involved with a little German hausfrau, no matter how pretty or engaging he found her.

Suddenly Klein recalled the young man who had accompanied me to the door.

"How did you get involved with him?" he asked, a look

of fear in his little bloodshot eyes. I told him I had simply asked where Klein lived.

"You know who he is?" Klein asked. "He's the local block warden, the party policeman. Now he will tell I have had contacts with the Americans and there goes my position as well."

For a moment I thought he was going to burst into tears again.

Although I found his lack of spunk disgusting, I still could not suppress the pity I had felt for him since the first time I had seen him trailing behind General Soloviev and Colonel Alexeiev like an obedient, spiritless dog. After all, he had compromised every principle he might have had, sacrificed every last touch of decency, in exchange for his pathetic home, his pretty, flirtatious wife and the security of a job. And now he had lost all of that.

It occurred to me that in his drunkenness he had not understood why I had come or the favor I had asked, and again I repeated it. But he simply shook his head. "I can do nothing for you," he repeated again. "There is nothing I can do." And once again he began to bemoan his fate. "There is nothing left," he said, waving his arm around the little room. "I have lost everything—and all for this—this—damned regime," he suddenly blurted out. "These swine who promised so much and all they've done is destroy our people, destroy our city, destroy our hopes." I was so startled by the outburst that I said nothing.

"I would help Dr. Dahlmann if I could," he went on. "She is a decent woman. I heard her testimony on the radio. What she said was right. So they are going to put her in jail, or perhaps shoot her."

He looked at me hard and for a moment there was a heavy silence. I had the impression he had suddenly come to a decision and was trying to work it out in his own mind.

Then abruptly he rose. "You must leave me now," he said. "Perhaps the warden has already reported you are here. Perhaps they are coming to arrest us together." Hastily he showed me to the door. "Hurry," he said. "But be careful; they may be following you. And for God's sake don't tell anyone you have seen me." He grasped my hand and shook it firmly. It was the first sign of strength I had seen him display. Then he said, "We shall be seeing each other again soon." He slammed the door in my face and I went back to my car.

For ten or fifteen minutes I drove about the area, twisting and turning through alleys and streets, my eye on the rear mirror. When I was sure that I was not being followed I hurried out to the Mueggelsee, where I found old Dahlmann alone in his big rundown villa. He looked even worse than when I had seen him before. He had heard the news about Annemarie and was in a state of despair about her.

I asked if he was not concerned about his own safety. He smiled sadly. "They are not interested in old men. Besides," he added, gesturing with his thumb toward the boathouse on the lake, "if they do come I have a back door, as you apparently noticed on your last visit."

"That was where Max was hiding?" I asked, and he nodded.

"He spent the night there usually," he said. "He came and went through the lake with Christl's old diving mask and they've never found out." He smiled almost gleefully.

"But they'll surely find out now that you're Annemarie's

father. And they may not give you any time to get away."

He smiled again. "If they come for me I will be warned in good time. I have a friend."

I must have looked skeptical, for he shook his head. "Harry, you don't know this regime. It's rotten from top to bottom. All you have to know is where the rotten spots are. For me that was easy."

He reminded me of his dealings with a police official when he wangled a passport for Annemarie when the Gestapo was after her. Like so many other German bureaucrats, Inspector Schwartz had returned to his old job when the Russians came.

"He's old now, and due for retirement, but he is still at the Alex, the new Alex. Of course he's only a deputy. The big boss there is a real party member. But he is useful in small ways—and he does what I ask him or else." And old Dahlmann passed his finger across his throat. "They're all like that. Every one of them has something to hide—bribery or murder or something. I'll call him tonight and send a letter to Annemarie," he said. I asked if he could take one for me but he shook his head. "My inspector friend is very timid. He would be annoyed if he thought you knew of him. And we don't want to annoy him at this point. But I'll send a message to her." Heavily he rose from his chair. "It is time you go, Harry. Some block warden or Vopo might spot your car."

When I finally returned to Miquelstrasse, Geoff was talking with General Patman. I daresay I must have been looking rather haggard as I walked into the study, for Geoff rose and came over to me and grasped me by the hand. "I'm sorry, Harry. Terribly sorry," was all he said. But even that was a great deal, for he was not given to emotional outbursts, and I knew then how deeply he felt about his part in the entire affair. But then he seemed to get hold of himself and his voice was normal when he spoke again.

"We were discussing our friend Samson," he said. I looked at Patman: "What are you going to do with that bastard?" I asked, recalling the tape recording. "It certainly was his voice."

Patman frowned. "I've no doubt about that," he said. "But we have to go slow. You know the army—and besides, with all his friends back in Washington and on the West Coast you can't move too fast. I've started an investigation. It'll take a day or two at least. We'll have to wait until we have the complete story."

"Let's leave the colonel be for the time being," Geoff said. "Frankly I'd rather not be reminded of his ugly face at the moment, and anyway there are more important things to do. The press relations office just called to say there were a bunch of journalists waiting to see me and I told them to come over here in half an hour. Now what am I going to tell them?"

The question was more or less rhetorical, for Geoff already had worked out what he would say. Briefly he told us.

When he had finished I spoke up: "I think it's very important to emphasize that you, Geoff, had no part in this whole affair."

"That would hardly be accurate, Harry. After all, I did

speak to Soloviev and he'll probably publish the fact before the day's out. He seems to get pleasure out of kicking me around," he added, smiling bitterly.

"But he can't prove it," I protested.

"Look, Harry. Everyone in West Berlin—in all Berlin for that matter, is going to look to me to save Annemarie and Max if that's possible. I'm not going to dodge my responsibilities. It's up to me."

For ten more minutes we talked as I tried to persuade him that he was in no way to blame and that he should not get himself personally involved. But I made little impression. From the West Berliner's point of view he had permitted the East Regime to take another bite out of them, as he put it, and it was up to him to call a halt. "The West Berliners expect it of me and quite rightly. We've been pushed around too long. We've allowed one encroachment after another. Now I must put a stop to it."

From back in my memory I recalled our conversations in Washington. Geoff's views had come a long way since he had spoken of putting the Berliners in their place.

But then the doorbell rang and a dozen newsmen filed into the room. I knew most of them, Americans, British and French, and four or five Germans. Among them was Hal Birding, an energetic, quick, somewhat emotional newsman who had been living for years in Berlin. He fancied himself as a champion of the Berliners and was generally highly critical of what he called Washington's pusillanimity.

While Matusek passed drinks among them, Geoff made a few opening remarks. He said that of course Colonel

Samson's efforts to use Annemarie had been completely unauthorized. General Patman added that the colonel had been relieved of his responsibilities pending a full investigation. Then Geoff gave his opinion of the whole affair, ending with the trial.

"I think we can do no better than subscribe to the statement Dr. Dahlmann herself made, that it was a cruel, tragic, wicked farce," he concluded.

"But apparently she was the leader of Bureau X, Mr. Schuyler," a German newsman said. "Could you tell us what you think of that organization?"

"Apparently she has admitted a role in Bureau X," Geoff said. "Personally I have never believed in the objectives of Bureau X, and in fact have done all I could to prevent its activities. I shall continue to do so. But that doesn't mean I condone Dr. Dahlmann's arrest and conviction, both of which were flagrant violations of elementary justice, and I shall do all I can to see she gets justice—real justice. The same applies to Herr Ebers."

"How do you propose to accomplish that?" an English correspondent asked.

"Frankly, I'm not sure yet," Geoff said candidly.

"Have you any instructions from Washington?"

"There's hardly been time for that," Geoff answered. "But I daresay the department will be giving me its ideas soon enough," and he smiled as though he were not too eager to get them.

After a few more questions the journalists started to file out, but Hal Birding hung back.

"Could I have a few minutes alone?" he asked in a low

voice, and Geoff reluctantly agreed. He waved Birding to a chair and wearily sat down beside him.

I knew Birding well and was determined not to leave Geoff alone in his hands. Unobtrusively I took a chair in the corner of the room. But when Birding saw me he made no effort to hide his displeasure.

"I said I wanted to see Mr. Schuyler alone, Harding. Do you mind?"

I said nothing but looked at Geoff.

"If Mr. Birding wants it that way, Harry, perhaps you'd leave us," he said. Angrily I stomped from the room and waited in the big, gloomy hall until the interview was over. When Birding had left, looking very pleased with himself, Geoff told me what had happened with that uncanny faculty he had of remembering every word, every gesture of an interview.

Birding had begun by asking if Geoff had known Annemarie before the war. Geoff admitted he had.

"He asked if I had known her intimately and I said 'fairly well.'

"He asked if I had helped her escape when she got in trouble with the Gestapo and I said I had had a part in it. Then he asked if I'd known Max Ebers too and I told him I'd known him well. He intimated that I had tried to keep Max from getting a fair trial by preventing Annemarie from defending him."

"And you replied?"

"I merely said I had not been enthusiastic about Annemarie's going to the East Sector but that when she had insisted I had obtained a safe conduct for her from General Soloviev."

"That must have shut Birding up," I commented.

"On the contrary he immediately took another tack and said: 'You mean you took a Russian's word for it that Dr. Dahlmann would not be arrested?' and then he added something like: 'Wasn't that sort of naïve, Mr. Schuyler?'"

"I said that at the time there were several reasons for accepting Soloviev's word and that we did not know certain things that we know now."

"Did that satisfy him?"

"I don't think so. He had a rather superior smirk on his face when he left," Geoff said, shrugging his shoulders. "I daresay we'll soon have his story. The Berlin papers will get it off the press wires."

"I wonder where Birding picked all this up," I said half to myself.

"I've been wondering about that too and about some other odd coincidences. It's almost as though someone had been listening in to some of our talks with Annemarie. If Patman hadn't assured me that the house had been so thoroughly checked by Security, I'd wonder if it wasn't still wired."

Geoff's prediction about the press reaction was all too accurate. That very evening the Berlin papers carried the story of Geoff's previous friendship with Max and Annemarie and his acceptance of Soloviev's promise of safe conduct.

We were about to go to bed later that evening when the red line phone flashed and Geoff picked it up. Then he passed me the receiver. "It's a Washington call for you, Harry," he said, looking as surprised as I.

The call was from old Nelly Larsen. Briefly he told me that the story of Geoff's acceptance of the Soloviev safe conduct was headline news in the evening papers.

"I didn't want to tell Geoff straight out but the reaction is pretty critical. So I thought you could break it to him a bit gently. I know he must be damned harassed. We're doing everything here to keep the record straight but it's not too easy."

When I hung up I was silent for a moment trying to figure out what I was going to tell Geoff, who was staring at me questioningly.

Finally I decided there was no point trying to deceive him and as mildly as I could I told him what old Nelly had said. Geoff took it very well, at least outwardly. He shrugged and smiled. "They're doing their best, I guess. But they'll never understand Berlin."

XIII

EARLY NEXT MORNING BILL Harmsworth reported that the students at the university were up in arms over the trial. Apparently they were planning some sort of demonstration.

"Are they angry at us Americans?" Geoff asked. Bill looked uneasy.

"As a matter of fact they are, and your name seems to have been mentioned rather frequently." I looked at Geoff's face, but he managed to conceal his emotions as usual.

"Christl could tell you more about it. She was at one of the meetings. They flatly refused to let me in." Geoff asked him to find Christl and bring her to the office. "And if you can find that fellow Sepp bring him along too." Obviously he was concerned about public reactions, and, recalling the meeting at the Rathaus, I could hardly blame him.

When Christl turned up an hour later she told us that

some of the more violent students were planning a rally at the Victory Monument on the Street of June 17, the extension of the Unter den Linden west of the Brandenburg Gate. It had recently been renamed in honor of the uprising in East Berlin in 1953.

Geoff frowned. "But don't you see that's the worst possible thing they could do for your mother, Christl?" he asked sharply.

"That's exactly what I told them, Uncle Geoff. I said we shouldn't do anything until they publish the sentence tomorrow. Most of my friends agree but there are some pretty wild ones still beating their drums, and if you don't mind, I'm going back to the campus now just to be sure they don't go crazy. They seem to listen to me," she added, and her face flushed. "I mean—after all—I'm her daughter." Geoff smiled and asked her to keep her eye on the campus—especially when the sentence was announced—and to report back to him at once.

When she had left, Geoff and I went around to see General Patman.

"There may be some pretty serious trouble when they pronounce sentence," Geoff said. "Can the Berlin police handle it?"

Patman rubbed his chin thoughtfully. "The Berlin police are as good a bunch as I know but they have just one small defect. They're a bit softhearted when it comes to handling their own people. If the Vopos try anything they're terrific, but the West Berliners—"

"Well, there's nothing to worry about yet," Geoff said, stressing the last word.

On the way home Geoff turned to me: "I've been trying

to get Soloviev on the phone all day but his aide says he's out of town for the weekend. If we could only get to him, there might be a chance he could, as he puts it, 'use his influence' with that bastard of a presiding judge. Besides," he added, "it might be as well to warn him that the West Berliners are in a dangerous frame of mind and that we can't be responsible if there's an incident at the Wall."

"What about Alexeiev?" I asked. "I might be able to find him." I recalled that Klein had once told me that Alexeiev's regular office was in the Soviet embassy on Unter den Linden and that he only went to Potsdam when Soloviev needed his political advisor. Geoff agreed to my seeking him out.

I got across the checkpoint without too much delay when I told the Vopos I was on my way to see Alexeiev at the Soviet embassy. He was not in his office but a flunkey promised to fetch him.

He appeared about half an hour later. He obviously had made a night of it on Saturday evening, for his face was swollen and his eyes inflamed. But that hardly surprised me.

Nor did it surprise me that he was curt, downright rude, when I told him what my mission was.

"You are asking me to interfere in a purely German matter," he said pompously. "No doubt the United States tells its puppets in Bonn what to do but that is not the way the Soviet government acts toward its allies. You can tell Mr. Schuyler that Dr. Dahlmann will be given precisely the sentence she deserves." Barely able to keep my temper, I went on to tell him of the unrest among the university students.

"If there are any incidents along the Wall or elsewhere,

Colonel," I said, stressing the title, which I knew was a purely honorific one, "you will understand that it is due entirely to the justified repugnance of civilized people for the type of justice your so-called allies administer." I had rehearsed my little speech carefully and was not surprised when Alexeiev rose angrily from his chair. "I am not prepared to receive such insulting messages from you or Herr Schuyler or anyone else. Our interview is ended."

When I told Geoff what had happened he laughed. "The little son-of-a-bitch. They can insult us as much as they like but apparently we must treat them with old-world diplomatic courtesy."

It was obvious that Geoff's earlier hopes of taming the Soviet officials had long since evaporated.

For the rest of the day Geoff and I sat about the Miquelstrasse villa waiting for time to pass. Geoff had been reporting to Washington the developments as they occurred, but neither of us expected to get any official reaction before late the next day. For one thing, Washington, unlike its missions abroad, abhorred working on Sundays. Besides, the Secretary of State was in New York attending a UN meeting on the South American crisis and the President was out in the West on a fence-mending tour.

But our enforced inaction while we waited for the explosion we knew was coming did not help our nerves, and I for one was relieved when after a nightcap we both went up to bed.

When I arrived in my office with Geoff next morning, a news announcement from the East German radio said that the sentence in the case of Citizen Dahlmann would be announced at noon. A few minutes later my telephone rang and an unknown voice asked me if I would come down to the exchange depot near Checkpoint Charlie at once. I asked what it was all about but the voice just mumbled that it was urgent.

When I arrived at the exchange depot where mail, packages and other shipments from or to the East Sector were sorted, examined and dispatched, I picked my way through a yard cluttered with mail sacks, boxes and crates to the shack which apparently served as an office. As I approached it I passed two coffins and then a third. I stared at the last for a moment, for the top was open.

Then as I entered the shack I saw sitting on a wooden bench, looking worn and disheveled, the little figure of Herr Klein. His ashen face beamed when he recognized me and he leaped from the bench. "Herr Harding, at last." I looked from him to an old sergeant who was in charge.

"It's sort of unusual, sir," the sergeant began. "But when they delivered those coffins this morning that one out there was making a hell of a noise." I could scarcely suppress a smile. "So we unscrewed it and this guy gets out. He's no more dead than you are, sir." I glanced at Klein, who was smiling proudly.

"It's very irregular, sir," the sergeant went on. "I mean there's nothing in regs about it. The coffins are supposed to have corpses in them—and only corpses. No packages, no contraband, no written materials. That's all in regs, sir. If there's anything else we're supposed to turn it over to the security officer, Colonel Samson. I called him but he isn't functioning, he says. We couldn't put the guy back in the box. Hell, he's not dead and we couldn't ship him back. Next exchange isn't till tomorrow, sir. So we had to call you—like the guy asked."

I no longer tried to hide my amusement as I turned to Klein: "Well?"

Klein beamed proudly. "I told you I would see you soon. It was easy enough. General Soloviev himself put me in charge of this corpse exchange business. So when you left I called the East German Funeral Trust and told them my brother who lived in West Berlin had died. They sent around a coffin and a truck. I made out the regular certificate and gave the truck driver two hundred marks and he screwed me in and delivered me this morning."

I told Klein to come with me, and was about to leave the shack when the sergeant intervened. "But, sir, I can't let him go. Have to have a receipt for the corpse but there ain't no corpse."

I said I would sign a receipt and would report fully to General Patman in person. At the name of the general the sergeant seemed mollified. "But tell him it wasn't no fault of ours the guy wasn't dead," he called after us as I took Klein to my car.

As we drove toward Clayallee, Klein's initial elation began to subside. Anxiously he asked if he would get asylum and I said "possibly."

"I had to get out, Herr Harding," he pleaded. "You know about Ilse and all that—and then this Dr. Dahlmann business. They're all a bunch of swine over there." He jerked his thumb over his shoulder.

"What'll they do with me now?" he asked. I said I

wasn't familiar with the refugee procedure, but I would turn him over to Harmsworth, who doubtless would take him to the refugee center at Marienfelde, where he would presumably be processed, and, if accepted, shipped to Western Germany.

"If?" Klein asked, and his eyes turned to me in panic. "You mean perhaps they won't?" I said that remained to be seen.

"But what about my statement?" he asked, and I asked what he meant.

"All refugees make statements," he said. "I've heard dozens of them on the RIAS broadcasts." (RIAS was the American-sponsored station in Berlin, more formally known as the Radio in the American sector.) "I have to make a statement, Herr Harding." I could scarcely conceal my contempt for this little man seeking his tiny share of glory. "What's so important about your statement?" I asked.

"But that's the whole point," he sniveled. I asked what he wanted to say. "About Ilse, of course. I'm going to tell them it wasn't her fault and not to blame her."

"Do you really think that'll help her? It'll just make them suspicious."

"And her friend," Klein went on, ignoring my remark. "I have to thank him too."

"Thank him?" I said. "Have you lost your mind?"

Klein said nothing, and as we had already reached headquarters I let the matter drop. Obviously the little man was slightly unbalanced for the moment, as who would not be who had escaped from the East Sector posing as a corpse in a coffin.

I took him to my office, called Bill Harmsworth, and when he appeared turned Klein over to him.

As Klein and Harmsworth left I looked at my watch. It was eleven-fifteen. In three quarters of an hour we would know the worst. None of us, I think, had any hope that the sentence would be less than ten years. I tried to read some reports on my desk but my mind would not take in what my eyes read. I went out and for half an hour paced up and down the long tree-lined driveway between the headquarters building and the main gate. Once when I turned suddenly I caught a glimpse of Geoff watching me from his window. Then I went back to my office.

My radio was already switched on and tuned to the East German station when Geoff came to my room, ostensibly to show me a letter he had received from Nelly Larsen with some gossip about a friend in the service. I read it, trying to appear interested in its contents. Geoff meanwhile slipped onto the sofa across from my desk. The radio sounded the time signal for twelve o'clock. A woman speaker with a high-pitched, rasping voice started reading the news. There was an item about a meeting of the East German Communist party, "the Unity Party" they always called it, which was to take place the following week. Then an item about a speech by Ulbricht given in some small provincial town, the name of which I missed. A government factory announced it had overfulfilled its monthly production of electrical equipment. From Moscow came the summary of a speech by Khrushchev on how to plant corn or something of the sort.

All the while, Geoff sitting facing me was smoking a

cigarette, his knees crossed, his eyes fixed on the ceiling. For a moment the announcer's voice seemed to fade and I bent over the radio set to readjust it. I must have turned the knob the wrong way for the voice disappeared entirely. I hastily spun it in the other direction and the voice came in startlingly clear:

"The People's Court of the District of Pankow has just announced the sentence in the case of citizens Max Ebers and Annemarie Dahlmann. Ebers was sentenced to the highest penalty of people's justice—death. Annemarie Dahlmann was sentenced to the highest penalty of people's justice—death. Appeal by the defense counsel has been rejected. The sentence will be carried out within the next forty-eight hours."

I slumped forward on my desk, my head on my arms. How long I stayed there I have no idea. But then I heard Geoff's secretary come in and tell him Bill Harmsworth was on the telephone. He took the call at my desk and after listening for a moment or two said: "I suggest you bring Sepp and some of his pals here at once. Keep the group as small as you can but be sure you get Sepp." He hung up and then I felt his hand on my shoulder:

"Come on, Harry," he said. "We've work to do." I rose and followed him to his office next door.

Berlin's Free University is for the most part not far from the U.S. headquarters and within a half hour Bill, Christl, Sepp and a half-dozen young men filed into the room, looking pale and determined. Christl's eyes were red and puffy as she came and sat beside me on the couch.

I could not trust myself to speak and just managed to force a smile of encouragement to her.

Geoff motioned Sepp to take a chair beside him but Sepp shook his head and planted himself directly in front of Geoff's desk, his feet apart, his shoulders thrown back. His voice when he started to speak was deep and the raw Bavarian accent marked: "Herr Schuyler, as chairman of the Student Union's emergency committee I have been asked to speak to you on behalf of the people of Berlin." He paused; Geoff nodded for him to go on.

Evidently he had rehearsed his words for they came out fast and emphatic.

"Sir, the sentencing of Dr. Dahlmann and Herr Ebers is intolerable to every decent German. We demand that our Western allies take every possible measure to prevent their execution and restore them to the freedom they as heroes of the German people deserve. If our allies fail us," he went on and now his words were slower, more deliberate, almost belligerent, "we Berliners will take justice into our own hands, whatever it may cost."

He stopped and glared at Geoff.

Geoff had faced other crises in his long diplomatic career. He had stood up to more violent threats, sometimes delivered at the point of a gun. But none of them had been directed so sharply at him, and not just physically but intellectually, morally. He paused longer than usual before he answered and his voice was low and even.

"Your reaction and that of the people for whom you speak is fully justified," he said slowly. "I share it and so does everyone in this room—some with more reason than you." His eyes fell on Christl and myself. "I have informed my government and have requested it to take every step in Moscow and elsewhere to prevent the executions. I am confident not only Washington but London and Paris and every other free nation will do what they can. But," he paused again and looked straight into the eyes of the young man in front of him, "but no life, no two lives, no matter how dear they may be to you Berliners or to anyone else," and again his eyes fell on me, "can justify the ultimate calamity that could turn not just you and your city to ashes but could destroy the entire civilization for which Dr. Dahlmann and Herr Ebers have been struggling." He paused again and looked around at the other young people.

"And may I say the form of their struggle was not one that had the approval of myself or of my government." The big young man in front of him stiffened and his jaws tightened angrily.

When Geoff began again his voice was softer. "You have my complete sympathy—much more than any of you realize. I knew Annemarie Dahlmann and Max Ebers before most of you were born. I admire them. I admire their courage and their principles if not their judgment. But," he paused once more and rose to his feet and leaned across his desk, "I am not prepared to risk the ultimate confrontation for their sakes or for the sake of anyone else, myself and my closest friends included." He sat down and there was a long, tense silence.

It was broken by Christl, and her high, hoarse voice so close to me made me start. "Uncle Geoff, isn't there some alternative? Isn't there some other way? I think many of us here thought perhaps there was another way."

Geoff looked at her hard: "Precisely what do you have in mind?"

"There's the Water Tunnel, for instance. Couldn't we open it and rescue them that way?"

Geoff looked puzzled: "Do you mean by force? That is just what I cannot allow."

Sepp broke in. "Not exactly, Herr Schuyler. If we have your full support we can get her out of the Alex. We have connections inside. The Vopos can be bribed, and then if the Water Tunnel is opened we can smuggle her across. But we need your full cooperation. Will you promise it?" His voice was hard and almost threatening.

Geoff stared at the inkwell in front of him. His face was drawn, the muscles of his jaws taut. Here was his decision. He could not appeal to Washington. There was neither time nor, in his eyes, any reason to shirk the responsibility. Ever since he had come to Berlin—in fact, ever since we had first discussed Berlin back in Washington—he had been determined never to let the Berliners risk a conflict. Since then he had come a long way to accepting their point of view, partly out of sympathy for their sufferings and admiration for their courage, partly under pressures that few men could have withstood.

At last he looked up at the big blond man. "My answer," he said slowly, "is no." He had made his decision. His voice was clear, firm and incisive, but as his eyes swept the room and rested on me they seemed troubled, as though for the first time in his life Geoff was not sure. He rose to indicate that the conversation was ended. Silently and sullenly the

Germans filed out of the room. Christl was the last to go, and as she was about to leave he called to her to wait. Then he came around the desk and bent down and kissed her on the forehead.

"I'm sorrier than you'll ever in your long life know," he said, and his voice was husky with emotion.

Early next morning Geoff left for his office. Knowing that I'd be in the way I stayed home. Around noon I got Matusek to fix me a sandwich, and, after I'd eaten, went on down to Clayallee.

When I walked into Geoff's office Bill was reporting once again on the state of the students. Since the group we had seen the previous evening had reported the conversation with Geoff, making no secret that they'd been thwarted by the American Representative, the campus had been seething with anger, he said. Plans were already under way for a giant rally. Not only the students were being mobilized. Squads were being sent through all West Berlin announcing the meeting.

"They mean real trouble then?" Geoff asked when Bill had finished.

"Yes, sir. I'm sure they do."

Geoff looked at him silently for a moment, as though trying to judge whether he was exaggerating, and apparently decided he was not, for he reached for the desk telephone and pushed the red line button.

"General Patman, please," he told the red line operator.

A moment later the general answered. "Pat," Geoff said, "I understand there's trouble brewing. Have you any dope from your people?" I couldn't hear the reply but then Geoff spoke again: "Anyway, I'm afraid it's pretty serious. Would you like me to come over or—"

Then he hung up and came back to his chair.

"If you can wait, the general is on his way," he said to Harmsworth.

A few minutes later Patman appeared, looking brisk and businesslike.

Briefly Bill Harmsworth repeated what he had told Geoff and the general listened intently. When Bill finished Geoff broke in: "Can your men handle them if the police can't?" he asked.

Patman smiled. "I've been giving them riot training for the past three months and if they can't handle a demonstration no one can. I'll put the provost marshal on the alert, though," he added, and walked to the phone, but just then it rang and he picked up the receiver and listened. Then he handed it to Geoff. "It's the governing mayor."

For several minutes Geoff listened to the rough, booming voice, which we could hear across the room.

When he finally put down the receiver he turned to Patman. "The mayor seems pretty worried. He's called the senate together, and as soon as he's through with them he's coming out here."

Patman nodded. "If you'll excuse me, Geoff, I'd like to put things in motion in my shop." Brisk as ever he hurried out the door.

Geoff said he wanted to draft another telegram to the department and Bill and I went out to my office.

"What do you think they're going to do, Bill?" I asked.

"They're talking again about storming the Brandenburg Gate."

"That's what they said the other day at the Rathaus."

"But this time I think they mean it." And he repeated to me snatches of the harangues he had been listening to all morning on the campus.

A few minutes later Geoff's secretary came out and told us we should go back in. We were soon joined again by Patman.

"Has your G-2 anything to report?" Geoff asked.

"Nothing," Patman said. "And while I don't want to disparage Bill here, or the mayor, for that matter, I'm not too worried myself."

"Just the same, Pat, I don't think we should treat it too lightly. When Berliners get mad they get damned mad, especially the students—they've been through too much in the last few years. Their patience is pretty thin. And remember they're not so docile as their parents were. Personally, I can't blame them. In fact, if I were a student here now I'd—well I don't know what I'd do, but I'm inclined to believe it wouldn't be just yelling. They're sore—and with damned good reason. For seventeen years they've been under those Communist guns, looking down those barrels every day, waiting for someone to pull the trigger and blow them sky high—or worse still, to pour a few thousand Vopos across the boundary some night and take the place over."

Patman started to protest but Geoff cut him short.

"Yes, I know, Pat, your soldiers are brave and determined and well trained and they all have the latest weapons. But you know as well as I, and every Berliner knows too, that you couldn't hold out against an all-out attack more than a few hours."

Patman started again, but Geoff kept on, his face flushed, his voice more vehement than I had heard it in a long time.

"Yes, I know, we'd retaliate with our A-Bombs and H-Bombs and storm the Fulda Gap or somewhere. But where would these poor Berliners be by then? Either ashes or on the way to Siberia."

He stopped and stared for a moment at the green blotter in front of him. Then he sat back and passed his big thin hand over his face. "But I guess this isn't getting us much further. The question is, what are we going to do?"

"I've just alerted the entire command and given orders to stand by for riot duty. They're breaking out the tear gas and tanks right now."

"Tanks? Will they be necessary?"

"That's standard procedure for mob action. It's chiefly for psychological effect," he added.

Geoff smiled wryly. "We're going to need all the psychological effect we can get if what Harmsworth reports is accurate." Bill shook his head in earnest agreement.

A moment later the governing mayor was announced and he bounced into the office puffing, shook hands, and half fell into a big armchair by Geoff's desk.

Geoff looked at him and waited for him to catch his breath, and then he said simply: "Well, Herr Mayor, how bad is it?"

"It is pretty bad, Herr Schuyler," the mayor said in a

heavy accent. "People are worked up. I've just got reports from various districts. The crowds are already gathering up in Charlottenburg. The chief of police is worried. Up till now he has handled every demonstration pretty efficiently. But he says he simply hasn't enough men. He'll have to have allied troops—"

"Well, you can count on us," Geoff broke in. "General Patman has his men on the alert. What about your British and French colleagues, Pat?"

"I've just talked to them. They're going on the alert too. They're a bit reluctant, though, to face a West Berlin crowd. We have a contingency plan all worked out ready to put into operation."

"Can't say I blame them one bit," Geoff said. "Especially as this seems to be largely of our doing—" he hesitated a moment and added more softly, as though he were talking to himself—"my doing, perhaps."

The mayor began to protest but Geoff silenced him.

"You know as well as I that the Russians have it in for me—personally." I rose from my chair and went over to him. Speaking as gently as I could I said: "Let's not get into that. It can wait for a post-mortem."

Geoff laughed. "All right, Harry, but I want to make one thing clear: if our troops have to go into riot action against the crowds I'm going to be with them."

Now Patman protested: "Sorry, Geoff. I don't think that would be possible. It's a military action and no place for civilians."

Geoff stiffened. His voice was hard, his eyes fixed on the general. "I'm afraid you can't stop me, Pat. If our troops move I'm going to be out there. If you'll provide me with a jeep and a loudspeaker I'll be much obliged. But if you don't I'll go on foot—with a megaphone."

"I shall be with you," the mayor suddenly interjected quietly. "They are my people, Herr Schuyler."

Geoff looked at him solemnly. "Yes, they are. But I feel as though they were mine too, and I'm proud of them."

"But they are angry, Herr Schuyler, and if you don't mind my saying so, it would be best if you kept away."

"That question is settled, Herr Mayor. We need not discuss it. If someone wants to pelt me with an egg—or a stone—it's their privilege. Perhaps I deserve it."

The remark annoyed me and I made no attempt to hide it: "For God's sake, Geoff, don't take this so damned personally."

Geoff looked at me as though I'd slapped him. He paled but said nothing.

Patman broke the awkward silence that followed: "I think I'd better get my staff together—and talk to the British and French."

He was halfway out the door when the telephone rang again and Geoff answered. "It's the chief of police for you," he said, handing the receiver to the mayor. While the mayor listened we were silent. At last he said, *"In Ordnung.* Okay," and put down the receiver.

He turned to us. "It is as we expected," he said calmly. "They are rallying at the Victory Monument and plan to march down the Street of June 17 to the Gate."

"That's the British sector, isn't it?" Geoff said.

Patman answered, "Yes, but our contingency plan calls

for our troops to hold between the monument and the Gate. I better get going."

As he went out the door Geoff called after him: "I'm expecting a jeep and loudspeaker outside in five minutes, Pat."

The mayor put in a call to the city hall and reported his plans. Then he turned to Geoff. "I think it is time," he said.

Downstairs outside the elaborate stone-columned head-quarters building the jeep and two motorcycle escorts were already drawn up. The men were stiff in their bullet-proof vests, and beside the driver rode a soldier with an automatic rifle and a walkie-talkie.

The mayor suggested we ride as far as we could in his car with the jeep and escort behind. "It will be more inconspicuous," he said, and Geoff added with a grin, "And a hell of a sight more comfortable." I was amazed at his calm at that moment.

Near the Tiergarten the crowds were so thick that we left the car and Geoff, the mayor and I squeezed into the back of the jeep. There was a loudspeaker rigged to the windshield and the driver gave Geoff the mike. Geoff told the rifleman with the walkie-talkie to get in touch with General Patman at the emergency operations headquarters.

The motorcycle escort darted ahead, but soon the crowds on the approaches to the Victory Monument were so tightly massed that we turned the jeep down a walk through the park and wound our way among the shrubbery until we emerged on the great avenue which leads from the monument to the Brandenburg Gate.

We got as near to the monument as we could and parked the jeep inconspicuously in the shrubbery. The mayor had planned to make his way to the speaker's platform but the crowd made it impossible. A squad of Berlin police officers offered to force a way through but the mayor wisely declined. "If trouble starts I want to be between them and the Gate," he explained.

For some minutes we watched anxiously as the crowds surged forward. Some were waving banners with slogans but others were carrying clubs and staves. A police officer reported they had already picked up some carrying arms and even plastic explosives.

Just as it was growing dark a voice blared out over a makeshift loudspeaker. The speaker was Sepp.

"Berliners!" he roared. "We have had enough!"

He paused and a roar went up from the crowd: "Enough and too much!"

"And we have had enough promises," he continued when they subsided.

"Too many promises," the crowd responded.

"Promises from the Russians," and an angry cry of derision filled the air.

"Promises from the Allies, the French, the English and the Americans."

Again a deep sullen roar answered him.

"Our own people, our own mayor has told us to be patient," and again the crowd roared derisively, "Patience!"

"We have been patient but what good has it done us? One after another they have taken our fellow Berliners—

all our comrades in the East—from us." Another booming shout swept across the big square.

"And now they have taken our beloved fellow Berliner Annemarie Dahlmann."

I felt a pang and turned to Geoff. His face in the light of the floodlights that lit the whole avenue was gray. His lips were pressed tightly together, his jaws set, and in his eyes was a look of despair.

By now the crowd was beside itself. Sticks waved in the air. The shouting was deep and ominous. A police officer came toward us.

"The Russians are massing troops behind the Gate," he said in a low voice.

"And what have they done to rescue her?" the speaker shouted.

The response was immediate: "Nothing! Nothing!"

"Not even her old friend, the American Representative has raised his little finger." Geoff's face was ashen. The muscles of his jaws bunched.

"Remember her words today to the hangmen across the Wall: 'Let no one accuse us Germans again of allowing another tyrant to destroy our nation.'"

The crowd cheered and began to move restlessly. The police officers and soldiers moved the jeeps and their cars onto the avenue. Behind us I heard a rumble, and in the dusk made out the low silhouettes of American tanks emerging from the park shrubbery. Beside them columns of soldiers were marching slowly, grimly, in single file. Geoff took the radiophone and demanded General Patman. "Not yet, Pat, not yet. Hold them back." A minute later the rumble behind us ceased. But ahead the crowd was roaring angrily and against the pink western sky their sticks and pikes waved.

"Action! Action!" they called.

The shouting subsided for a moment and Sepp's hoarse voice went on: "We are not the cowards of the Third Reich. We must take action now, now before it is too late. Before we are enslaved again. Now, citizens!"

The chant was taken up: "Action! Action! Now!" Sepp gestured for silence but the chant continued: "Action! Now!"

Unable to silence them, Sepp leaned into the microphone in front of him and in a bloodcurdling roar shouted: "To the Gate," and his hand pointed down the avenue over our heads to the great stone arch, its four horsemen just visible against the darkening sky. Then suddenly the mob started to move with a rush and a sound like water bursting through a dam.

One of the American soldiers seized Geoff and pulled him into the back of the jeep. The mayor followed, while a German policeman lifted me bodily and set me down in one of the German riot cars. Behind me I could hear the backfiring of the motors in the tanks as they started up. Above our heads the floodlights glared down. The crowd surged forward. Slowly the German riot car started to back away. But the jeep stood fast and I watched as Geoff and the mayor rose in the back seat, gesturing futilely. The mayor took the microphone in his hands and shouted: "Citizens of Berlin. Wait, stop." His words, amplified by the speaker, carried far back into the crowd.

Startled by the sound of the familiar, deep booming voice the first wave slowed and then stopped hardly thirty yards from the jeep. But the pressure behind them pushed them forward, and at last the jeep driver began to give ground, slowly moving in reverse. For a moment more the mayor continued to shout through the loudspeaker, but now the roaring crowd seemed to pay little attention.

The rumbling behind us grew louder and suddenly the leading tanks, three abreast, spread out across the wide avenue and slowly, grimly, moved ahead. Crouching beside each tank, the American soldiers, their helmets down around their ears, fanned out in Indian file, their bayonets thrust forward, and advanced in slow funeral-march cadence. At each step they let out a throaty, terrifying shout, and their heavy boots pounded the pavement in unison.

The surging crowds were only a few yards away when suddenly they saw the great steel monsters and the crouching phalanx of American bayonets shuffling slowly toward them.

Two high-pitched screams rose above the low roar of the crowd. Then there was deathly silence. The front ranks halted, their faces in the weird floodlights contorted with surprise and anger, as though unable to believe what they saw. Then the pressure of the crowd behind pushed them forward until only a pace or two separated them from the glistening steel bayonets. Again they halted and again they were pushed on from behind and stopped again.

At some unheard command the tanks had halted, and beside them the troops stood fast, still crouching, their bayonets at the ready. A policeman beside me with earphones leaned forward to the officer beside the driver: "The Russians have brought up their tanks to the Gate." The officer, his eyes glued to the faces staring at us across the few feet of pavement, merely grunted.

Then suddenly the crowd split, running to the sides of the avenue, trying to outflank the troops. With a wild shout they poured around us through the shrubbery of the park. But then they stopped abruptly. From the shrubbery a solid front of soldiers backed by jeeps moved in through the brush. Frustrated, the crowd stood motionless, shouting furiously and brandishing their sticks. For a moment I thought it was all over.

But one look at the tense, anxious faces of the police beside me told me I was mistaken. Then out of the crowd emerged the curly-haired young Bavarian, Sepp. A German flag in one hand and what looked like a grenade in the other, he marched boldly up to the tanks.

"Make way." He paused for a second and the crowd took up the chant again: "Make way." Then he pulled back his hand holding the grenade, ready to throw it.

Just then a voice roared out over a loudspeaker and I recognized Geoff's, whose jeep was hidden from me by a tank.

It was hard and cold. "You're not going through," he said.

The young man looked startled at the familiar voice, but he kept his hand high. Geoff's voice roared out again: "You're not going through. Unless you want a massacre, drop that hand and make sense." Slowly Sepp's hand came down. A sullen murmur ran through the crowd. Geoff had won the round but that sea of faces, fury written on every one, showed the battle was not over.

I stood up in the seat, where I could see Geoff over the front of the tank between us. He was standing on the hood of the jeep, the mayor behind him.

Then a stone crashed with an angry clang against the jeep's fender and the soldier with the automatic rifle rose, and took aim at a young boy in the front rank whence the stone had come. Geoff swung around and knocked the barrel down.

"All right, throw your stones this way, if you want," he shouted. "My name is Schuyler. I am the American Representative." Another loud murmur of anger rippled through the crowd. "I knew Dr. Dahlmann in the Nazi days. And I respect her just as much as every one of you here. For I know her courage, not just against those gang-sters across the Wall. I knew her courage against Hitler." He stopped for a moment and the rumbling in the crowd seemed a shade less hostile.

"But is this the way to honor her courage—by behaving like maniacs?"

Back in the crowd someone shouted, "Take away those American tanks and we'll show you."

Once again the muttering rose to a roar and another stone crashed harmlessly against the leading tank.

"And if we let you through, do you know that fifty Russian tanks are standing back there?" Geoff said, point-ing to the Gate. "And beside them are hundreds of Soviet soldiers with their guns loaded. You know—or your parents know—they won't talk before they shoot."

Then the mayor seized the mike and turned to Sepp. "They might miss you," he said, "though you're a damned good target, but they won't miss the people you're leading into their trap." For a moment the crowd was silent and once again I thought we had won, but then the shouting began again in the rear of the crowd: "Make way! Make way!" The crowd surged forward under the pressure from behind until only a step or two separated it from the bayonets of the crouching soldiers. The soldiers in the front rank looked up anxiously at their troop commander in the cockpit of the center tank.

The commander called to Geoff and the mayor: "Another foot and I'll give them the tear gas," he said.

"Not unless you have enough tear gas for two million Berliners," Geoff called back angrily.

The shouting in the rear of the mob grew stronger. The leading ranks tried vainly to hold back.

Someone shouted, "Go through! They won't dare shoot! They're our brave Americans!"

I could see Geoff was about at the end of his strength. His face was white and sweat was streaming down his cheeks. His eyes roved over the crowd as though seeking a friend. But there were no friends in that hostile mob. He caught sight of Sepp and their eyes met. They had once been friends and had respected each other. But now they stood on opposite sides of the line.

Geoff gave Sepp an appealing, pained look. He gestured to the stocky Bavarian to come forward. But Sepp stood where he was, his feet apart, his hands on his hips, defiant, belligerent.

Geoff hesitated a moment and then he leaped from the hood of the jeep to the ground and, pushing his way through the soldiers, crossed over to where the students stood. Every eye on both sides of the line was on him as he walked up to Sepp. He leaned forward and spoke low into his ear. The big Bavarian face frowned, bewildered. Then he took Geoff by the arm and led him out of the crowd, into the darkness of the Tiergarten.

Less than a minute later they emerged. Geoff went straight back to the jeep. His face was still taut, still worried, but it had lost that look of panic he had had when the crowd had surged forward the last time.

Sepp went back to his group of students and a moment later was talking in low tones to his friends assembled around him. The rest of the crowd stood silent, watching them intently. Sepp gestured toward them and his friends turned and fanned out among the crowd, speaking to them quietly, calmly, but, it seemed to me, with self-satisfied confidence. The crowd seemed bewildered at first but then gradually they became less belligerent and in little groups turned and started back up the avenue away from the soldiers and the tanks. Whatever the word Sepp had sent out, they had accepted it and now like good Germans they were ready to go home—and not trample the grass on the way.

I climbed from the police car and hurried over to Geoff. He was slumped in the back of the jeep alone. The mayor, looking thoroughly mystified by the whole procedure stood off at a little distance, staring at him. I climbed in beside him and impatiently asked what he had done.

"I . . . I . . ." he began uncertainly, reluctantly. "I agreed," he said at last. "I agreed to help."

I looked at him in amazement. A few minutes before he had been angrily, defiantly berating the crowd. Now he had crossed the lines and joined them, capitulated.

What had possessed him? I thought anxiously, for, no matter how he expressed it, he had in effect pledged his cooperation in the students' mad scheme to free Annemarie from the Alex. What was more he had declared war—a private, personal war no doubt—on the Russians. Soloviev might never learn what he had said to Sepp, but from his agents who must have been mingling in the crowd he was sure to learn that Geoff had changed fronts and now stood facing not the rioting crowds but himself, the Soviet commander. From now on no matter what Geoff did, what happened, it would be interpreted by his suspicious Slav mind as a hostile act.

I looked at Geoff unhappily as he sat huddled beside me, his face now blank and expressionless, a defeated man. Then abruptly he shook his shoulders, sat up straight and leaning forward told the driver to move off.

The motorcycle escort emerged from the darkness. A siren screamed. The silent mob gave way and we drove slowly homeward.

Geoff was amazingly calm when we reached Miquelstrasse. Though subdued and silent, he seemed in complete command of himself as he picked up the telephone and called the duty officer and asked that a secretary be sent over at once. Then he added: "Tell the code room to stand by for an urgent message."

When the secretary appeared he started dictating a detailed account of the riot. I was amazed at the concise, vivid and balanced language that flowed articulately with scarcely a pause. When he reached the end he repeated word for word the statement he had made to the crowd. Then he stopped and looked up at me: "Is that absolutely accurate, Harry? Have I left out anything?"

Then he turned to the secretary: "Paragraph," and then he started again:

"The department will, of course, appreciate," he dictated, "that the arrest of Dr. Dahlmann, the trial and the ensuing riot are all directly attributable to General Soloviev's breaking his solemn pledge given to me personally. In other words, the entire action was basically an attempt to destroy my position. For this reason I had no choice but to take the unusual step of pledging my own word to retaliate. While I realize that my assurances were unusual, the department will appreciate the exceedingly delicate circumstances under which I was required to act. Had I not done so there is little doubt but that widespread bloodshed would have resulted from a clash between our troops and our Berlin allies with repercussions not just in Berlin but throughout the world. Therefore, until we can reassess the situation tomorrow morning I urgently request that the department renew my assurances and refrain from further comment." He stopped again and looked up at me.

"Is that fair, Harry?"

I hesitated for a fraction of a second.

"What I mean is, there would have been bloodshed, wouldn't there?" he said.

I was relieved that the question was thus narrowed down and readily enough I agreed.

While the secretary transcribed the cable we sat in silence. Then Geoff carefully went over the message, changing hardly a word, and initialed it.

"See that they get it moving at once," he told the secretary as she said goodnight. When the door had closed behind her, Geoff's long, lank frame seemed to go limp. His shoulders drooped and his face muscles were slack, almost puffy. "I guess I've had it for today," he said. "I'm turning in."

In bed at last I tried to sleep but Geoff's last words kept echoing in my mind. "I've had it." They were perhaps a better assessment of his position than he had meant. No matter how I looked at it he had made a mistake—and a serious one. He had not, of course, openly threatened the Russians or presented them with a public ultimatum he could not back up. Geoff was far too experienced, too familiar with the Russian mind to make any such stupid blunder. But by his ill-concealed gesture to Sepp he had challenged them and set the stage for the events that were to come. Though at the time I confess I never imagined they would come so swiftly, so catastrophically, I was uneasy—uneasy and frightened.

Yet, etched on my closed eyelids was the picture of Geoff in the glaring lights tonight. My ears still rang with those shouts of "Action! Action!" Who could have withstood those terrifyingly desperate pleas?

XIV

PROMPTLY AT EIGHT NEXT
morning, Sepp and his committee, including Christl, came
to Geoff's office. Geoff was calm as he began to speak:
"Last night I promised you my help. I am going to keep
my promise but I cannot guarantee you will be successful.
What do you now propose, the Water Tunnel?"

Sepp nodded, smiling.

"All right, I'll have the guard withdrawn. I am told it
will take at least eight hours before it is passable." Sepp
nodded agreement.

"But how do you propose to get the prisoners from the
Alex?"

Sepp started to speak but Christl interrupted. "They're
being moved to the maximum security prison at Pankow
at midnight tonight. Our friends will divert the prison van
and bring them to the tunnel entrance."

Geoff looked skeptical: "Is that a hope or are you sure?" he asked.

"We have a friend in the Alex," Christl said. She was sitting beside me again and I leaned over and whispered: "Inspector Schwartz?" She looked up surprised. "Have you talked to Grandfather?" she asked and I nodded.

Geoff was speaking again.

"If you are sure of it, then let's not waste time. I'm going to ask Mr. Harding to work with you. That will be all." Once again the Germans filed out. Now their mood was anything but sullen and jubilation was written on every face.

When they had left Geoff turned to me: "Harry, I'd appreciate your keeping an eye on them. I'm scared to death of that Water Tunnel. But there's just one stipulation," he added emphatically. "I don't want you taking part in any theatrics in the East Sector. You had your share of that twenty-five years ago. Let the students do it this time. Besides, it's a cinch that by now the Vopos have their eyes on you and you'll be watched like a hawk whenever you go across the boundary."

I was about to leave when Bill Harmsworth, who had remained behind, broke in. "There's another matter I have to ask about," he said. "It's about this fellow Klein." My heart sank. That Klein should be causing difficulties at this crucial stage was almost too much. Impatiently Geoff asked what was wrong.

"It's this statement he wants to make, this broadcast. He seems to think it's very important. We put out the usual statement to the press yesterday. It's in the papers today."

He pointed to a small item in a newspaper he was carrying. Geoff and I glanced at it hastily. It was the usual comment of escapees, explaining that he had defected because he could no longer tolerate the iniquities of the Eastern regime. At the end was a plea that the Eastern authorities take care of his "beloved wife Ilse who is in no way to blame for my actions."

That was a stupid thing to say, I thought, if he really meant it. But I made no comment.

Geoff also said nothing but smiled as he read it. Then after a moment's thought he said, "And now he wants to broadcast something?"

Bill nodded. "Then let the little son-of-a-bitch go ahead. He may not be so dumb," Geoff said and turned to me. "Go with Bill and help arrange it with RIAS." RIAS was under Geoff's direct control, and after I had talked briefly with the director I went to the refugee center and saw Klein and told him he could record a statement which would be broadcast at six that evening. Klein was jubilant. "Could you do me one small favor?" he asked. "It's not hard but it's terribly important—for you," he added with a mysterious and, I thought, evil grin. I asked what it was.

"Go to Unter den Linden, see Alexeiev, and ask him to listen to RIAS at six," he said. Annoyed, I told him I was far too busy with other more important matters and left him.

From the refugee center I went straight to the Water Tunnel with Bill. The students were already at work. A powerful pump they had borrowed from the Siemens Electric Works was churning away. Already, they told me gleefully, the water level had dropped three inches. By three or four o'clock it should be passable. But it was not so easy as they supposed.

While I waited some gravel got into the pump, and with an angry grinding sound the blades of the turbine stopped. Frantically the students disassembled the pump, put it to rights, and started again. In the interval the water level had once more begun to creep up. But then it began to fall again. Feverishly they worked on. Again the pump choked up and they had to take it apart once more. But slowly the level dropped: Four inches, then five and six. It was nearly four o'clock when it had reached a level which Sepp thought was enough to allow someone through. Then he assembled the students working on the outlet and told them someone must go through to check the East Sector entrance, spot whatever Vopo patrols would have to be by-passed or otherwise dealt with and prepare for the actual operations later that night.

He himself volunteered to be the first, but a thin young man even taller than he claimed precedence. He had started the tunnel, the tall boy said, and besides, being taller, he could manage better in the deep spots. The group sided with him and, stripping to the waist and holding a flashlight above his head, he slipped into the opening. A moment later he disappeared and all we could hear was an occasional gentle splash.

As we stood silently staring into the forbidding hole the sounds of the splashing faded away. Ten minutes passed and then fifteen. Suddenly from the mouth of the tunnel came the dull sound of a muffled explosion. The young men around me exchanged startled glances, their faces paled, but for a full minute they said nothing, waiting and staring down into the pit.

At last Sepp spoke up. "I'm going in," he muttered and before anyone could stop him he slid into the hole and a moment later he too had disappeared.

For fifteen more minutes we waited anxiously. No one spoke. No one took his eyes from the black pit. Then at last we heard the sound of splashing water. Finally Sepp's grimy face appeared, his long blond hair falling over his mud-streaked face. As he emerged we saw he was dragging something behind him. A dozen hands reached down to help him as they dragged the limp body of the tall student to the surface. We stretched him on a blanket near the tunnel. His body was coated with mud, but through it on his chest a stream of bright red blood spurted at short intervals. His eyes opened and he looked around at the faces leaning over him.

His mouth opened. "Vopos," he murmured and then his eyes closed.

I don't know how long we stood there staring down at the long, lank body. At last in the distance I heard the wail of a siren and a moment later an ambulance drew up. Two attendants laid the body on a stretcher and gently eased it into the back of the vehicle. As the car drove off all we heard was the churning sound of the pump coming from the pit. Sepp slowly let himself down beside it and threw off the switch. Then, in the dull, heavy silence that followed, the group broke up.

Bill Harmsworth took Sepp in his car and I took Christl.

Half an hour later we met again in Geoff's office. I told him what had happened. His head drooped forward on his collar for just a moment but then quickly he straightened up.

"I never trusted that damned Water Tunnel," he muttered. "It's been there too long. They always locate them."

Sepp turned on him. "It's no one's fault, Mr. Schuyler, no one's except the Vopos, and if they think they can stop us—"

Geoff smiled grimly. "You still want to try?" he asked and scornfully Sepp nodded. Geoff stared down at the blotter in front of him and said nothing for a full minute. Then he raised his head and looked hard at Sepp. "There's still one possibility," he began, but then he hesitated as though he were trying to make up his mind. Finally he went on, his doubts apparently resolved.

"You remember when I traded the Sankt Jakob churchyard for the Bluecher Palace there was a good deal of opposition. Perhaps some of you shared it. But when I first saw that ruin again I remembered that back in the first days of the war, when they were digging air raid shelters all over town, they built one right behind the palace—near the Foreign Office. It was for Foreign Office officials and, incidentally, for us foreigners. It had an entrance from the Bluecher cellar, another from the Foreign Office and a third from the Adlon. I remember that because in those first days when they had practice alerts we were ordered into the cellar a couple of times."

Sepp and Christl were listening intently. "But does it still exist?" Sepp asked skeptically. "After the war the

Russians pretty well destroyed all those shelters around the Reichs Chancellery—Hitler's bunker and all that."

"It was quite separate from those," Geoff said with a sneer. "It was for us ordinary folk. It had no connections with Hitler's staff or Goering's or Goebbels' next door."

"But when they bombed the palace, wasn't the entry destroyed?" Sepp objected again.

"When we made the exchange," Geoff said more patiently now, "I sent in surveyors ostensibly to make plans for rebuilding it. They found the entrance still intact, which is not surprising, since it consisted of a heavy steel door. I presume the doors to the Adlon and the Foreign Office were also steel. What's more," he went on, "the surveyors even found the key. I guess when we went to war and the embassy staff was interned they simply left it in the door." He reached into his desk and pulled out a long, heavy iron key. "Here it is."

I had listened puzzled, wondering why he had never mentioned a word of all this to me. But I soon guessed why. Whenever Geoff had opposed any more tunnels he had always added "under present circumstances." Obviously he had not ruled out the possibility of those circumstances changing, but it was a possibility he did not relish and would not mention even to me.

"But what about the other end—the Adlon entrance?" Sepp asked.

"Yes," Geoff agreed. "I've been worrying about that too. The entrance must have been in the wing closest to the shelter—the south wing, which is still standing. Someone's going to have to explore it." He looked and several

of us including myself volunteered. At first Geoff objected
to my going across the boundary again on the ground that
by now the Vopos would be following me. But then I
recalled Klein's request that I go to see Alexeiev.

"If I tell the Vopos at the checkpoint I'm going to see
Alexeiev they'll certainly let me through. They may tail
me but what the hell? I'll see Alexeiev and then I'll drop
into the Adlon bar for a beer." Geoff pondered a moment
and finally consented.

I glanced at my watch. It was five-thirty. I said I would
have to go at once. We agreed to meet again at Miquelstrasse when I got back from the East Sector.

As we started to go, Geoff motioned us to wait.

"There's one more thing," he said, looking at Christl.
"What about old Herr Dahlmann? When Harry saw him
a few days ago he seemed fairly confident but that's plain
bravado. The East Germans are bound to catch on to him
in the end." He turned to Sepp. "Are you going to let him
get caught?" Sepp shook his head vigorously. He admitted he hadn't thought of him and agreed that he must
be included in the escape.

Geoff turned to Christl. "Can you get hold of him in
time? Could you tell him to meet you at the Adlon around
eleven?" Christl nodded.

"Then let's get going," Geoff said and smiled for the
first time that day.

The Vopos at the checkpoint let me through without
delay as soon as I told them I was calling on Colonel
Alexeiev. I suspect the riot the night before had unnerved
them and they could sense that the situation along the
boundary was tense and uncertain.

Alexeiev by good luck was in his office. He looked tired and worried when I came in but he was still not too tired to be his rude, surly self. "I suppose you're coming about that Dahlmann woman," he began, "and I can tell you now that it's useless. General Soloviev has already told you he will not interfere and that should be the end of it."

I said I regretted that the general took his word so lightly, but added that I had not come to talk to him about that. I said I had a message from Herr Klein. Alexeiev started. "That little bastard!" he said between his teeth. "Did you read what he said about his wife?" His eyes flashed furiously. I said I had, and added that Klein was about to make another statement, this time by radio. "It will be on RIAS at precisely six o'clock," I said. Alexeiev's red face lost its color and his eyes, their arrogance.

"What will he say?" he asked, his voice small with fear.

"I honestly don't know, Colonel. But he was particularly anxious that you hear it." The colonel looked at me for a long moment, his face tense and now quite pallid. He glanced at his watch. It was five minutes to six. Then he tried with partial success to regain control of his reactions. "Just five minutes. Then perhaps you would like to listen with me," he said. For a moment I wondered what Klein's statement contained and whether it might provoke Alexeiev to take revenge on me, for there in the Soviet embassy I was completely in his power. But I dismissed the thought and agreed. He rose from his desk and went to a cabinet in the corner of his office.

"While we wait, perhaps you would care for a glass of brandy." Without waiting for my reply he took out a bottle and two glasses.

"Good Georgian brandy," he said, trying to act jovial, though his manner was anything but that.

He poured the glasses and for once he proposed no toast. I took a sip. It was strong and hot. He tossed his glass off in a single swallow and refilled his glass. Then he turned on the radio by his desk and twisted the dials. A moment later the RIAS announcer was coming in clearly. He turned down the volume till I could just make out what was being said. There were several unimportant announcements that took less than a minute and then the announcer introduced Klein. The thin voice was precise and cutting.

The first part of his statement coincided with the press report I had read and for a second Alexeiev seemed to relax as he slumped in his chair, his uniform wrinkled around his collar. But then Klein went on:

"And finally I want to thank my benefactor who was so kind to me and for whom I worked so happily in the past year. My wife and I will always be deeply indebted to our mutual friend, and should he choose to join me I am sure he will be welcome. God help him."

Alexeiev had risen to his feet. His face was ashen, his mouth compressed with rage and fear. "That—that—that—" and there followed a Russian word I had occasionally heard Russian workmen use but which I shall not attempt to translate. I rose with him. "I shall be leaving you," I said, and made for the door. But he was beside me. He snatched up his military cap and together we hurried out of the building. Without a word to me he almost ran to his car parked across the street and the last I saw of him he was driving the car at full speed down Unter den Linden.

I got into my car and drove in the opposite direction, to the Adlon Hotel. A gravel driveway from Wilhelmstrasse led up to the entrance of the surviving wing of the once luxurious hotel. I parked the car in the drive and as I got out I saw another car drive in and park beside mine. There were two men in it. When I reached the entrance to the hotel I looked over my shoulder and saw they were still in their seats trying futilely to look occupied. Suppressing a smile I went in and straight to the bar, which except for the old waiter was again empty.

Remembering my five-dollar tip he greeted me profusely and seemed disappointed when I ordered nothing more than a glass of lemonade. He hovered over me as I drank it and, as almost all East Berliners do when no one in authority is present, began to complain bitterly about the regime.

"I just heard on RIAS that another of the rats has left the ship," he said, gesturing to the radio on the bar. "Fellow called Klein. I'll bet he's a real swine. Asking the government to protect his wife! What does he want to do, see her murdered?"

I said nothing but listened to his complaints about his tiny salary and the high cost of food, the wretched school his child attended.

"If they gave us half a chance I'd be out of here so damned fast they'd never see me. But how can you get out with a wife and child?"

When I'd finished the lemonade I asked him where the men's room was and he pointed to a staircase leading to the basement. He switched on the light as I started down. A wide whitewashed corridor led through the basement. Off it were the washrooms. At the far end of the corridor I saw a big steel door with L.S. written in yellow letters. *"Luft-schutz"*—the wartime symbol for an air raid shelter.

I tried the door handle. It was locked. I stooped down to examine the keyhole. Perhaps a skeleton key would open it. Then I heard the scuffle of feet on the concrete floor and turning around I saw the old waiter watching me, his hands on his hips, his head cocked on one side.

I stammered something about looking for the men's room but the waiter simply smiled.

"Would you expect to find it in the air raid shelter?" he asked sarcastically. "You won't get anywhere that way," he added. "The door at the other end is locked. I've tried it myself."

"Then you have the key to this door?" I said. He nodded and patted his trousers pocket.

"Suppose I had the key to the other end?" I said.

His eyes lit up. "In that case we might make a deal," he answered.

I wondered whether I could trust him? But it was obvious that if I didn't the whole scheme would fail.

"Look here," I said. "There'll be one or two guests here this evening. If you open this door for them I'll see that the other end is open too."

"It's pretty short notice," the waiter said. "Couldn't we wait till tomorrow?" But I shook my head. "It's tonight or never." He thought for a moment. Then he stretched out his hand and shook mine. "It's a deal," he said.

Back at Miquelstrasse I reported to Geoff what I had

done and we debated whether we could safely trust the waiter. But again we realized we had no choice. Carefully we went over our plans again with Bill Harmsworth, Christl and Sepp. Christl had already notified her grandfather and would meet him and bring him to the Adlon at eleven. Sepp with his Bavarian passport was to cross and notify Inspector Schwartz to divert the prison van to the hotel. Bill Harmsworth was to wait in the Bluecher Palace ruins.

I suggested that I too go to the Adlon by car just to be sure the old waiter lived up to his agreement. But Geoff would not hear of it. "You said yourself you were followed this afternoon and you'd just attract attention. We'll simply have to take a chance with the barman." So in the end it was agreed I should go with Bill Harmsworth to the Bluecher Palace.

When the young people had left, Geoff glanced at his watch. It was eight-thirty now. "Just one more chore, Harry, before you go," he said. "We've plenty of time." I looked at him questioningly.

"It's Samson," he explained. "Patman has just finished the investigation. It seems even worse than we'd thought and he wants us both to talk to him before he leaves."

"Leaves?" I asked.

"Yes, Patman has ordered him back to Washington on the first plane." Then he called Patman on the phone and asked him to come around to Miquelstrasse and have Samson sent for. A few minutes later Patman appeared, tired, drawn and angry. Geoff offered him a drink but he refused. Then Matusek announced Colonel Samson.

He walked into the room diffidently, and bowed as though he were the butler himself. Patman asked if the arrangements for his departure were completed, and in a low, almost inaudible voice he said they were. His plane, he explained, left in two hours, from Tempelhof.

"Well, don't miss it," Patman said sternly, and the colonel bowed again, his fat neck folding into a half-dozen rippling chins over his necktie.

Geoff straightened himself in his chair: "Colonel, have you any idea on how that tape they used at the trial could have been made?"

"Yes, sir. I made it myself," the colonel said, and we all started. "I always tape such talks—for security reasons." He drew a small green case from his pocket. "It all fits right in here. The mike's a fake cuff link," he went on, pulling a thin wire from his pocket and beginning to demonstrate just how he wore it down his sleeve, as though eager to show his own ingenuity. But Patman stopped him.

"Then you have the complete recording—not just the cuts they played at the trial?"

But the colonel shook his head. "I'm afraid not. It was the only tape I had. I didn't make any copies. It's too dangerous."

Patman snorted: "Dangerous? Then how did they get the tape at all?"

"They must have stolen it from my personal files."

There was a long pause: "Colonel, have you any other such tapes that were stolen?"

"I haven't had much time to make sure yet, sir. I've given a quick check. There are only one or two others I can't find."

"What were they about?" Patman asked, leaning forward again, his face inches from the sweating features of the colonel.

The colonel drew back as though to avoid his superior's angry gaze. He coughed and cleared his throat.

"Perhaps I should first explain—"

"Explain all you want but make it fast—" Patman snapped.

"Well, you see, we keep an eye on everyone around here. Just checking on their security. Particularly when they talk to outsiders—to prevent leaks. It's been standard procedure ever since I came here." The colonel drew back again, twisted in his chair to face Geoff and with his tongue moistened his lips.

"Occasionally, sir," he said at long last, "we've taped some of your visitors."

"Where? In the office? Is my office bugged?" Geoff asked.

"Yes," the colonel said, and then added, "And so is this room. It was pretty easy. You see it always was bugged." Now his words came faster as he explained. "They always had wires here. It was just a question of connecting them up to Matusek's room."

"Matusek?"

"He's been our man here right along, sir," Samson said.

"Then he was the one who stole that galley," I broke in.

For the first time Samson turned toward me. He seemed nettled. "Well, how did we know who you were? We had to be sure."

Geoff interrupted. "Tell me about other conversations you took down, are any of them missing?"

Again Samson seemed to shrivel in his chair. "There were some talks with Dr. Dahlmann, sir."

"You mean you recorded my conversations with my personal guests? Are they missing?"

"We had our eye on her long before you came," Samson said. "There was material suggesting her connections with the East. So we were pretty careful to cover her."

"I hope to God you haven't lost those tapes?" Geoff said.

"So do I, sir," Samson said, his voice again a whisper. "But they were among those I didn't readily find just now when I was checking."

Geoff leaned back in his chair. His eyes searched the ceiling and his fingers clasped together. A low murmur escaped his lips. It was almost like a moan.

Finally Patman spoke again. "That'll be all!" he snapped, his voice trembling with anger.

Samson rose and slowly left the room.

When he had gone the general turned to Geoff. "I guess you know how I feel about this," he said. "I suppose it's my fault for tolerating the ass." Geoff stopped him.

"It wasn't your fault, Pat. What could you do against those eager-beaver witch hunters at home? Anyway, it's all over now and there's nothing we can do."

The general rose and said goodnight. When he had left I glanced at my watch. It was nearly ten o'clock.

"It's time," I said and tried to force a smile. Geoff looked unhappy as he held out his hand. "Well, good luck to you. And we'll be seeing each other later—here."

I picked up Bill Harmsworth and together we drove through the Tiergarten to a clump of shrubbery as near to the Gate as we dared go. We left the car and slipped across the street to the ruins. When the Communists had made their deal with Geoff, they had not built a new cement-block wall but simply strung a three-strand barbed-wire fence along their side of the palace plot. Through it they could dimly see any movement within the plot from the reflection cast by the floodlights in Pariserplatz, the big square just east of the Gate itself.

Crouching we silently picked our way through the shadows cast by the heaps of rubble and the great blocks of upturned granite. Geoff had described just where the shelter door was and we had no trouble finding it. The engineers had bulldozed a trench about ten feet deep down to it and once inside the pit we were safely hidden from the glare of the lights.

With the key we opened the great iron door. Bill wanted to explore inside but I warned him not to, lest the Vopos had guards stationed underground in the shelter area. So we sat and waited, wondering anxiously what was taking place at the other end of the tunnel. It was our last chance, I knew, to free Annemarie, and I felt sick at the thought of how many things might go wrong.

Only later did I learn what had happened.

The Vopos had stopped Christl at the checkpoint and at first refused to let her through, saying that on orders of General Soloviev the crossing point had been closed for the night. But after she told them she was only going over to visit her boy friend they eventually let her through. After making sure she was not being followed, she hurried to the Adlon bar. There she was surprised to discover an older woman wrapped in shawls sitting with a small boy near the bar. However, she quickly realized that these were the bartender's family. A minute or two later an old man supporting himself on a stick limped into the room. He had on dark glasses and was wearing the black-and-yellow armband which in Germany denotes a blind man.

He sat down at a table near Christl's and imperiously summoned the waiter by tapping his stick. Only then did she recognize her own grandfather and barely suppressed a smile at his strange disguise.

When the waiter came to take her order she passed him a five-dollar bill, which I had given her, and told him it came from the same source as the last one he'd received. He nodded slightly and pointed questioningly to the old man. Christl whispered: "He's one of us."

"Then let's get started," the waiter said.

"But there are some others. They'll be here any moment."

The waiter looked uneasy. "It's too risky having you all waiting about like this. I'll take you down to the shelter and wait for the others myself," he said.

Christl motioned to her grandfather to follow the waiter as he led his wife and child downstairs. But she herself remained seated, determined to wait for her mother herself.

A minute later the waiter reappeared. "I left them just inside the shelter," he said. "They'll have to wait there till I show them through. Otherwise they're bound to get lost in all those tunnels."

Another ten minutes passed. Then two strangers came in and each ordered a glass of beer. The waiter eyed them unhappily and after serving them pretended to write out a bill and laid it in front of Christl. On it was written the one word "Police." Christl started, horrified, but the waiter motioned to her to stay calm.

She began to tremble with fear, but just then she saw the lights of a car swing into the driveway. It stopped near the door and several people got out. Through the window she saw them huddle in the shadow of the car while two of them went into the hotel. A moment later the barroom door swung open and Sepp, followed by Inspector Schwartz, entered jauntily.

The two strangers looked up at the newcomers.

"Hello, Schwartz," one of them said jovially. "What brings you to this joint?"

The inspector stared at the two in horror and mumbled something about looking for a friend. "But he's not here," he said and turned and rushed outside. Sepp followed him. Christl, no longer able to control herself, went after them.

Outside the inspector was whispering hoarsely: "It's a trap! A trap. I'm sure of it. They've found out! The deal's off!" He started toward the police van, pushing Annemarie in front of him. But Sepp caught him by the arm and held him fast. "You can't back down now," he said. "We can deal with those two in there," and he patted his hip pocket.

The inspector hesitated, but just then Max, who was standing dumbly behind Sepp, panicked and started running across the driveway. Sepp did not see him until he had reached Wilhelmstrasse and had turned toward the Brandenburg Gate. He started after him but Max had a long head start.

The inspector, terrified, seized Annemarie again, thrust her into the van and started the engine. As the van sped off Christl stood frozen, staring after the disappearing van and the two figures running toward the Gate. Just then the waiter appeared beside her: "Either you come now or I'm leaving you," he whispered. Dumbly she turned and followed him into the bar, and while the two strange policemen sipped their beer unconcernedly she and the waiter walked down the stairs and through the shelter entrance. The waiter turned and carefully relocked the door from the inside. Then with his flashlight he found the other three and they all started through the labyrinth of corridors.

Bill and I had been waiting uneasily for what seemed an hour when we heard a Vopo shout, "Halt!" We raised our heads above the trench and saw two figures running through the floodlit square toward the Gate. From the limp of the first and the bulky silhouette of the second we recognized them at once. There was another shout and then a shot followed by a second. The first figure fell and the second stumbled but staggered on. A third shot echoed across the empty square and the second figure sprawled on the pavement.

We exchanged horrified glances, but before we could speak we heard the shuffling of feet in the shelter. A moment later in the dim light I recognized the figure of the waiter emerging from the doorway leading a small boy by the hand. Behind them came a woman half dragging the weeping, stumbling figure of Christl, and behind her, old Dahlmann.

"Annemarie?" I asked in horror. Christl did not answer but simply shook her head. Then she turned toward Bill and collapsed in his arms. Slowly we crept through the shadows back to the car.

As we drove back to Miquelstrasse Christl managed to control her sobs just enough to tell us what had happened. When we reached the villa at last Bill offered to take care of the waiter and his family as well as Christl and old Dahlmann.

Alone I entered the library where Geoff was waiting. He must have seen at once from my expression that we had failed again. Straining to keep control of myself I told him quickly what I had learned from Christl. Then, I confess, I simply collapsed in a chair, my mind whirling in a confused nightmarish kaleidoscope of images: Max running across the square dragging his crippled foot, the hulking figure of Sepp behind him; the two bodies sprawled on the asphalt; Christl, her hair clotted to her tear-covered face, stumbling from the shelter entrance.

I don't know how long I sat there but finally I felt Geoff's hand on my shoulder. "Here," he said, "take this," and he offered me a long glass of whiskey.

I took it and drank it down almost in a single swallow. Suddenly I was feeling desperately tired. Up till then the tension that had been built up by my harrowing hour at the Adlon had kept me going, but now—perhaps it was the whiskey, perhaps just plain exhaustion—all my muscles seemed to go slack. Even my eyelids drooped. Slowly I rose. "Geoff, I'm all in."

It seemed as though I had hardly dropped my head on

the pillow when I felt a hand shaking my shoulder and Geoff's voice was calling me from my sleep: "Harry, I'm sorry, but you've got to wake up. I need . . ." Slowly I opened my eyes and sat up.

"Soloviev just phoned," Geoff was saying. "He's coming around at once and when Soviet generals call at 1 A.M. it's not a social call."

I dressed quickly and joined Geoff in the library. For the first time since Annemarie's arrest his voice was cheery, his eyes were bright, and on his face was the slightest trace of a smile. At last he seemed to see some hope in the whole appalling affair, and frankly I too was suddenly a little less depressed. Perhaps there was a way out.

The doorbell rang and I let the Soviet general in. To my surprise he was alone. He was in dress uniform; his chest gleamed with medals. But his big, rugged face was gray and troubled. He sat down in the chair Geoff indicated. Geoff offered him a drink but he brushed the offer aside. Then he leaned forward: "Well?" he said in German, and stared hard at Geoff. The hopes that I had tentatively entertained sank, for there was no friendliness, no sign of conciliation in his expression.

Geoff said nothing. Better than anyone I knew he understood these tough, hard, shrewd Slav peasants. The general sat rigid for a long minute, his hands tapping his knees.

"Mr. Schuyler," he said at last, "this is a dangerous game."

"I agree completely, General. You have only to keep your word to me and the danger will pass."

"My word?" the general seemed taken aback. "My word?

It is not for me to decide." He paused and watched Geoff for a sign of reaction.

"General, it was you who promised a safe conduct for Dr. Dahlmann. Release her and the matter is settled."

"Dr. Dahlmann you talk about! That is nothing! Who is Dr. Dahlmann? Just a German! You must realize the colonel is a Russian—and, in case you are not aware, the brother-in-law of Comrade Volkov, the Deputy Chairman of the Supreme Soviet."

"What colonel are you referring to, General?"

"Ah, you propose to deny it; you pretend you are not aware!"

"General," Geoff said, bewildered, "I have no idea what you're talking about. What colonel has got you so excited?"

"Alexeiev, of course. My political advisor. Don't pretend you have not lured him across, kidnaped him." Both Geoff and I started half out of our chairs.

The general raised his hand: "Do not deny, it will do no good. I have all the evidence.

"I have witnesses that Herr Harding here called on Colonel Alexeiev in the Soviet embassy this evening— around six o'clock. The colonel left his office with Herr Harding and has not been seen since."

Geoff looked at me in astonishment.

"The general's quite correct," I said. "I saw Colonel Alexeiev, as you know, and he did come out of his office with me, but then he drove off in his own car. That's the last I saw of him myself."

The general glared at me. "So you deny you arranged to meet him this evening? You deny you lured him into the little hotel—what is it called—the Adlon? You deny you abducted Colonel Alexeiev through an old air raid shelter?" His voice had risen as he spoke, and he finished in an almost hysterical shout.

Geoff looked from him to me.

"Yes, General, I flatly deny it. The last time I saw Alexeiev was on Unter den Linden." I was about to add that when I left him Alexeiev had not, to my surprise, returned to his office, but that was not my business. As for the Adlon, I had no intention of going into that.

Geoff turned to the general: "General, if Colonel Alexeiev has entered the American sector, and perhaps he has, I have no knowledge whatever of it."

"You make believe, Mr. Schuyler. It is no good," the general said. "You must have him somewhere. Your security officer must know where he is."

Geoff half smiled: "General, perhaps your security section under similar circumstances would know where he was—if he ever crossed the border. But I can assure you our security service is—" he hesitated a moment—"is less, shall we say, less thorough. Perhaps Colonel Alexeiev has crossed the boundary, but I can promise you I haven't the slightest inkling of it; nor has Herr Harding."

The general twisted impatiently in his chair and his two hands were enormous fists pounding on his knees. "Do not play with me, Mr. Schuyler. This is serious. His brother-in-law—"

"Yes, yes, General, you told me about his brother-in-law. But that doesn't help. Could you give me a little more information: was he alone?"

"Mr. Schuyler, you are not a serious man. You are playing with fire and still you try to make me a fool. You know, Herr Harding knows, there was a woman too. She has disappeared too—undoubtedly with him."

"A woman, General? Do you know who this woman was?"

The general was now beside himself with rage.

"Mr. Schuyler, I am no fool. I will not be made one. You know the woman: Frau Klein."

"God almighty!" The words burst from me so suddenly that I scarcely knew I had spoken them. The general whirled in his chair. Geoff looked at me and the flicker of a smile crossed his face as though he were laughing at my slowness in catching on to Klein's trick. Then I recalled that curious passage in Klein's radio statement. Seeing the smile, the general's fury seemed to galvanize him. He sat upright for a moment, staring malevolently at Geoff. Then suddenly he rose and started toward the door. On the threshold he stopped.

"Make no mistake, Mr. Schuyler. Last night in the Tiergarten you made a promise to those crazy West Berliners. I do not know precisely what it was but I am no fool and I can guess. Now I make a promise. If Colonel Alexeiev is not returned before tomorrow at midnight, I shall fetch him myself, and you and General Patman's forces, yes, and the British and the French—you will not stop me." He started again, but then turned back, his voice lower and more controlled: "Mr. Schuyler. For your own good I warn you not to say anything publicly. If Comrade Volkov—" He decided he had said enough and strode out of the room. When he had left Geoff called General Patman. Briefly he told him of Soloviev's visit.

"I think he really means trouble," he said. "What's more, I'm inclined to believe Alexeiev has indeed skipped. I wonder if you'd get a report from the checkpoint and see if anyone answering the colonel's description did cross over, sometime this evening. And I'd suggest you may want to order some sort of alert—though that's your business. I'm going to call Washington. Perhaps you want to tell your boss in Heidelberg, General Price. But don't get him all excited. He's enough of a warhawk as it is."

As soon as he'd rung off he flashed the red line operator again. "I want Mr. Larsen in the State Department—or at his house." Geoff glanced at his watch. "It's nine o'clock in the evening there."

In a matter of seconds Larsen was on the phone, and quickly but fully Geoff described the new turn.

Then Larsen asked a question I couldn't hear.

"No, of course not. We're perfectly cool at this end. We'll do nothing rash. But please don't you fellows interfere."

Then abruptly he rang off.

Hardly ten minutes had elapsed before the red line flashed again. It was Patman and he reported that around seven-thirty in the evening a Russian in civilian clothes with a Soviet officer's pass had driven through the checkpoint. As of a few minutes before he had not yet returned.

"Was there a woman with him?" Geoff asked.

"The MP's didn't see any," Patman said, "but that doesn't prove anything. They don't search Russian officers' cars and she might have been concealed."

"Pat, I'd appreciate it if you could mobilize every last MP and G-2 man you've got and comb this town. I know it's a needle-in-haystack job, but perhaps with a bit of luck—and if we could find him a lot of our troubles might be over." He paused and just before he hung up he added, "But I wouldn't relax your other precautions. Soloviev is scared to death and a scared Soviet general with a dozen divisions under him is nothing to joke about."

When he'd hung up Geoff slumped in his chair.

"Harry, would you mind pouring me a drink—a light one." When I'd mixed it and given it to him he took a long sip and then looked out across the room at me over the top of his glass. "If we could just find Alexeiev, perhaps—"

I knew what he was thinking and nodded. "But West Berlin is a very easy place to get lost in."

"And that little bastard Klein." He smiled. "What a hell of a trick to play on anyone."

Geoff covered his face with his hands. It was not a gesture of despair, merely one of deep, heavy concentration. "If only we could find him."

Once again, Geoff was back to normal, his depression gone or at least momentarily forgotten as he wrestled with his problem.

He looked up: "Harry, you had that crowd out dancing somewhere—"

I started and put down my glass: "The Bird Cage—it's a possibility," I muttered, "but a damned slim one. Not exactly where a fugitive or a refugee would go."

"No, but—do you suppose your old friend and namesake has a phone?" I said that he did, and began searching through my phone book.

"No, don't bother," Geoff interrupted. "It's not exactly the sort of thing to discuss on a Berlin telephone line."

"Do you want me to go down?" I said, and looked at my watch. It was a little after two in the morning. "He'll be open for some time yet."

"Let's go together," Geoff said.

The Bird Cage was packed when we arrived. I looked around carefully but saw no one I knew. Geoff went to the bar and asked for a Scotch. Old Harry started at the sound of his voice and the cocktail shaker in his hand seemed to freeze, his blind eyes peering at Geoff. "A Scotch?" he repeated.

"Yes, Harry, make it fairly light, please."

Harry put down the shaker and leaned across the bar. "You couldn't be—Herr Schuyler?"

Geoff grasped his hand and shook it. "Yes, Harry, I'm Schuyler. Sorry I haven't been in to see you since—"

"Yes, since 1939, I guess."

There were no free tables so we stood at the bar. Another couple was standing there but when they left I leaned across the bar. "Harry, do you recall those people I brought here a few weeks ago?"

"A Russian, wasn't it—at least he had a Russian accent—Leningrad, I think—and a German couple—Berliners—right?"

"Right, Harry. You haven't seen—I mean—they haven't been in here recently, have they?"

"No," Harry said so positively that I was astonished at his certainty.

A stranger came up to the bar and we fell silent. When

he had left Geoff said, talking almost in a whisper: "Harry, if by any chance he should turn up—would you get in touch with me—or with Mr. Harding here. And in a hurry."

Harry nodded: "Okay, Mr. Schuyler."

We finished our drinks and headed home.

XV

WHEN AT LAST I WENT TO BED FOR the second time that night I fell asleep at once. But within a couple of hours I woke up, my mouth parched, my head throbbing dully. From then on I dozed fitfully. Dreaming that I was in a New York subway station, I kept hearing the roar of passing trains. At last I got up to get myself a glass of water and afterward went to the window. Dawn was breaking, and in the leafless trees outside a flock of starlings were calling in their whining, rasping voices.

Then overhead I heard again that noise of rushing trains. The clouds were hanging low over the city, but suddenly through them I made out the squat form of a helicopter streaking over the housetops. A few minutes later a second roared by. Helicopters were common enough in those days in Berlin, but I had never seen or heard them maneuvering over the city so early in the morning, and I wondered sleepily what was up. Then I went back to bed and soon I was sound asleep again.

It must have been around seven or eight when I woke suddenly and saw Geoff, already dressed, standing at the foot of my bed.

"Sorry, Harry," he said apologetically, "but I thought you ought to know what's going on."

I sat up and blinked: "Yes?"

"It seems Soloviev is raising the ante on us. A formation of Soviet tanks have been moved into the East Sector and are heading toward Checkpoint Charlie. Our choppers are keeping an eye on them. They also have moved some ground troops in—Russians, not just Germans—and Patman has indications that there's a general concentration going on all along the border."

Trying to take in what he was telling me I blinked confusedly. My first thought was, what the hell could I do about it?

"I thought you ought to know, just in case Soloviev really means to let the balloon go up. There's a flight out to Munich in an hour if you want to get on that."

At last I realized what Geoff was driving at and snapped indignantly: "What the hell are you suggesting? That I duck out at this stage? You're nuts," I said and fell back on my pillow. Geoff left and I got up and dressed hastily. Downstairs in the dining room my breakfast was waiting and Matusek hovered over me. I noticed when he poured the coffee that his hand was trembling. I looked up at his face and it was white and pinched.

I heard voices in the library, and as soon as I had finished went in to find Bill Harmsworth talking to Geoff.

"They're pretty jittery," he was saying, "but then they're used to crises by now." Then he turned to me: "I was telling Mr. Schuyler about the state of mind of our friends."

The phone rang and Geoff picked it up. As he listened I could see his eyes squint with displeasure. Once or twice a "damn" or a "hell no" exploded from his lips. Then he put down the receiver and sighed deeply.

"General Price down at Heidelberg thinks this is it, and he's on his way up here to take command," he said. I knew that General Price was a fire eater of the give-the-Russians-the-works school, and I fully appreciated Geoff's anxiety.

"Pat tells me Price has sent ahead orders to put a battalion of tanks at Checkpoint Charlie. They're on the way now."

Then Geoff picked up the phone again and dialed: "May I speak to the governing mayor?" he asked. A moment later he repeated to the German the information he had had from Heidelberg. Then he added what Bill had told him.

"Could you ask the chief of police to send every last man he can scrape up to the checkpoint to keep it clear of any mobs? If there's trouble with the Russians it'll be plenty without a roaring crowd of teenagers back of the tanks," he explained.

He hung up. "I'd better get over to headquarters. Price

will be blowing in any minute and I'd better be there to back up poor Pat—and keep Price as cool as we can."

As he started out the door he turned to me.

"Harry, you might go down to the checkpoint and see what's going on. If you don't like it give me a ring over the red line."

Bill and he left together. I was putting on my top coat when Matusek appeared and told me I was wanted on the phone. A woman's voice answered. Though it sounded vaguely familiar I could not place it.

"I must see you quickly," she kept repeating. Finally I managed to get her to identify herself. It was Frau Klein. I started in my chair. Perhaps now we could find Alexeiev.

Not daring to mention his name I asked: "Are you alone?"

Between the sobs that answered me she indicated that she was. She gave me the name and address of a hotel off Kurfuerstendamm and I promised to come right over. Then I phoned Geoff's office and told his secretary where I was going. I'd call back if I learned anything interesting, I promised.

As I headed toward the center of town, I passed a formation of troops in personnel carriers. They were all in battle dress, and behind them followed an ambulance unit. The ambulances, rather than the troops, gave me a start. Evidently General Patman—or was it General Price? —meant business.

I must have been driving fairly fast, for suddenly I heard the wail of a German police siren. A little blue car drove up beside me and waved me to the curb.

Politely the policeman pointed out that I was going fifty miles an hour in a restricted zone. "We can prove it—" he began, but I cut him short.

"I'm sure you can," I said, trying to keep my patience. "But I'm in a hell of a hurry. It's important. It really is."

The police smiled politely. "I'm not denying it, but I'll have to give you a warning fine and ask you to obey the law. You know even our American allies must—" I cut him short: "O.K., O.K., what's the charge?"

"Two marks," he said, and I fumbled in my pocket for the change, cursing under my breath. I told the policeman I didn't need a receipt, but he insisted that it was the law, and slowly and deliberately he wrote down my name and license and at last handed me a scrap of paper. I wanted to toss it back at him, but I restrained myself, crumpled it into a ball and stuffed it in my pocket. Perhaps, I thought, there was a fine for not accepting a receipt for a fine. I wouldn't put it past the German police.

But at last with a courteous salute he told me I could go on, and as long as he was in sight I kept the speedometer well below the legal speed limit.

The hotel Frau Klein had named was one of those dingy "Hotel garni" which give you a room and breakfast. It was in a narrow back street, and next it was a gaping ruin where nearly twenty years ago an allied bomb had knocked out a block of houses. But in this second-rate district no one seemed interested in rebuilding. As I walked past it toward the hotel I saw a sign: "Ruins for sale." I wondered if in a few hours there might not be a great many new ruins for sale.

Frau Klein's room was a tiny cubicle with a single brass bed, a washstand and a bidet. A loving couple could doubtless rent it by the hour, I thought to myself.

Frau Klein, despite her pretty figure and soft blond hair, was far from her best. In fact, her round face was puffed and tear stained. Her full lips, unpainted, were a washed-out, pale pink. Her eyes were red and swollen and her hair, though combed, seemed to have lost its luster in the dim, gray light that seeped through the little window from the light well outside. Her dress, which under different circumstances might have shown off her trim little figure, hung unpressed and shapeless around her.

She motioned me to the only chair, a straight-backed wicker one, and she seated herself on the hastily-made bed.

She brushed her hands over her face and tried to straighten her hair, and then without preliminaries she blurted out: "Where is my *mann?*" In literal German, of course, she could only be referring to her husband, but with my concern for the colonel I thought for a second she was speaking of Alexeiev, and I shrugged my shoulders.

"But you must know," she insisted. "He would only come to you."

"If you mean Herr Klein," I replied, "I suppose he is at the refugee center."

"Can I find him there?" she almost shouted.

"Of course. You must go there yourself eventually. Everyone who crosses must go."

"But will they let me talk to him?"

"I don't see why not—that is, if he wants to see you."

It was an unnecessarily cruel remark, and she burst into

a fit of sobbing. But I felt little sympathy for her, and let her cry for several minutes.

"I should very much like to find Colonel Alexeiev," I said at last. "Where is he?"

"I've no idea. He left me last night."

"Left you last night?" I repeated incredulously. "But you just came over yesterday evening."

Through her sobs she told me that they had gone to a cheap café in Wilmersdorf.

"He got very drunk," she said. "I finally got him out onto the street and we walked half the night. I wanted to get him sober. But the soberer he got, the meaner he became. He said I had ruined his career—and then he ran off and I haven't seen him since. Luckily he gave me some West money—or rather I took it when I paid the bill at the restaurant."

The words had come out in a burst, and when she stopped I was silent, hoping she would give me a clue, but she obviously knew no more. Alexeiev was still lost, wandering the streets. With plenty of money he could hide away indefinitely in one of the thousands of hotels or pensions in the West Sector. But then a thought struck me:

"Do you think he would go back East?"

She looked at me wide-eyed: "East? You mean the Democratic Republic?" she said incredulously, and I smiled at her use of that pompous and meaningless title. I nodded.

"But he can never go back now," she said. "He would be arrested at once. His brother-in-law—his wife's brother—"

"You mean he's married?"

Once again she burst into tears and when at last she stopped crying I urged her to go on.

"He only told me about her, his wife, yesterday—after you'd seen him and heard the broadcast," she said, talking through her tears. "He came right away to the apartment. I'd gone there to get some clothes. He was frightened and so was I. The block warden said an American had been visiting my man the day before."

I nodded. "Yes, I'd gone to see him," I explained.

"We thought it might be you. We thought maybe he'd tried to get you to help him get away. But we didn't know. It was awful."

I pictured to myself the two terrified creatures huddled together in that tiny, smelly apartment.

"I had listened to the radio too." She began to wail again. "It was awful, I mean that part about his benefactor and 'our mutual friend.' Everyone knew who that was, even the block warden. If he had just said something awful about me, just denounced me or something, no one would have paid any attention, but when he said, 'God help them'—that was when Alexeiev told me about his wife." There were more tears and then she went on.

"You see she's in Leningrad, having a baby." A faint pink blush came over Frau Klein's pale, tear-stained face and I felt a wave of disgust at her contemptible, petty shame.

There was nothing to do but get away then, Alexeiev had told her. Otherwise his brother-in-law . . . "So we got into the car and we came across right away. I hid in the back."

"And no one stopped you or searched the car?"

"The Vopos never stop a Soviet officer," she said. "And the Americans didn't seem to care." She stopped and mopped her eyes with a tiny, wet and dirty handkerchief.

"And you've no idea where he might have gone?" I asked.

She shrugged her shoulders and I was afraid of more tears, but instead she answered indignantly: "I don't know and I don't care—all I want is my man."

I knew there was nothing more to be gotten out of her so I told her to get her things together, and put her in a taxi and sent her off to the refugee center at Marienfelde. Then I called Geoff and told him what I had found out. After that I set off again for Checkpoint Charlie.

XVI

AS I APPROACHED THE CHECK-
point I found that the police had cordoned off the streets
several blocks from the sector boundary. With the aid
of my identity card I managed to get through the outer
cordon, but the closer I came to the checkpoint the more
reluctant the police were to let me drive through. Eventually I parked my car in a vacant lot and went on to the
boundary on foot.

Two large American tanks had occupied the street on
either side of the guardhouse. Their big guns, poking out
in front, were only inches back from the white boundary
mark. From their turrets black-helmeted heads protruded,
and watched the scene around them with unconcern. Behind them stood two personnel carriers, as big as freight
cars, their rear gates down. Inside, soldiers were lounging

about, reading comics, eating chocolate bars and playing cards. They were as peaceful as though they were in their own snack bars.

But across the boundary the atmosphere was less relaxed. Two large Russian tanks stood with their guns pointing straight at the American tanks, their muzzle covers removed, their crews sitting rigidly at their posts, their faces grim and, I thought, just a little frightened.

Between the two Russian tanks, East German Vopos were maneuvering a hose truck equipped with a powerful water pump.

The scene was not reassuring, especially when you realized that a single nervous hand on the trigger of one of those cannon could set off a reaction that might leave our world in ashes. I walked up under our own guns toward the white boundary strip. A young lieutenant, his face half hidden under his big steel helmet, hurried toward me.

"Excuse me, sir, but would you step aside? You're directly in the line of fire of one of our machine gun emplacements in that ruin behind us," he said diffidently. Only then did I realize that there were not just four triggers but perhaps a hundred loaded weapons trained on that little patch of asphalt. Along the white stripe that divided it Vopos in their long gray-green overcoats stood inches way from another rank of West German police and American GI's, their machine guns held tightly to their chests, their eyes directed straight to the front, into those of their opposite numbers.

Behind both ranks, milling about among the tanks and personnel carriers, were MP's, officers, messengers, and here and there someone in civilian clothes—a plainclothes agent or a newspaperman perhaps. Occasionally, a Russian officer would raise his field glasses and peer across the boundary. But, except for those glances, nothing penetrated the invisible wall that separated east and west.

I drew back into the doorway of an abandoned shop and watched the scene. Except for the low, ominous rumble of the tanks' engines, it was strangely silent. Even those who were moving about seemed to tread softly as though they might jar loose one of those triggers. When they spoke to one another their voices were low and almost inaudible.

Here at last was that confrontation which the war hawks, as Geoff called them, had been crying for. I wondered how they would enjoy the awesome sight if they were here now sandwiched between the muzzles of the rifles, machine guns and cannon.

Once the silence was broken as an American helicopter swooped down over the checkpoint. Angrily, the Russians and East Germans glared up at it through their field glasses. One Vopo raised his rifle and aimed at it, but at a low, guttural command from an officer beside him he lowered it shamefacedly. How many, I wondered to myself, among those on both sides of the line were so stupid that they did not realize the holocaust a single shot might set off? And how many did not feel that chilling draft along their spines that sent a shudder through my entire body?

Half an hour of that unearthly silence went by. Then a staff car drew up behind the American personnel carriers and a general leaped smartly from it, followed by a tall, athletic-looking aide. I recognized General Price even before I saw those archipelagoes of four silver stars that shone from each of his shoulders, from his glistening steel helmet and his puffed-out chest.

For a moment he looked about eagerly, not at the tanks or the troops, but at the civilians cowering in the doorway. A single photographer ran out and knelt to take a picture, and the star-spangled chest seemed to expand and a proud smile lit up the general's face. That smile, it seemed to me, was the most incongruous thing about the whole weird scene, and I had an almost irresistible urge to yell at the general and ask what in God's name there was to smile about here at Checkpoint Charlie. But I managed somehow to hold my temper.

The general stalked toward the white line, and as he did so the Vopos across the way closed ranks so that they stood shoulder to shoulder. As though he had not noticed the maneuver, he turned and stepped into the guardhouse. Through the windows we could see him exchanging a few words with the lieutenant in charge. Then he emerged, did a quick turn around each of the tanks and walked back to his car. As it backed out of the street and disappeared I seemed to hear a sigh coming from a thousand chests on both sides of the line, as though for all their belligerent appearance they had one thing in common—a dread of those generals.

But when the general was gone I asked myself if he alone was responsible for this monstrous confrontation. Surely there were similar generals on the other side, Soloviev and his superiors. And was either set of generals really responsible, or were they simply reacting? Reacting to what? The disappearance of a Soviet colonel, the brother-in-law of the deputy chairman, or the arrest of Annemarie and the mob animosities that had aroused?

Suddenly I felt tired and sick to death of the scene. Quietly I slipped from the street and went through the police lines.

But the farther I walked from the Wall, the more I felt a magnetic pull to come back. It was the appalling fascination of staring over a cliff at the bottom of which lay the ashes of a world in ruins, the smoke of the atomic bombs curling upward so that one could almost smell the acrid fumes.

Even when I got to my car the pull continued, and though it had been my intention to go back to Geoff and urge him to withdraw the troops, I drove instead along the Wall. First I stopped at the Brandenburg Gate. Four British Centurion tanks were drawn up across the square from the Gate itself. Under the arches the Russians had put up great earthenware pots filled with geraniums, as though they somehow took away the ugliness of the barbed wire which they concealed. Between the flowers Soviet and East German soldiers watched every movement on our side of the line through long field glasses. Overhead an American helicopter wheeled and dipped.

As I walked up to the tanks, a British tommy wearing a black beret was lolling nonchalantly in the open turret of one of them. He called to a fellow soldier in the turret of the neighboring tank. "Looks like the brass has the wind up," he said in a strong Scotch accent. He was a young man—far too young ever to have seen action in World War II, and I smiled indulgently at his bravado.

Then I climbed back into the car and drove up to Bernauerstrasse in the French sector, where the boundary runs down the very edge of the street. Bernauerstrasse itself was deserted except for one or two West German police, which gave it a deceptively peaceful air. But directly behind the street in the alleys that led into it from the west, several columns of tanks manned by French soldiers were sitting waiting, their engines purring. As I walked by I smelled the pungent odor of black cigarette tobacco, and I had the strange feeling I was passing a peaceful Parisian sidewalk café.

Finally, I tore myself away from the Wall and headed back through the heart of new Berlin, the Kurfuerstendamm. Within a few blocks, the entire atmosphere changed. It was as though I had not merely moved into another city but into quite a different climate. Along the wide sidewalks Berliners were idly strolling, gazing at the shop windows with their latest models. A young man and woman, their hands tightly clasped, were staring at a display of jewelry in a sidewalk showcase. Oblivious of the ghastly confrontation only a few blocks away, they were, I imagined to myself, choosing an engagement ring. Would they ever, I wondered, enter that blissful state they were contemplating, or would they, an hour, two hours, hence, become charred skeletons, the bones of their hands still twined together as they lay on the smoking asphalt?

In the bars and cafés on either side, fat burghers were sitting reading their papers, the latest football results, the dreary debates in the Bundestag in Bonn, perhaps a sensational murder trial. It was as though Checkpoint Charlie were off on some other planet and of no earthly concern to them.

An impatient taxi driver blasted his horn behind me as I drove slowly up the street. I edged the car toward the curb and the taxi flashed by. Why, I asked myself, was he in such a hurry when only a few miles separated him from his last stop?

When I reached Geoff's office in Clayallee, he was alone, his desk was bare, and even the in- and out-going boxes, usually piled high with pink and yellow telegraph forms, manila folders and mimeographed bulletins were empty. The absurd thought flashed through my mind that he alone realized that the end was at hand and in his neat and orderly way had finished off his work in good time.

But when I looked at him closer, the illusion disappeared. He was calm enough and apparently relaxed, but his drawn mouth and deep-set eyes revealed that inside, despite his exhaustion, he was tense and very much on the alert. Without waiting for him to speak I launched into a detailed, and I fear somewhat excited, account of what was going on at the checkpoint. I ended with a despairing plea:

"Geoff, can't you pull back those tanks, if only a block or two? Surely they'd be just as effective there if the worst comes to the worst?"

He smiled a tired, helpless smile. "Harry, they've taken it out of my hands. General Price is in full charge—on orders from Washington. They're trying to keep me from finishing my own fight."

His own fight—there it was again. Even at this last

moment he saw it all as "his" fight.

"If only they could find Alexeiev—I still think I could pull it off."

"But they won't find him," I said.

"We've got all the MP's we can spare out looking."

"Have you talked to Harmsworth?"

"Not in the last half hour—" He reached for the phone and dialed. "Bill," he said, "anything new?" Harmsworth said something I could not hear, but from Geoff's expression it was not hopeful.

"Well, keep on looking," Geoff said. "We've still time." His voice was calm, even encouraging, and I marveled at his self-control.

We were silent for several minutes and then abruptly he rose.

"Let's go down to the checkpoint, Harry. There's nothing I can do here. And when it comes, if it comes, I want to be on the spot." He seemed resigned now. The last shred of hope was slowly disintegrating. But still he was calm.

Little had changed at the checkpoint, though now it was growing dusk. The Provost Marshal, a good friend of Geoff's, was in the guardhouse when we arrived. Harmsworth was with him.

"We've spotted Soloviev across the way," he told Geoff. "He's back there next to that big staff car," he said, pointing, and I could just make out the tall, powerful frame of the Soviet general surrounded by officers.

Some Vopos were maneuvering the big hose truck and apparently testing the water pump. Suddenly a powerful jet of water shot out of the nozzle and struck one of the American soldiers standing on the white chalk line in the stomach. Just as quickly, the jet was turned off, but the GI doubled over, then recovered himself. In the glare of the lights his face was twisted with anger. He brought his rifle down to the ready and aimed from the hip at the Vopo by the pump.

The entire scene seemed to freeze. Every eye was on that taut soldier but no one spoke a word, as though any sound might jolt his trigger finger. A young lieutenant standing a yard or two behind the GI stepped quietly forward, and in the unearthly silence I could hear his low, soothing voice as though he were talking to a child.

"Easy, Bill," he coaxed. "Hold it."

Slowly the soldier raised the muzzle of his gun.

Geoff had been watching, transfixed with horror, but as the soldier put up his weapon his face relaxed.

An hour went by, hushed but tense. Now only the glare of the electric lights lit up the little patch of street. I was standing outside the guardhouse smoking one cigarette after another. Geoff was inside. The field phone rang and a soldier came out and touched my arm. I jumped and wheeled around.

"Sorry, sir," the soldier said, "but you're wanted on the phone."

I hurried inside and seized the receiver.

An operator said there was an outside call for me. "The man says it's urgent—he's a German."

There was a click and I heard a voice I recognized at once.

"He's in here now," the voice said in a whisper which

I could barely understand. I tried to make him repeat but again he whispered.

"He's here—"

I dropped the receiver and turned to Geoff. "It's Harry at the Bird Cage. Alexeiev's there."

Like a shot Bill Harmsworth was out of the guardhouse and had commandeered an MP jeep. General Price, who had driven up a few minutes before, looked bewildered. "What's going on here?" he asked, but Geoff simply smiled, and the general looked angry.

It could hardly have been twenty minutes but it seemed like two hours before we heard the wail of the siren on the MP jeep. It stopped back of the personnel carriers and Bill Harmsworth ran through the tanks to where Geoff was standing.

"We have him, sir. He's back in the jeep."

Geoff's face lighted up. "Keep him there," he said. Then he turned and started toward the white boundary line, but General Price, who was beside him, spoke up: "Mr. Schuyler, where are you going?"

Geoff merely pointed across the line.

The general stiffened: "No one is going across without my say-so, Mr. Schuyler. I'm in command here." The mysterious events going on under his nose without a word of explanation had obviously angered him.

Geoff paused and turned to him: "General, you may be in command of the troops. But no one is in command of me." And without another word he headed through the rank of soldiers.

Across the line the Vopos shuffled together as though

to bar his way. But he paid no attention and walked straight at them. A Russian officer barked an order in broken German. The line parted and Geoff disappeared behind it.

General Price turned to me: "Do you know what he's up to?" he asked belligerently.

"I wouldn't have the vaguest idea, General," I said in a tone hardly likely to convince him. He stalked off, grumbling into the gloom.

And then we waited. A half hour went by, and another half hour. Bill Harmsworth stood beside me but we hardly spoke.

Then at last the rank of the Vopos parted again and Geoff re-emerged. He stopped on the line and called for Bill.

"Bring him across," he said in low tones. Bill disappeared.

The general walked up into the light again: "Mr. Schuyler, I'm ordering you to return to this side."

"All in good time, General," he said soothingly. Bill appeared with two MP's, between whom stood Alexeiev, disheveled, pale, his eyes bloodshot and wide with fear. They took him to the line and stopped. Then a Soviet officer stepped forward, seized him and dragged him through the Vopo ranks.

Suddenly I had an awful pang of doubt. Did Geoff have any right to deliver that helpless human being into the vengeful hands of the Russians? I knew as well as Geoff that he was no legitimate refugee seeking asylum, but a cheap little wife stealer, a fugitive from criminal law, not a seeker of political asylum. But who else would understand that?

At that moment, the Vopo rank parted again and out of the darkness a woman appeared.

I recognized Annemarie at once. Her face was chalk white and she walked unsteadily even though Geoff held her firmly by the arm as he led her toward me. She raised her head and seemed to smile faintly as she saw me. Without thinking what I was doing I stepped across the line and hurried to her side. It had not occurred to me that the Vopos might seize me. But it apparently did not cross their minds either, for instead they stepped back to make way for me.

I took Annemarie's other arm, and as Geoff released her she turned and kissed me. At that moment I wanted to take her in my arms again as I had so many years before, but I managed with difficulty to restrain my emotions. We recrossed the line and started through the maze of tanks and jeeps. Just then someone behind the Vopo ranks shouted a command in Russian. With a burst of backfiring, the engines on the Soviet tanks started up.

General Price, who had been standing at the white line glaring about him, puzzled and bewildered, whirled around to give a command to the American tanks but Geoff seized him by the arm.

"Take it easy, General," he said quietly. "They're withdrawing." Startled and still angry as though he had been cheated out of a headline, the general watched as the Soviet tanks slowly went into reverse.

XVII

GEOFF HAD INSISTED THERE be none of the traditional departure ceremonies for him. He had also let it be known that he wanted no one to see him off. Only General Patman and his wife came by the house to say good-bye. The general was in an angry, unhappy mood. As he shook hands with Geoff his voice was thick and rough.

"I remember I once warned you that if things went well I'd get the medals and if things went wrong you'd get the blame. That's what happened but I'm still goddamned mad." He tried to smile but his face wrinkled up in a wry grimace. "I'm sorry, Geoff, sorrier than you . . ." His voice broke and his wife tugged him by the sleeve. Geoff smiled and shook him by the hand. Then the couple turned and hurried out the door.

A few minutes later we climbed into the car and Geoff told the chauffeur: "Tempelhof—the side entrance." The chauffeur nodded and we drove off from Miquelstrasse for the last time.

At the airport the car stopped at a small gate beside the main building and the chauffeur murmured something to the guard. The gate swung open and we drove out onto the apron where the big airliner was waiting to take off for Frankfort and New York. A stewardess showed us aboard and I sat with Geoff until the other passengers had been shepherded on and shown their seats.

For a moment there was an awkward silence between us. I broke it by once again trying to cheer Geoff. "No one could have licked that situation," I began but Geoff broke in with a wry, humorless laugh. "Skip it, Harry. I did what I could to fix things but it just didn't work. Perhaps I pulled a boner or two and took a chance I shouldn't have. But what else was there to do?" He paused staring out the porthole at the lights of the airport.

"But one thing I have learned. The Berliners are as great a bunch of allies as we have anywhere and we've got to defend their rights—the rights they have won by just plain stubborn, fearless loyalty. That's one thing I'm going to try to explain to the boys in Washington—though I doubt if anyone can ever understand the Berliners without living among them." He stopped again, evidently thinking about how much and how quickly he had learned from living among them. "But still," he went on, "still I am convinced that no city, not even Berlin, is worth blowing the world to pieces for. And that's our dilemma."

He sighed and laced his long, slender fingers together in that familiar gesture. "I wonder how it's going to work out for them?"

He expected no reply and I kept silent. Finally he spoke again: "And I wonder what old Nelly has in mind for me." This time he looked searchingly into my face. But I still remained silent for I was sure that Nelly had nothing in mind for Geoff but a quiet, quick retirement. No one was going to risk asking him to fix things ever again. As I returned his gaze I suspected that he too knew that his trouble-shooting days were over.

The stewardess called attention to the No Smoking sign and then nodded to me that it was time to leave the plane. I rose, and as I shook hands with Geoff my throat choked up again. Without a word I walked down the aisle and off the plane. Outside a clear, coppery-blue sky lit by a full moon hung peacefully over Berlin.

Inside the airport Annemarie, Christl and Bill Harmsworth were waiting for me. As I approached, Christl and Bill discreetly wandered off, leaving me alone for a moment with Annemarie. Often in the last day or two I had considered asking her to leave Berlin with me, but I knew that it was silly even to propose it. Despite all that had happened she still believed that her job, her post, was in Berlin. Whatever her feelings for me, they would never take the place of her devotion to her city.

"You'll come back and see us?" she said affectionately. "After all you and I have to look after those two," and half laughing she nodded toward Christl and Bill.

Then the loudspeaker announced the departure of the

Munich flight. Annemarie took both my hands and kissed me again just as Christl and Bill came up. I kissed Christl too and she looked as though she were going to burst into tears. Bill's gruff voice broke the silence. "Thanks, Harry," he began. "If it hadn't been for you I don't know . . ." But I did not wait for him to finish and, shaking his hand, hurried to the departure gate.

A few minutes later I was staring down at the bright lights of Berlin as the plane circled for altitude. The glare of the floodlights along the Wall cut like a flaming knife through the very heart of the city and, I thought, through the hearts of its brave citizens, killing some, maiming all of them. I thought of that big, rugged Sepp and the crippled Max sprawled on the asphalt behind Brandenburg Gate, and the scores of others who had died trying to destroy that knife. I thought of Annemarie and the others whose lives were dedicated to quenching that flame. So long as those floodlights blazed they would never stop trying, perhaps not by such nefarious methods as Bureau X's but by their constant, stubborn refusal to accept it or live with it.

The stewardess went through her little welcoming speech. "Our altitude . . . our air speed . . . our estimated flight time . . ." The words came in snatches to my ears but scarcely penetrated my mind, for my thoughts were on another plane just ahead of us and on its lonely passenger.

To many, like General Patman, Geoff's abrupt recall after the confrontation at Checkpoint Charlie had come as a shock and had provoked indignant, often angry surprise. After all, they argued, Geoff had prevented what was perhaps the most serious crisis since the Wall had gone up. He had done so despite a Russian general terrified of his tough Kremlin taskmasters and an American general terrified for his public image as a fearless warrior.

Both Geoff and I did our best to still the criticism, for as old Foreign Service hands we knew and understood the code under which he had operated. The fact was Geoff had blundered. Indeed he had blundered twice. The first time was when he had let Annemarie go across to defend Max. He was quite right to try to provide Max with an effective defense, but in doing so he had out of ignorance become an accessory of the notorious Bureau X. No doubt he had done the right thing, but unwittingly, for the wrong reason.

And then, when he had put a stop to the riot by his capitulation to Sepp, he had risked the one thing he had been determined to avoid—a confrontation with the Russians at the Wall itself. At that moment he had done the wrong thing for the very best of reasons—to avoid an open clash between the people of Berlin and their American defenders.

Of course it had all worked out more or less in the end— thanks largely to the devilish little mind of Herr Klein. But that hardly excused Geoff's mistakes.

Why, I kept asking myself, had he made them? No one I knew was more experienced, better qualified for the difficult Berlin job than he was—with one small reservation. Again I recalled Nelly Larsen's remark, "The only trouble with Geoff is he personalizes his job too much."

It was true. Geoff had always identified himself personally with whatever task he was given. Whenever he was accredited to a foreign government, for instance, he seemed to think that its relations with him personally were equivalent to its relations with Washington. Or whenever our own government confronted a problem of concern to him, Geoff felt that it was his personal problem and that he had a moral obligation to solve it whether it was solvable or not. He had never accepted the basic limitation of every professional diplomat: that he is only an impersonal instrument or a tool—sometimes a delicate device, but sometimes too just a hatchet or a hammer.

In other assignments the defect had not been noticeable —except to Nelly. But in Berlin it had been fatal. Perhaps, I thought, it had been unfair of Nelly to assign him there in the first place. Perhaps the pressures he had inevitably been exposed to from that first walk through Grunewald to the riot in the Tiergarten had been too great for any man of his sensitivity and temperament.

And the Berliners themselves had done little to alleviate the pressures—particularly Annemarie and her senseless Bureau X. I thought of her now back in her apartment in Charlottenburg, her schemes shattered but her devotion undiminished. She had made use of Geoff, deceived him and even brought about his destruction, but for a cause for which she herself was ready at any time to sacrifice her own life.

Now both of them had been destroyed but, I wondered, uselessly?

Someday the rulers of Russia would be persuaded that to hold on to East Berlin and East Germany was not worth the effort. To that end there was no more persuasive argument than the stubborn determination of the Berliners themselves and their allies.

The high-pitched voice of the stewardess jarred me from my reflection: "In a few moments we shall be landing at Munich-Riem Airport. Kindly fasten seat belts and observe the No Smoking sign."

ABOUT THE AUTHOR

Charles W. Thayer, after graduating from West Point in 1933, started his career as private secretary to the Ambassador and Attaché of the United States Embassy in Moscow. In 1937 he entered the career Foreign Service and transferred from Moscow to Hamburg. Thereafter he served in Berlin; a second tour in Moscow until 1942; in Kabul, Afghanistan, where he opened the first permanent U.S. Legation in 1942; then in London on the European Advisory Commission, planning the occupation of Germany.

In 1943, Mr. Thayer received a military leave from the Foreign Service. After attending parachute school in England, where he became a qualified parachutist, he was assigned to the U.S. Military Mission to Tito in Yugoslavia and soon was named head of the Mission. He later was transferred to Austria as head of the OSS Mission and Russian advisor and interpreter to the U.S. High Commander, General Mark Clark.

In 1946 he was named Political Commissioner on the U.S.–U.S.S.R. Commission for Korea and served six months in Seoul negotiating for the unification of Korea. Thereafter he attended the National War College in Washington. In 1947 he started the first broadcasts to the Soviet Union on the Voice of America and subsequently took over the entire Voice of America operation.

Transferred to Germany in 1949, Mr. Thayer was appointed U.S. Political Liaison Officer to the newly formed German Government at Bonn. In 1952 he was transferred to Munich as Consul General and Land Commissioner for Bavaria. He resigned from the Foreign Service in 1953. Currently he and his wife live alternately in Washington and Germany.

Mr. Thayer has written *The Unquiet Germans, Bears in the Caviar, Hands Across the Caviar, Diplomat, Moscow Interlude, Guerrilla* and *Checkpoint*.

Format by Gayle A. Jaeger
Set in 11/14 Linotype Janson
Composed, printed and bound by American Book–Stratford Press
HARPER & ROW, PUBLISHERS, INCORPORATED